——THE——
REBELS
— OF —
FLORIDA

—THE—
REBELS
— OF —
FLORIDA

LEAH K. OXENDINE

gatekeeper press
rethink publishing

Published by Gatekeeper Press
3971 Hoover Rd. Suite 77
Columbus, OH 43123-2839
www.GatekeeperPress.com

Cover design by JewelDesign
Back cover photo by Leah K. Oxendine

ISBN: 9781619846487

Printed in the United States of America

Acknowledgements

THROUGHOUT THE PAST TEN YEARS in which this novel was researched, written, and edited, I've been blessed with an incredible amount of help and input from some downright amazing human beings.

First off, I'm just thankful that everyone has been patient with me during the process. A project ten years in the works can become tedious to work on, yet still there have remained a faithful number that pressed on with me to the finish line.

Above all, I dedicate this book to the Lord Jesus Christ, my Creator and Savior. Without God I would never have been able to put this dream into reality. I credit the words on these pages to His inspiration and guidance. I believe He placed the passion to write this on my heart. I pray that The Rebels of Florida glorifies Him.

I want to express my sincerest gratitude to my parents, Butch and Kathy Oxendine. They taught me to have a love for writing and history, as well as for expressing my creativity and pursuing my dreams. I am the writer that I am today because of this remarkable couple. They were my first editors and critiques. They were my first cheerleaders. Thank you, Mom and Daddy.

To my beta readers and voluntary proofreaders: Sam Graber, Hannah Mummert, Mallory O'Steen, Alex Martin, Maddie Wilson, Andy Keener, Amanda Wikoff, Hannah Stewart, Marie Herman, and Em Parrow for reading through the early drafts and giving valuable insight. Thank you to my editor, Alexandria Mintah.

To James Permane and Thomas Fasulo for the tips and information provided early on regarding Florida's involvement in the Civil War, which I used to further my research and study.

To Daniel Cook, one of the finest reenactors and fellow Christians I have known: The Rebels of Florida would not have been possible without your dedicated research and input on Florida's military history, which is covered herein. The information Daniel provided was literally an answer to prayer, given how obscure this whole subject was to delve into. Daniel also recreated several maps showing the path which the 7th FL units took during the time elapsed in this story.

All in all, I am beyond blessed to have had such marvelous support behind me on this project.

Couldn't have asked for better.

FOREWARD

WELCOME TO NORTH-CENTRAL FLORIDA. To this day, my homeland of Marion County is composed of lush farmland, towering pines and simplicity. Not to mention humidity, most of the year. It is beautiful, and to me, it is paradise.

Here, circa 1863, is where we find a world untainted by development and untamed by mankind as a whole. Even though Florida had been in the Union since 1845, it would be years before it was looked upon as more than a muggy, mosquito-infested jungle.

Before I go any further, there are some points about this book that you ought to know.

The Rebels of Florida is fictional, but many of the characters are based on real people, although some of their names have been changed for privacy and the sake of creative license.

Most of the experiences you're about to read are real experiences. The details which pertain to both the 7th Florida Infantry and the Florida homefront are based on dutiful research. I attempted to recreate the most accurate picture possible of what life during the War would have been like—for both the Floridian civilian and the Floridian soldier.

When I was twelve years of age, and just starting to write this novel, it was a whole different book. More imagination than anything else, the characters were just figments of my daydreaming childish mind.

But the storyline evolved, changing bit by bit as the years advanced.

Like Marjorie Kinnan Rawlings in her earlier literary years, I had been writing about things I didn't have any idea about.

She wrote about Victorian romances, I wrote about a Victorian Union-sympathizing family in Pennsylvania. A state I'd never set foot in at the time.

My story was simplistic, yet I spent a lot of time working out the puzzles historical fiction authors must work around, in order to avoid being historically incorrect. I had my own vague idea of what Altoona, Pennsylvania looked like. But it's hard to write about something that doesn't apply to you, much less something you've never seen. So, I dropped the location and replaced it with something I could actually write about.

Like Miss Rawlings, I started writing about my home.

Florida.

The characters became people that I knew or have known. Or maybe it's been the other way around - perhaps *the people became the characters*. There have been so many interesting people and happenings that I couldn't resist writing a bit on each. I also developed a desire to shine a light on Florida's involvement in the War, specifically its military involvement.

I have always enjoyed creating. But in historical fiction, there are guidelines to follow and room for creating is limited by nature. That being said, I appreciate the boundaries which are bestowed upon me as I write about actual events. There is a satisfaction in abiding by these guidelines, but also, a challenge. I write freely, and according to my own desire and motivation, but I am always confronted with the reminder that if I'm going to write about history, I must do exactly that.

So as you hold this book in your hand, I hope that you not only enjoy the story but find yourself learning new things about Florida's past.

You are now in 1863, and you are about to experience something that historical fiction has never even touched before.

Not like *this*.

Chapter One

June 1ˢᵗ, 1863

Often the worst enemies fall closest to home. They don't have to exist miles away to be dangerous or haunting. They don't have to be menacing dragons spewing billows of smoke and fire.

No, most of the time the antagonist isn't clearly marked. Foes emerge in the place of friends, and allies turn out to be the ones you thought you should be avoid. Time changes people.

But some things never change. Some enemies never go away.

This was the case with a particular tale that sprang up in the wild, untamed lands of the Florida frontier. The tale you hold in your hands at this very moment.

There once was a girl named Zephyr. And Zephyr Darson was her own worst enemy.

***

It was hard enough that there were countless *other* struggles in Zephyr's life. The very place she called home was a harsh, wild realm, a place full of unexpected events and teeming with hostility. From the swarming mosquitoes to the wild coyotes and bears roaming free, one could never know what to expect.

Few people inhabited the rolling fields, endless woods and sunbaked prairies of north-central Florida. Those who did were either ingenious survivors - or dead. That was the bottom line. Pansies didn't make it in these parts.

Still, external struggles were nothing in comparison to what sixteen-year-old Zephyr battled. Her worst fears didn't lie in rattlers and coral snakes.

Zephyr envied the folks who'd been blessed with the gift of being able to hide their thoughts. She longed to hold the peace of those who felt pain and emotion, but were able to douse its treacherous flames. Because fact of the matter was, she possessed far too much emotion. She could have supplied the entire world with it.

And people with grit didn't let emotions get the best of them.

Zephyr walked along the dusty wagon tracks, making her way to the small Reddick trading post where she'd purchase some things her mother had requested. As she walked, her mind buzzed with thought and tingled with searing memories.

Emotions ran through her veins afresh, emotions she couldn't stifle. She clung to the memory of life before the war. Memories were things she held on to dearly; books she could read again and again and never tire of, reminding her of a time when life happened at a slower, easier pace and evil didn't seem to dominate all of mankind.

It felt like an eternity ago. In reality, only a year that had passed since that fateful day when the Confederacy took Pa away.

Zephyr's stomach turned as her bare feet moved along the hot, barren path. A certain hollowness filled her, as if she were reliving the moment. She hardly noticed the sun's glare as she walked, or the sweat trickling down her back and moistening her bodice.

She recalled an event which occurred at supper one sultry, airless evening. She could still feel that oppressive humidity lingering on her skin. Everyone was going about in typical conversation, finishing their supper, when Pa raised his hands for silence.

The eight-year-old twins Rudy and Royce, and five-year-old Lemuel stopped their incessant chatter about spade-foot toad tadpoles. Thirteen-year-old Clarence stopped boasting about how much work he'd done that day and fourteen-year-old Lydia quit elbowing him.

Ma's demeanor was calm as she observed her children and husband.

"I have some news for you all."

Pa inhaled deeply. A somber expression was written across his profile.

Zephyr's mind raced with dread. Those words had an unpleasant ring to them, and she immediately sensed that they implied a grave sort of news.

Anticipation fell over the children as they waited.

"I've been ordered to join the Rebel army."

Zephyr's worst fear come true...the one thing she'd prayed would never happen was now becoming a reality. She felt her body go numb.

Clarence's mouth dropped open, and his blue eyes grew wide. "What?!"

"What's that mean?" Royce blurted out.

"It means I'll be going away to fight. For us, and our freedom. The Feds desire to take more money from us than they should. They want too much control over our lives. Someone has to fight against that."

Zephyr's skin tingled and her cheeks flushed. Pa didn't want to go, but he took the command awful well. He made the draft sound honorable when in truth he knew it wasn't. The Confederacy had good reasons to fight, but Zephyr knew Pa disagreed with the way they were going about it. She knew he despised the notion of forcing men to enlist, especially when it came from folks who said they were in support of the freedom of the individual states.

Now Rudy was the one with a concerned look on his face.

"But if you're gon' away, when you comin' back?"

Pa exchanged a knowing look with Ma, who remained completely unruffled. He must have told her beforehand.

"Only God knows that, son," the middle-aged man replied.

"Does God want you to go fight, Pa?" Royce asked.

"He wouldn't set this path before me if He didn't want me to walk it. I'm hoping to try and evangelize some of the men I meet, if I get a chance. Surely God has a reason for this."

"It's not right." Clarence's face was getting redder by the minute, and his blue eyes burned with anger.

Mr. Darson exhaled, as the teen boy continued fiercely, "Can't the Rebs find some other man? Just tell 'em you won't do it! It's just not right that they can come an' make you go. I'd stick a rifle barrel right up in their faces if it were me."

"Clarence, if I don't go, they'll shoot me and burn the farm. That's a direct quote."

Nothing else came from Clarence's mouth. Pa's grim eyes and daunting words silenced any further outbursts.

Zephyr wanted to hate the Rebels for making her father leave. But she would've hated it equally if the Federals had drafted him instead.

Upon learning the horrific news, Zephyr found herself in a daze, a state of mental and emotional confusion. She found herself crying out to God inside, beseeching why He was allowing this to happen. Despite the fact that her mind felt like a raging ocean, she couldn't bring herself to utter a word. A thousand sentences flashed through her head, but it was as if her mouth had been sealed shut.

How had this all happened? Had Pa been out in the fields when the recruitment officers rode up, or, had he been at the trading post with the other men? It didn't matter. The bottom line was that Harold Darson had been stolen away from his family. No questions, no allowances for time, long discussions, or fitting goodbyes.

Zephyr found herself fighting back tears, as she said good-night to Pa that evening. She could barely leave the room before wetness overcame her eyes.

She still didn't know what to make of all this. The war had felt so distant, but now it was snatching her father away.

Her heart ached at the consideration that he might never return. A million bullets pierced her heart at the horrific thought.

Oh Lord, please don't let anything happen to him…please don't.

The sound of strange voices reached the girl's ears, pulling her back to the present.

Zephyr let out a short sigh, staring ahead as the buildings of the trading post came into view. Maybe it was time she thought about other things.

Reddick didn't qualify as a town, and it could barely even be called a trading post. It was merely two buildings in the middle of two hundred acres of citrus trees. The dusty wagon-trail road ran into a large clearing, where several wagons and horses were tied to hitching rails in front of the lonesome two structures.

Zephyr glanced about herself, observing the surroundings as she always did. She'd never had trouble walking to the post by herself, but one could never be too careful.

The central building of Reddick was the Faircloth mercantile. It was the only two-story edifice to be found for miles, and it was where Zephyr was headed now. On the other side of the street was the Gaultney consignment place, a meager shack with a tin roof.

Several men stood outside on the mercantile porch, and Zephyr looked them in the eye as she trotted up the steps. She only recognized one of them, the middle-aged son of elderly Mrs. Gaultney across the street. The other two were probably grove workers.

As Zephyr entered the store, tempting aromas tickled her nostrils. A new saddle caught her eye on the wall, and several belts were draped across it. The scent of the new leather always made Zephyr feel good. Several sacks of coffee beans were leaned against a table, and the dark, rich scent that rose from the sacks was the near equivalent of earthly perfection. Zephyr almost wished for a cup of the stuff right then. But coffee wasn't what she'd come for, and today was too hot for coffee anyhow.

Zephyr smoothed the skirt of her faded green homespun dress. Her eyes searched the shelves and boxes, taking in all the fascinating and useful items for sale. So many things filled the room...so many distractions.

Salt and white sugar. That's the goal.

More voices reached her ears, and she remembered that both the salt and sugar were purchasable in the back of the store, where the register counter was. There was no need to wander around – she certainly didn't bring money for leather goods or coffee.

"Afta'noon, Zephah!"

She glanced up as one of the Faircloths' slaves greeted her from behind the counter.

"Winnie!" Zephyr smiled at the cheerful brown-skinned girl who was roughly her own age. "How are you today? Can you ring me up some sugar and salt? A pound each, please."

The short young woman nodded. "Sho' thing. And, I'm alright, thank ya." She turned to fetch a scoop, and kneeled beside a row of sacks against the back wall. Zephyr watched as she measured out the foodstuffs.

"Anything new happen 'round here lately?" She asked, hoping to continue in some form of conversation. Zephyr couldn't stand awkward moments of silence or idleness. Even now as she waited, she unconsciously twiddled her fingers, and cracked her knuckles, habits she'd developed years ago, her excuse for being that they kept her fingers limber for piano playing.

Winnie rolled her shoulders as she stood back up, placing two brown sacks on the counter. "Not really, 'cept that…" She lowered her voice a notch and glanced across the room. "..Mistuh Faircloth done gave a feller the sack jes' now. Don't tell nobody, neither."

Zephyr's brow furrowed slightly as she peeked over her shoulder to follow Winnie's gaze. The Faircloths didn't approve of the slaves making conversation with customers. But what that obnoxious couple didn't know couldn't hurt them.

"Well, who got kicked? What did..." Zephyr stopped mid-sentence as the sight before her answered her own questions.

In the back corner of the storeroom, a dirty-looking young man stood a few feet from a middle-aged fellow dressed in a white half-apron. The older man had his back turned to Zephyr, but she could make out the face of the other...

"Anson?" She mouthed the young man's name under her breath.

Little bits and pieces of the conversation floated to her ears, and she could tell just from those fragments that things weren't going well. Zephyr sighed.

Anson Whistler, you always did have a big mouth.

Winnie raised a brow, staring at the two men and then flashing a look at Zephyr. "You know dat feller? And yer total's a dollar n' seventy-five cents."

Zephyr forced herself to pull her gaze away from Anson. She shook her head dismissively and rummaged around in her basket for the change.

"He and I used to be best friends when we were little. But I don't see him much these days."

First time I've laid eyes on him in years and my, he sure hasn't gotten any taller.

Winnie shrugged. "Well, he sho' got a mouth on 'im, but don't mention I said dat."

Zephyr shook her head again, handing Winnie the money. "No, I agree with you whole-heartedly. But I guess there's nothin' I can do about it. It's his life."

Anson's domineering voice echoed across the pine floorboards, causing Zephyr to stop and listen.

"You know how that blasted tariff destroyed everything; don't even try to mosey around it. That's the whole damn reason we're in this war. It seems to me you're just sittin' on the fence, Mr. Faircloth. Well, 'round here fence-sitters don't fare so well. Seems to me you need to make up your mind who you're sharin' sympathies with."

Zephyr cringed. No wonder the fellow was getting the sack. And the Morril Tariff, *really*? That was years ago, for goodness' sake.

Pa used to shake his head in disgust as he recounted the details of the mandated tax on southern imports and exports. It was an unjust thing, he'd say, as it laid most of the taxation on southern civilians, even though more people populated the north than the south.

But still, what was the use of bringing that up now with one's employer?

"Boy, I'm three times your age. I don't need to be told what to do with my life. If you're so dead set on serving Jeff Davis, you best get yo' rear on out of here and go enlist in his army."

Zephyr looked back to Winnie and sighed. "Well, I guess I should get going. I've stuck around long enough to hear too much."

Winnie rolled her eyes. "Jes' figure what *I* hafta put up with. You take care, anyhow!"

"You too." With a parting nod and smile, Zephyr grabbed the two brown bags and turned to leave. She didn't look in Anson's direction. The two hadn't carried a conversation for years and as much as she wanted to talk to him right now...

Nope. The girl set her jaw and marched out of the building.

She was halfway across the road when she heard her name being called.

"Zephyr!"

Anson.

Pink flushed across Zephyr's cheeks. She stopped walking, and sucked in a breath. Her heart raced, as she stood motionless for a second before turning to face the seventeen-year-old.

He was about her height now – 5'8". Ever since they were young, Zephyr had been taller than him. She was surprised that he'd finally managed to catch up. He was wearing denim overalls, a short-sleeved shirt, and boots. Zephyr noticed the development in his upper body since she'd last seen him– his arms were muscular, and even though he had small shoulders they looked equally worked-in. Anson's hazel eyes met hers, and for a moment, they just looked at each other in silence.

It was hard to believe that this was the boy she'd spent most of her childhood with. Now, they were both of marriageable age. Where had the time gone?

Finally, Zephyr managed to clear her throat. "Hey." She tilted her head, eyeing him somewhat suspiciously.

Not awkward at all.

"I just saw you leaving the store and thought I'd say hi…it's been a while." The corner of Anson's lip curled up slightly, forming a half-grin. His eyes looked steadily into Zephyr's, unfazed.

Zephyr forced a smile.

"I heard you got the boot."

Anson exhaled loudly, and his half-grin faded. "Yeah. It's a mess. But I'll find something else; it's nothin'."

Memories flew through Zephyr's system. Was this really the kid who had tried to kiss her when they were all of twelve years old? That rascally redhead who was always flirting and joking around?

"You sure were telling it to Mr. Faircloth…you know, you only made yourself another enemy there." Nothing that came to her mind presently was encouraging, but at least it was honest.

"Well, having enemies sure ain't gonna kill me. I've got a hold on things." Anson shifted his weight from one foot to the other. "And since you must've been listening…well, you agreed with what I was saying, I know you did. You're no Yankee sympathizer." Each word was drenched in arrogance.

"No, of course not. I just think there's a better way to get your point across than cussin' out a body."

Anson's nose wrinkled, a frown crossing his face. "I'd say it don't really matter. Whether or not a feller cusses don't change the facts."

Zephyr placed a hand on her hip. "Maybe this isn't my place, but you do call yourself a Christian, don't you?"

Anson nodded.

"Christians watch what comes out of their mouths."

The young man grimaced and shook his head.

Zephyr hated sounding preachy, but wasn't it best to just be upfront?

"I'm just saying it like it is. Nothing towards you, but people are watchin' and it's best to make sure one's example is acceptable."

Zephyr hated sounding preachy, but wasn't it best to just be upfront?

"Honestly, Zephyr, this isn't the kind of discussion I was hopin' to get into with you today."

Ain't that too bad. Well, life doesn't go the way you want all the time.

"I'm sorry." She didn't intend for her response to sound so flat and wry, but that's how she felt. She tried to force a smile but somehow that too felt false. "I'm just pointin' this out for your own good. Somebody would've told you sooner or later. And, if you claim to be a follower of Christ, well, it's your duty to live up to it."

Anson stared at her in disbelief. "I can't believe we're even talkin' about this." He coughed. "It might just be the most substantial conversation we've ever had." His tone was sardonic, matching the half-grin pasted across his profile. Now he kept fidgeting, shifting his body position every few seconds.

"What's that supposed to mean?"

Anson shrugged. "Whatever you take it to mean."

"Considerin' we were only kids the last time we talked...maybe it is." Zephyr felt her brow furrow a little. She realized all too late that she was taking on a defensive tone.

Anson smirked slightly, but it wasn't a very pleasant one. Clearly, things had gotten off to a bad start here. But had they ever truly been on a good note to begin with?

Zephyr tried to resist thinking about the sheer amount of time she used to spend with this boy – er, man. *Too much.* He didn't deserve it.

"Look, it doesn't change the fact. I know it's not my business, but...I just..." Zephyr let out a sigh, her cheeks burning bright crimson. "I think it's important to make sure you present yourself in the right fashion."

Anson took a few steps away and lit a pipe. Now, he turned, looking Zephyr in the eye coldly.

"You're damned right...it's not your business. It never was and never will be." He paused, and then shook his head, muttering, "Women these days."

Zephyr's stomach dropped.

"Excuse me?"

Anson grumbled something else inaudible as he walked away. His footsteps fell heavy on the dusty path, making dull thuds that echoed in Zephyr's ears as he stormed off. He didn't even turn to look back.

I guess it's safe to say I've officially made an enemy.

Chapter Two

THE WALK HOME WAS A lonely one.

Not because there were no human beings to be found for miles - that was something Zephyr had gotten used to.

This was a different kind of lonely. This isolation was the sort that seared deep into the soul, filling its victim with regret and despair. Also, in this case, major frustration.

Zephyr kicked at the dusty road, gripping the salt and sugar tightly. She felt like a kettle -bubbling with hot liquid and threatening to overflow any moment.

What on earth just happened?

Anson's angry words burned in her mind. She still couldn't believe he hated her after those few words she'd spoken.

I've never had an enemy before. The thought was daunting. But the knowledge that somebody you knew all your life now abhorred your existence…that was even worse.

Steaming in a mixture of confusion and frustration, Zephyr found herself replaying the whole event, trying to figure out who had been in the wrong.

I was just being honest. He ought to have known by now that I don't hold things in. With that filth that came from his mouth earlier? No wonder he was given the sack. Oh, Anson…

All Zephyr had done was to point out Anson's bad habit with cussing, and how it didn't reflect well on his character. Has she been wrong to do this? Was he right that it was not her concern?

Maybe she should've just kept her big trap shut. Silence sure never got a soul in trouble the way speaking up did. Then again, if everyone was silent, nothing would ever happen.

Zephyr's turquoise eyes smarted. She swallowed, her mouth painfully dry. The summer heat penetrated every crevice of her skin. She wanted to rip off her clothes and jump into Orange Lake where an escape from the smolder might be possible.

But Orange Lake was seven miles north, and that was too far to walk today, what with so much work to finish on the farm. Zephyr's pace increased. The sooner she could get out of this oppressive sun the better.

Lord, did I just close a door that was meant to be open? Was speaking up worth turning Anson away? He'll never want to talk to me again...I won't ever be able to point him back to You.

If it weren't so blisteringly hot, Zephyr would've felt numb inside. As it was, she felt overcome by guilt and haunting questions of what-if this, what-if that. What if she'd never said anything? What if she'd just smiled curtly like a lady, and ignored the boy's language?

She'd never know. It was over now, and the two had parted ways for good.

Maybe it was for the best.

Anson was never husband material, anyway. Not even great friend material. How were we ever best friends?

Zephyr took a deep breath and pulled her broad shoulders back, almost in defiance to the thought processes that demanded to linger on young Whistler. She would move on, continue with her life like nothing ever happened. She could live with having an enemy.

The young woman jogged the rest of the way home. She didn't flinch as her bare feet pounded the uneven path, and sharp, small rocks met her weathered soles. She was fed up with social interactions for the day.

Lydia's freckled face was the first sign of human life she saw as she entered the large Darson property.

Lydia. A sigh of antagonism escaped Zephyr's lungs.

The redhead was high in a sweetgum tree, staring down at the world with hawk-like green eyes. If not for her dirty, cotton boys' pants, the girl could never have gotten that high without being terribly immodest.

What on earth is she doing climbing trees at this hour of the day?

"Heeeeey Zephyr! Jealous? I bet ya couldn't get up here worth beans if ya wanted." Zephyr's adopted sister shouted from the tree's branches.

Zephyr stuck one hand on her hip and glared up at the smirking girl. "You get down here right this minute, Lydia Ruth! You know very well that we don't have time for foolin' around."

Time.

Ugh. Thinking about time was depressing. Zephyr preferred not to dwell on it at all if she could, but it was unavoidable. There was so much to be done and never enough time to do it.

It was hard enough that Pa was gone, leaving an immense load of work on Ma and Zephyr in particular. If Zephyr didn't pull her weight, the family might go hungry, or broke. So, with Clarence and Lydia being fully capable, functioning adolescents with strong bodies, there was no reason they couldn't pitch in and carry some of the burden.

Lydia stuck her tongue out, pulling back and forth on the tree's boughs, making the whole thing sway precariously.

"I'll come down when I feel like it." She tossed her head defiantly as a slight breeze ruffled her stained, oversized cotton shirt and ginger hair.

Zephyr didn't possess the energy to argue with the little imp that somehow was her adopted sister. Rolling her eyes, she exhaled and stomped toward the house.

It was no cooler inside than outside. Without any drafts or breezes, the house felt like an oven. Zephyr scurried through the four-room home to the kitchen, a completely separate building in the back.

The kitchen's screen door slammed, and Clarence emerged from inside the small building. This was the first time Zephyr had seen him since breakfast, and he should have been out working in the garden… but whether or not he had been doing so was questionable.

With one look at Zephyr's hands, he huffed.

"As *usual*, no letters from Pa," he muttered, stomping dirt off his shoes at the doorstep into the house.

Zephyr grunted, pushing past him with the sugar and salt packages. "Can you expect a letter every week?"

The boy grumbled something but followed his sister back into the kitchen, sweat trickling down his head, neck, and arms. He let out a weary sigh and rested his elbows on the pine counter.

"Any news in town?"

"Not really." Zephyr put the store goods away, not looking up. She didn't want to talk about Anson if it could be helped.

"I sure wish we had a telegraph office there or somethin'." Clarence's voice carried a shade of frustration. "You never know what's going to happen. I mean, there could be armies marchin' down here this very moment and we'd never know."

Zephyr inhaled slowly, staring for a moment at the grimy-looking wall across from her. "Well, Micanopy doesn't even have telegraphs. So you'd best give up the thought of seeing one of them things ever."

Clarence wiped his moist face with his shirt sleeve, and shook his head. "I don't like it. Too much could happen out of nowhere."

Zephyr knitted her brows together. She picked up a stack of clean plates and put them away in the cupboard. Then she took the scraps tub outside, where she carried it to the goats' food trough and emptied it.

Clarence followed her. "You think Mr. Faircloth is hirin'?"

Zephyr sighed again as she trudged back inside the kitchen.

"Clarence, the groves are full of fellas that would eat you for breakfast."

Clarence kicked at a stray rock in the grass. "That's balderdash. I could take on any man easy. You didn't answer my question."

Zephyr opened the screen door and returning to cleaning the kitchen.

"Don't you have work to finish?"

Work in the groves my foot. As if there's not enough to do around here.

Clarence rolled his eyes, shuffling his feet.

Wiping down the flour-dusted counters, Zephyr glanced up to see her mother at the woodstove, checking a pot that was boiling.

"Zephyr, did you forget to check the stew?"

"Uh, no, I just…" Zephyr bit her lip, and narrowed her eyes at Clarence. "…got distracted."

Clarence glared back at his sister.

"I just wish I'da gone with Pa, then I coulda been there to do something firsthand." His tone had taken a dark, bitter ambiance. This chilled Zephyr inside, because she knew he couldn't possibly understand the depth of his words.

"What does *that* have to do with anything?"

Mrs. Darson eyed Zephyr, and the girl threw her hands up to display her confusion and aggravation with her brother.

"What's going on between you two?" Mrs. Darson's eyes found her son's.

Zephyr relocated to the woodstove where she could monitor the stew that she had almost burned. She moved it to the back of the stove to let it cool.

"Nothin', Maw. I just…I just think Zephyr's not in the best of moods today…which isn't new."

"That's not so in the least." Zephyr snapped, releasing the words before she could stop herself. "You just wanna go on and on about how there's nothing we can do and we're so isolated and you'd rather go take part in the bloodbath yourself. All you want to do is complain."

"I just wanna see some action, that's all. I just wanna see stuff get finished… Maybe if I were there myself, I could help that happen."

Zephyr sprinkled some pepper into the pot. "If you were there yourself, you'd just get yourself killed."

Mrs. Darson looked at her eldest children, her brow furrowing in disappointment.

"Enough, you two. That's all I want to hear about the war. No more discussing this, Clarence, you hear? No more."

Silence engulfed the humid summer air for several moments as Clarence stared back at Mrs. Darson, frozen by her words.

Finally, he turned and stormed away.

Ma wasn't finished. "Zephyr, you're a grown woman. I know how Clarence can be, but he's also three years younger. You need to set a better example."

Zephyr sagged against the counter and closed her eyes, clenching her teeth beneath her lips in humiliation.

"I know."

Why was it so hard for her to keep her mouth shut?

Chapter Three

June 10ᵗʰ, 1863

HAROLD

Seek the Lord and His strength, seek His face continually.
Harold Darson adjusted his spectacles as he read silently from an old black book, his most valued possession. Those words from 1 Chronicles 16:11 lingered in his mind– they were the ones he'd memorized earlier this week.

Scripture was one of the few things that refreshed his soul these days. Over a year of campaigning miles from home had a way of wearing on a man's spirit.

As the morning sun beat down upon the canvas material of the small A-frame tent, beads of sweat formed on Harold's forehead and neck, and he wiped his cotton shirt sleeve across his face.

The middle-aged man closed the book cover gently and brushed it off, running his calloused fingers over the two words engraved in the leather. *Holy Bible.*

"Thank you Lord for giving me your Word. Sometimes it feels like it's all I truly have anymore. I guess it's all I really need," he murmured, rising from his simple bedroll and putting the bible away in his knapsack. He willed his mind not to focus on the pain lingering in his back from yesterday's drills.

His looked over the little makeshift room, the less-than-standard regulation tent which he shared with his brother Ezra and a few others. The shabby thing was hardly a proper living space, and it was always leaking during rainy periods. It made the bedroom he shared with Cecelia seem so luxurious in comparison.

Home was a luxury, period. If there was one thing he had learned from these last two years, it was how to truly value the simple things he'd taken for granted back on the homestead in Reddick.

And not just the things, but the people. Things were nothing in the great scheme of it all, but one's family? That was another matter entirely.

I'm a father, but my very own children and wife may never see me again. The thought was a bitter one, and Harold bit his tongue in stifled anger toward that Confederate recruiter.

Ever since he'd been mustered into the Florida 7th at Camp Lee in Gainesville, his body was only one of thousands, unnoticeable in a sea of human beings. The Army of Tennessee was like a colony of ants.

And Harold and Ezra were just privates. As a natural leader, Harold didn't care much at all for this position. It was difficult for him to take orders from another man.

6:36 AM. Harold flipped his pocket watch close and tried to set aside his steaming thoughts as he ducked beneath the tent flap door and out into the morning air.

The sun peaked through the trees, barely risen above the eastern horizon. The massive red globe illuminated the acres of rolling hills with its warmth. Unlike in north Florida, there were no pine trees to cast long shadows. There were few trees, period. This was Eastern Tennessee.

He looked about the camp, where soldiers went around doing morning chores such as chopping firewood, cleaning their weapons and preparing rations to put in their stomachs before drills.

The smell of coffee tickled his nostrils, and he turned to see where it was coming from.

"Mornin' Harry." A russet-haired young man smiled, poking at a campfire with a stick. Above the fire was a small grate, upon which a tin mucket gurgled.

Harold forced a small smile in response to his brother's greeting. "Coffee done yet?" He stretched his long arms for a moment, groaning.

"Fresh as the air you're breathin'," the twenty-eight-year-old responded, pouring his older brother a cup.

Harold popped his knuckles and creakily sat down on a washtub beside the tent, a grimace splintering across his grizzled face.

"You keep that up and folks'll think you're seventy."

"Ezra, when you get to be my age I think you'll sympathize. I ain't no spring chicken anymore."

Ezra raised an eyebrow as hr handed Harold the tin cup.

"Not as bad as yesterday's." Harold took a sip.

Ezra smirked. "I thought the same thing myself."

The two chuckled quietly. Both knew how horrible the coffee was, but it was an ongoing joke that somehow the beans acquired a better taste with time.

A moment of silence fell on the brothers, as each man quietly drank his coffee. Amid the lack of conversation, the crackling fire and other soldiers' muffled conversations filled the air. Flies buzzed, creating a monotonous underscore of annoyance.

Ezra stretched his arms for a minute, and cracked his big knuckles in a similar fashion to what his brother had previously done. Then he reached into a small leather pouch and retrieved a stiff, cardboard-colored object. With a bit of effort, he snapped the square into two pieces and offered one to Harold.

"Care for a bite of filet mignon, sir?"

Some comparison. Harold looked distastefully month-old hardtack. "Your optimism is admirable, youngster."

Ezra shrugged, his hand still outstretched with the unpleasant bit of ration in it. He gnawed a chunk off his own section with great effort.

"Well, somebody's gotta look on the bright side," he retorted through an arduous mouthful. "Want it or not?"

Rations weren't bountiful in the least, and what existed of them hardly qualified as fine dining. But it was still food. A substance to fulfill one of the most basic bodily needs.

"You know it must be pretty awful when not even the bugs touch this stuff," Harold grumbled as he took the crusty object from Ezra's fingers, and examined it briefly. An ugly monster, it was about as colorful as a piece of cardboard, hard as a Cyprus knob, and no easier on the taste buds than it was on the eyes. Absolutely no flavor whatsoever.

Down the hatch. After dunking the wretched thing in his coffee, he crammed it down his throat in two bites. The sooner it was digested the better. Even though it had been softened in the coffee, Harold feared for his teeth as he crunched down on the painful meal.

With a final gulp, it was done. The man took a couple swigs of coffee to clear his mouth of the stale taste. He didn't want to know how long that section had been sitting around in some supply wagon. At least there hadn't been any weasel infestations yet. The last thing Harold wanted to think about was biting down on a mouthful of worm-filled hardtack.

Once again, silence overcame the brothers. Ezra continued to sip from his cup, vacantly staring out at nothing in particular.

Harold's blue-green eyes drifted from the gritty cup in his hands to the stretch of tents and make-shift shelters surrounding them as far as the eye could see. He let out a short sigh. So many souls, all crammed together in one place. Harold wasn't a chaplain by trade, but he believed it was his God-ordained duty to minister to these men and boys. In April, the 7th's chaplain resigned, leaving the men without a designated pastoral leader to turn to. That was when Harold felt the tug of the Holy Ghost, and he began taking over the chaplain duties non-officially. He knew this was what God wanted him to be doing. If he had to spend several years of his life away from his wife and children, the people he valued most on earth, he would make it worth something eternally.

Ezra finished his hardtack and wiped his mouth of a few remaining crumbs. He glanced up at his brother and the two locked gazes for a moment, their eyes meeting in the weary silence.

There were times when there was simply nothing to be said.

EZRA

Night fell on the camp, and it came none too soon.

After a long, laboriously boring day of drills and idleness, uninterrupted sleep was welcomed as both an escape and a source of rejuvenation. If you were blessed enough to fall into a decent slumber, that was.

All throughout the army, the soldiers began to settle down for the night, adding more wood to their campfires to help keep away the mosquitoes and provide a small sense of home-reminiscent comfort. There was something about looking into a fire that helped relax a body.

Sitting on an overturned crate, Harold puffed on his pipe. The flames danced across his blue-green eyes. A small group of fellows now accompanied him now around the fire that he and Ezra had shared that morning.

"I'll be darned if I'm not running out of elbow grease," twenty-seven-year-old private Damascus Hayden muttered, cleaning his rifle for the fifth time that week.

"No surprise there." Ezra propped his leg up, his long body sprawled across the grass. He looked at the Cook & Brother muzzle-loading gun in Hayden's hands. "That must be the pertiest gun in the whole unit."

Hayden shot Ezra a look of mild distaste. "I don't clean this thing just for its looks. A weapon ain't any use if it ain't functional."

Harold inhaled, sucking a breath in and then releasing a ring of smoke into the air. His lip curled slightly in amusement at the ostentatious Irishman.

Hayden was one of the night sentries and always on edge, even during the day. An open package of .57 caliber cartridges sat on a bucket next to the short man. With his skill in shooting, he ought to have known whether a gun was functional or not. His aim was impeccable...he could've been in Berdan's Sharpshooters if he wanted.

The unit surgeon, thirty-one-year-old Carter Pratchit grinned slightly, eyeing Hayden's rifle. "Well, if any of them Yanks sets foot down here, they'll get a good taste of what they need to know... I guess we can all rest assured of that."

Fifteen-year-old William Dade made his hand into the shape of a gun and pretended to fire it. "That's right as hell, they'll know."

Harold looked up from the flames at Will. "Boy, who taught you such language?

William's grin grew bigger as Hayden chuckled.

Ezra looked at his brother, whose face was calm and solemn. A serene dance of shadows and flickering flame-light licked across Harry's unshaven face, and his eyes sparkled every time the light touched them.

He is every bit the leader this group needs, the man thought to himself. Ezra always looked up to Harry, ever since they were youngsters. Now that they were both grown men, Ezra respected him even more. And even though they were hundreds of miles from home, it could've been worse. It was almost like having a taste of home right there, with your own flesh-and-blood to brave the hardships alongside you.

Hayden and Pratchit stayed by the fireside nearly the whole evening, even after all the other fellows had gone off to their tents or to join some other party's campfire. The four were sitting next to each other, each lost in his own thoughts and listening to the popping and crackling of the fire.

Finally, Hayden interrupted the silence, running his fingers through his mop of dirty red hair. "Anybody been to town to hear the telegraphs?"

Pratchit shook his head, spitting tobacco juice into the fire. "There's nothin' to hear. If you're expectin' some compensation for all this wasted time…"

"Please, for the love of heaven. Let's not get into *that* again," Ezra grumbled.

"There's rumors…and listen, I ain't one to go around high-tailin' after old wives' tales and goose stories. But, well, rumor has it we've got our heels inches deep in inflation. The CSA, I mean." Pratchit's blue eyes were somber as he swished his tobacco around under his bottom lip.

Hayden shook his head and cursed, raising his rifle and squinting down the barrel. "I'd be damned if that's not already obvious."

Removing his spectacles and cleaning the lenses on his shirt sleeve, Harold exhaled, a frown etching itself into his weathered face. Ezra couldn't help but notice the weariness in his brother's eyes. Putting up with Hayden and Pratchit's political remarks was far from enjoyable, and Hayden's filthy language was downright tedious. He was like a misbehaving schoolboy who never got a lesson in proper etiquette.

"I reckon that's enough squabble for the night." Harold's back hunched and his eyes sagged. On an evening of higher morale Ezra knew he might've attempted a discussion with these wayward fellows, try to talk some sense into them. More importantly, get them thinking about their salvation.

But that would have to wait another day.

Chapter Four

June 19th, 1863

ZEPHYR

"I HATE DREAMS."

Zephyr groaned, slowly pushing herself up to a sitting position in her bed. She placed a hand over her sweaty forehead and let out a long sigh.

A face lingered in her mind. Haunting brown eyes. A paradoxical half-grin.

Falling back onto the lumpy mattress, Zephyr gazed absentmindedly at the tin ceiling. How she wished she could forget those eyes. They were beautiful, in a tragic sort of way. Somehow, they spoke volumes, but Zephyr couldn't figure out what it was those volumes meant.

Eyes like those could only belong to one person.

"Who'd you dream about, Zeph? Somebody special?"

Lydia's taunting voice reached Zephyr's ears, interrupting her bittersweet thought processes.

The young woman rolled her eyes, ignoring the little imp lying next to her. She kicked the damp, thin sheets off her legs and continued to stare vacantly at the roof.

"Why does it have to be so stinkin' hot all the time?" she complained, trying to find some way to distract the girl from talk of her awkward dream.

Lydia flapped her chemise up and down, trying to get the still, heavy air moving against her skin. "Don't ask me. *I* never asked to live down here in this oven. Northern folks get it so easy."

"I bet it's going to rain," Zephyr grumbled, feeling sweat beads roll down her neck. She willed her sluggish body to rise. On days like this even the notion of sleeping in was ruined. It was still dark out, but the humidity was overbearing. The small bed the girls shared was unpleasantly wet from the moisture in the atmosphere, and the lack of air between the walls was stifling.

"So who'd you dream about?"

Zephyr's shoulders slumped as another voice broke the silence. A long sigh escaped her lungs.

Not Clarence, too. She beamed a hostile look across the room where her brothers' two beds were.

Clarence shrugged at her sleepily. "What?"

"Enough about the dream."

With an air of conclusiveness, Zephyr pointed a finger at her siblings and pretended to speak in an English accent. "Time to get up, children!"

"Who you callin' *children*?" Clarence rebutted, reluctantly pulling himself out of bed.

Zephyr unbraided and brushed her long, auburn hair, standing near the open window, looking out at the dark, gray sky looming above. A thunderstorm was certainly on the horizon, which would be good for the crops, as long as it didn't last more than a day.

After rebraiding her waist-length tresses, Zephyr tied the ends with a piece of string and let the braid fall down her back. She tossed a glance in her brothers' direction. "Well, what are y'all sitting there for? Up, up! There's work to be done!"

Lydia muttered something incomprehensible, curling into a fetal position.

Rudy was half-naked, pulling pants on his bony legs. Royce tugged on Clarence because the adolescent boy was still sprawled out in bed.

"Clarence! We'll be behind on the chores if you don't get your carcass out of bed!" Zephyr ordered, trying not to wince as she noticed Rudy's dressing skills.

"Rudy, for goodness sake, put your trousers on right for once! And I don't mean backwards – yes, that's right, put them on the normal way. Good."

Boys. Zephyr shook her head in amazement.

As to her own attire, she'd just wear what she'd worn yesterday. Chemise, corset, and cotton wash dress, with a single petticoat underneath the skirt. Work around the farm didn't require anything fancy.

She padded across the wooden floor, throwing Lydia another threatening glare. The girl ignored it.

Fine.

Zephyr exited the modest room and walked briskly into the hall. It was still fairly dark out, and she stubbed her toe against the doorframe, forcing her to limp through the main living quarters. A gentle drumming made her look to the windows again, and in the dimness she saw raindrops.

Thud, thud, thud, *thud,* thud, *thud.* Each drop was amplified as it hit the tin roof.

The aroma of oatmeal cooking brushed Zephyr's nostrils as she dodged raindrops and ducked into the kitchen.

"Good morning, Zephyr!" Mrs. Darson greeted her daughter cheerfully as she stirred a pot over the stove.

Zephyr forced a grin in response and sluggishly looked around the little kitchen. Boxes of tomatoes littered the countertops, reminding her that today all those nasty red things needed to be canned and stowed in the cellar. That would take a good chunk of the day. Delightful.

Mrs. Darson pointed toward two empty milk pails sitting besides the tomatoes.

"The McIntoshes are exchanging seed with us for milk again, so I need you to go take it to them, as soon as you eat."

Zephyr's eyes widened slightly at the mention of the McIntoshes. She nodded, snatching the pails.

Running from the little room, Zephyr found a knot working its way up her throat. A sudden giddiness came over her as she dashed to the front door to throw on some boots.

A trip to the McIntoshes would be no great excursion, if it weren't for one thing.

One *person.*

Haunting brown eyes.

Zephyr's heart skipped a beat. What if Silas came to the door when she showed up at his family's homestead?

The girl's mind buzzed with concerns and worries. *Perhaps I should change my dress? Maybe just fix my hair up a bit better instead. After all, it's just a Monday. Certainly no cause for dressing up,* she mulled over. *But then again…*

It *was* rather silly of her to make a decision based off of what one man might think.

Oh, but this one isn't like the rest. Zephyr swallowed, wishing her heart would stop pounding so heavily.

After retrieving her old black work boots she hurried to the barn to milk the cow and goats. The barn smelled of wet hay, mud, and animal manure. Zephyr let herself into the structure and immediately set to work, squeezing udders.

Flies buzzed in her ears, and mosquitoes hovered over her skin. She swatted a few away in annoyance. At least the sun was up now, providing some light to work by.

The young woman closed her eyes, continuing to squeeze methodically, offering a silent petition to the Creator.

Father, please help me to do what you would have me do. Thank you for this new day. Please help me to use it wisely. Also, please help me to be kind and exercise patience with my brothers, and Lydia. Protect Pa, wherever he is.

Zephyr strained the milk and secured lids on the pails. Then, she tossed a patty of hay into the cow's stall and threw some scraps to the goats.

Finally, the young woman turned to Daphne, a sleek brown Morgan horse. Her main purpose was to draw the Darsons' wagon, but she was also a great help in pulling the tiller when it was time for a new garden plot, and the mowing machine when the rye grass got tall enough for hay. And now, Zephyr would utilize her for quick transportation to the McIntoshes.

Coaxing the horse out of the barn and into the rain, Zephyr picked up the milk pails, stopping Daphne for a moment to secure them in the saddlebag. Then she reached her arm around, grabbed the saddle, and swung her leg over. It wasn't very ladylike to ride that way, but since nobody ever passed her out on the road it wouldn't matter.

She prodded the horse a little, and the animal trotted along in her even, steady, Morgan way.

Zephyr barely noticed as the rain fell more heavily. Her mind was overcome with a deluge of its own. Flashbacks from the encounter with Anson. All the things she wished she could ask Silas. Endless theological questions. Was hell located at the center of the earth, or somewhere out in ungraspable space? What about the human soul– did it become thus during conception or earlier? Oh, and what would she cook for dinner that evening?

Zephyr's mind was a mess. But she didn't bore easily, and maybe that was why.

The McIntosh farm wasn't too far away, only about three miles. Before she knew it, Zephyr found herself arriving at their front gate.

Here goes.

The girl wiped her wet forehead against her rolled-up sleeve, jumped down to open the gate and tied Daphne to a fencepost.

Looking about herself, she glanced curiously at the weed-infested garden and tall, wild looking grass that'd grown up nearly to her waist. There was still an old, worn path through the jungle-like turf, but anyone venturing in or out of the house would have to be on the lookout for snakes hiding in the brush. Zephyr thought of how Pa would've had this place tidy the first day it got out of hand- though he'd never let it get out of hand to begin with.

It seemed to take a long while to reach the little log cabin with its slanted roofs and pipe chimney. Zephyr straightened her parted hair as she ascended the front steps. Holding the milk pails firmly, she knocked on the damp cypress wood door.

Trying to compose herself, she rocked back and forth on her heels. Finally she heard a series of footsteps echoing across the wooden floor, and the creaky doorknob turned. The door swung open to reveal a dark-haired fellow Zephyr's age.

He peered out at her, still gripping the doorknob.

It was Silas.

Zephyr's mouth went dry and she had to force herself not to stare at him. Her heart whammed inside her chest; and she felt as though a thousand pounds rested on her diaphragm. To top it off, the sudden force of her heartbeat felt as if it was pulling her back and forth with each thump. She despised the feeling, yet it excited her at the same time. She tried to swallow the oppressive reaction and speak.

Get a hold of yourself, silly girl.

"He- hello." *Drat this person that I am!* The girl scolded herself. She swallowed pasted on the best smile she could.

Silas nodded, replying rather shyly, "Hello."

For a moment, the two shared eye contact. Then Silas broke his enigmatic gaze away, just as Zephyr did the same. Another reflex she'd found herself with; whenever around this young man.

"I-I'm here to give y'all your milk. Two, uh, two gallons...your father said you had, uh, some seeds..." She clumsily handed him the pails. A wave of self-consciousness caused her cheeks to flush bright pink.

"Yeah, I'll go get them now." Silas took the pails and stepped back into the house.

Zephyr's heart sank. Why did she feel so drawn to him? What was so amazing about him that he could affect her speech patterns and make her feel so discombobulated? He might as well have been a stranger, for the little she knew about him.

You're being ridiculous, you know that?

I know, but what am I to do about it?

He was back. Zephyr's eyes jerked up, her heart pounding as hard as it possibly could.

He's looking at me. I'm looking at him. What on earth are we doing?

The haunting brown eyes were staring into hers. Not a word came from his lips- or hers, for that matter. The two just stared at each other.

Maybe it was just her imagination, but Zephyr thought she saw a hint of remorse in those deep, reclusive eyes. They didn't laugh or sparkle. They were like an amber maze of crystal, both beautiful and confusing at the same time.

Zephyr felt a prick of pain seize her heart - Silas' eyes were purging into her soul, as if searching her thoughts. Gripping her heartstrings with a subtle fierceness that no other gaze could equal, something in that look made Zephyr wonder if... just maybe...

Naw, it couldn't be that. She was allowing herself to be too hopeful.

The young man coughed and handed her a small paper bag, while looking off into the distance.

Was it really that hard for him to sustain eye contact with her? Of course, she was no better. For some reason, whenever they locked gazes, she eventually had to look away just as he did the same. She couldn't help it. Sharing eye contact with Silas McIntosh was one of the most exhilarating things in the world - but also one of the most traumatizing.

"Thank you." Zephyr forced her lips to curl into an awkward smile, still very aware of her flushed cheeks.

"Nothing of it."

Zephyr exhaled through her nose. She couldn't think of anything else to say that would fit the moment, even though she longed to fill the silence with conversation. Awkwardness was choking out her line of thought, and her mind had become as clouded as the ominous sky above.

It was time to go.

"Well, I guess I should leave…I mean, I need to get going." Zephyr couldn't hide the tinge of reluctance in her voice. She found her hands fidgeting with the seed packet. She dropped her gaze, biting the inside of her lip, and then glanced back up at the boy who was easily four inches taller than she.

Silas met her gaze. His eyes looked into hers a second more, a second which seemed to last an eternity. Zephyr merely stared back, powerless against the force that was causing her to do so.

And then, quick as it had come, that wonderful yet paradoxical second was over.

Silas gave a quick nod and stepped back inside the house. "So long."

"So long," Zephyr echoed.

The door closed. Feeling as if she would explode, Zephyr turned and descended the steps to the walkway, never looking behind her.

Now the walkway didn't seem so long any more. The girl barely noticed that the rain had stopped or that the humidity had increased. She didn't notice the beads of wetness collecting on Daphne's coat or the thunder rolling in the distance.

If this had been a dream, it would've been another lousy one. Only unlike many of Zephyr's dreams, this didn't paint a picture of unrealistic optimism.

Was Silas a fellow believer? What was the story with his elderly parents? Did he have any siblings? Did he enjoy making music–playing piano–as Zephyr did?

The endless questions barraged Zephyr's mind. She ached to be around Silas, and was equally pained to be in his presence. The girl sighed. Sometimes it was hard to keep all the ponderings trapped in her head, the suspense and curiosity piled high within. And knowing that she was so transparent, it wouldn't stay trapped in there for long. She had to vent to someone–the key was to not vent to the wrong person.

Was it too much to wish for a decent, normal conversation with Silas McIntosh? Was it improper to plead for more than a few awkward words and broken sentences?

Pull yourself together and stop being so stupid. Why on earth did you have to let yourself fall for a total stranger?

Zephyr tried to shake the matter out of her mind. What a futile effort.

But, he's not a stranger.

She stuffed the paper bag into her skirt pocket to protect it from the rain.

It doesn't matter, because you know absolutely nothing about him. He's just a business acquaintance. And besides, you know it's not decent for a girl to initiate a courtship…

Zephyr groaned, weary of her internal conversations. The bottom line was this matter didn't merit spending so much thought and energy over.

And yet, deeming it all as innocent curiosity didn't suffice either. This wasn't a subject that could be shrugged off, as much as she wished that were possible.

What if things were to change though? What if, one day, Silas removed his shroud of clammy reclusiveness and somehow…?

Silly girl. What ifs are dangerous things, and you know that. Stop fantasizing. You don't want to disappoint Ma by being late to finish your work.

Zephyr blinked as rain dripped from her hair into her eyes. She bit her lip, her body tensing.

It was all so trifling, so silly. Silly optimism, silly dreams–silly, selfish notions.

And if there was one thing Zephyr didn't have time for, it was silliness.

Chapter Five

June 24th, 1863

EZRA

EZRA SIGHED AS HE TRUDGED back through the woods to the camp.
God, I'm so tired of this whole mess.

This last month had been simply the pits.

Ezra wondered how much lower the morale of the entire camp could drop. Nothing was happening. Boredom and idleness had swallowed the entire army, and it didn't look like things would be changing any time soon.

How he got immersed in the complaints of the others, he didn't know. He was just having a hard time finding any reason to stay in this hole. That was all there was to say.

The Army of Tennessee had engaged in a campaign to Kentucky and back last year, and then on the seventh of June, there had been a skirmish in Knoxville. But now, they were doing nothing but sitting around chewing tobacco. Between three regiments, at least forty men had died last fall from various illnesses. Now that another season of mosquitoes had come, everyone was in fear of catching malaria—one of the most notorious diseases of the south. Diarrhea and dysentery were also a major concern.

Ezra looked down at his dust-covered boots as he plodded on. *When would it all end?*

Voices reached his ears, and he looked up to see the camp ahead. A spirit of oppression seemed to engulf the congregation. Ezra wished he could get as far away from the scummy place as he could.

If wishes were horses...

He trudged through the stench-ridden place, feeling the energy sucked from him with every step.

Several fellows nodded gravely to him as he passed them sitting around their tents. Each set of eyes seemed to share in his weariness.

This army is full of people, but none of them are alive.

A young boy caught Ezra's attention.

The kid couldn't have been any more than thirteen, if even that. His dirt-covered, childish face portrayed a mixture of emotions. In his hand were a book and a quill pen. His small frame was propped against a tree, his legs crossed Indian-style in the dirt.

Curiously, Ezra ventured towards the lad.

As he watched the boy, Ezra wondered how such a young fellow had ever gotten here in the first place. He knew of at least fifteen enlisted boys who were fifteen or sixteen, but a twelve or thirteen-year-old?

He shook his head. Who in the world approved these enlistees? Had he been blind?

Insanity. It was plain insanity.

The boy looked up then. His blue eyes pierced Ezra's as the two stared at each other.

Ezra raised a hand in greeting and smiled.

"Hullo."

The youngster gave a slight nod in response. He didn't return the smile.

"I don't reckon I've seen you around the camp before." Ezra's gaze softened. "Where'd you enlist?"

"Jacksonvul." The boy's response was quiet.

Ezra studied him placidly. "What's your name?"

"Frances J. Cranston." He spoke the words with perfect enunciation, despite his heavy southern accent.

"Well, I'm Ezra Darson. Good to meet ya, Frances." Ezra extended his hand.

Frances stood clumsily and looked at Ezra's outstretched hand. Finally, he seemed to realize what to do, and stuck his own hand in Ezra's, pumping it up and down awkwardly.

The two stood there for a moment, analyzing each other. Finally, Ezra cut through the silence. "So where you from?"

Frances looked down at the earth beneath his bare feet. "Oh, well, uh, Jacksonvul…that's whar I guess we was closest to." He blinked his hazy-blue eyes and swatted at some buzzing mosquitoes. Suspicion...along with an unidentifiable emotion lingered in his gaze.

Ezra wondered what the skinny boy's story was. Did he run away from his parents, looking for adventure, and a relief from the doldrums of everyday life?

"Well, Frances, it was good to meet you. I'd like to talk to ya again sometime, hear more 'bout your family and all." He smiled. "—But now ain't the time. Drills in ten minutes, now, ya hear?"

Frances nodded. He gave a small smile and turned back to his book, pen, and Pokeberry ink.

Ezra watched for a few more seconds, but turned to head towards his and Harry's tent after Frances pulled the book closer to him so that Ezra couldn't see what was inside.

Frances J. Cranston. Ezra's brow furrowed. This boy didn't belong here. Not in such a grisly, wretched place. He was surely the youngest in the camp, and the thought of him going into actual combat...

Harry was talking to some of the men when Ezra found him. Drills were to start soon.

Drills. Something to do, at least, but Ezra already looked forward to the end with a fair amount of anticipation. Six hours of marching wore a fellow out. And it was the same thing, every single day. That was the most tiresome aspect of all.

Ezra hated so much about this camp. He didn't like to dwell on it, but he was growing less and less fond of the place each day.

Every day, he anticipated the end of this war more than he had the day before. And every day, he anticipated the time when he could return to a normal life. He knew the real heaven would be much better by far, but right now, the closest thing to it seemed like going back home and being done with this whole blasted war.

Harold's baritone reached Ezra's ears. "I'd ask you about your excursion to town, but we best be commencing onto the next task so nothin's out of order."

Ezra willed himself to nod. Inside, he groaned.

The sun beat down. It was directly over the camp, and Ezra swore it felt like it was a hundred and fifteen degrees out. His cotton shirt was thoroughly soaked in sweat, and his hair was sticky and wet as well. Not an uncommon thing. Though Ezra's body had been conditioned to this climate long ago, it was no less grueling.

Gonna be another long day.

***

Ezra's body ached as he bent next to the camp's make-shift well. His arm muscles twitched in soreness as he pulled the water bucket up the dark shaft. An hour or so after drills, some of the men got the idea that they wanted to play a game of ball. Somehow, they managed to convince Ezra to join them since he wasn't half bad at the sport.

They had played a full nine innings and Ezra had busted up his knee when diving on the hard ground to make a catch. He wondered why in the world he had ever consented to playing in the first place.

Groaning, he lugged the full bucket back. He watched longingly as some of the cool water splashed over the side.

A bath would be amazing right now.

Baths were hard to come by, and with the restraint on water use…Ezra was going on four weeks without a good washing.

It couldn't happen tonight, however. It'd have to wait a little longer.

He neared the camp. Fires were burning to ward off mosquitoes and to lend a bit of light in the thick darkness.

Ezra liked the sound of their crackling flames. They didn't help much with the rank stench that choked the air, but the sight of the flickering fires was halfway pleasant.

As he plodded through the camp, he looked around at the little groups that had formed around each fire. Some of the fellas were playing cards and gambling, others were talking. Some slept, others wrote letters or sang songs.

It was nice to see smiles when there were so many frowns abounding throughout the day.

Ezra wondered out of the blue where Frances was and what the boy was doing.

Still don't even know his age.

Ezra's pressed his lips together. A heavy feeling settled on his heart. He didn't know what it was coming from, but it was certainly there. Something about Frances tugged at him. He determined that he would find a way to learn more about the boy.

He wasn't far from his and Harold's tent when he saw a circle of men and boys sitting around the dwelling, with Harry in the middle. How could he have forgotten? It was time for chapel, as it was each night at six forty-five.

Ezra sat down nearby. He wanted to hear what his brother would talk about, but he also didn't want to mingle any more with the soldiers. He wasn't a preacher or an evangelist.

Then again, he had never tried either, so how could he know?

"Fellas, if any of you were to die tonight, where would you go? That is the question, brothers, because your whole eternity rests on your answer." Harry looked around at the men and boys.

"Ephesians 2:8 says that Christ's gift of salvation isn't bought through anything we can do on our own. To get to heaven, all you need to do is believe. You see, with hell, it's not because of anything you *do* that earns you a place there. It's what you *don't* do. And what might that be? *Not* accepting Christ as your Lord." Harry's eyes were deep, portraying a genuine care for each of the men's' souls.

Ezra wondered if the men were paying heed to what he was saying. Looking around at their tired faces, it was hard to tell. Ezra exhaled, resting his chin on his hand, propping his arm against his knee. He felt somewhat guilty for not trying to spread the gospel like his brother was. But speaking to people didn't come naturally to him. And perhaps he was just lazy. To be honest, he didn't feel strongly enough about his own beliefs to try spreading them to others.

His thoughts wandered back to the day's misfortunate events. More specifically, the incident which had occurred that morning in town.

How could such a tangle happen over one little thing? All he'd wanted to do was walk to the trading post to indulge in a change of scenery. It hadn't taken much to acquire a pass from Colonel Bullock.

A terrified Negro woman was on the ground, trying to retrieve a number of fresh tomatoes from off the pathway.

Ezra remembered her face. He knew as well as she did that tomatoes bruised easily, and that bruised tomatoes never sold decent. These tomatoes would have to have their prices reduced to half of what they could have been. The poor slave obviously knew she would pay for that.

While she still was trying to pick up the tomatoes, Ezra watched as a stout, short man, the store owner, came to the open door. He stared down at the woman, his eyes wide and his face red.

"Ada! What in tarnation did you do, you b---?"

Ada looked up at him, tears swelling in her eyes. Sheer terror was written all over her face. Not a word came from her trembling lips. She quickly got up and brushed off the last tomato, dropping her gaze to the ground.

Ezra walked by her slowly, up the steps of the store. He didn't make eye contact with the store owner. Resentment had already crept into his veins. This man smelt of nothing but trouble.

Walking further into the building, Ezra looked around at the goods for sale. He tried to push the woman's fear-stricken eyes out of his mind. But as he wandered, he couldn't help but listen to the events taking place outside. His insides churned.

He pretended to look at the new bolsters.

Then there were shrieks. The woman spoke no words, but that didn't mean she couldn't scream.

Ezra grinded his teeth.

It sounded like the man was killing her. Ezra didn't want to know what exactly he was doing, but he could tell by the yelling and curses that he wasn't a gracious master.

Ezra's heartbeat increased, as his fists clenched. He wanted to do something, but what could he do? Technically, that woman was only a piece of property, as much as Ezra hated to admit it, and her master could do whatever he wanted to her. Ezra's intruding couldn't change that.

Finally, the wails and cries stopped, and all Ezra could hear was faint whimpering.

Then it was quiet.

Ezra turned to look loathingly out the door and saw that the street was empty.

Footsteps echoed across the room, and Ezra looked up, steely-eyed.

It was the store-owner.

You sure have a thing coming to you, mister.

"G'day sir! What can I do ya for?" The plump man nodded to Ezra as if nothing ever happened.

"That... depends."

The man took a handkerchief from his pocket and wiped his bald forehead with it. "Well, don't idle 'bout, mister. Tell me what yer hankerin' for an' I'll get it." He turned and started opening crates behind the counter.

Ezra's jaw tightened.

"What's your name?" He glowered at the man's flabby back.

"George Hallison." He didn't look up from his work.

"Mr. Hallison, do you mind me askin' you something?"

Hallison still didn't look up. Whatever unpacking he was doing must've been awful important. "Why not? You got mah full attention."

I will, when you hear what I got to say.

Ezra took several steps away from the counter, toward the door. He clasped his hands behind his back, and turned around, looking at Hallison.

"Mr. Hallison, I'm not one to pry into people's business, neither do I advocate being a busybody, so ya understand. But...perhaps this is an exception."

Now this got the fat man's attention. Hallison looked up, eying Ezra suspiciously. "What's an exception?"

Ezra continued to look the storeowner in the eye. "I saw how you treated that slave of yours. You oughta know, that wasn't no way to treat a woman. No gentleman talks to a female like that and... and...that's just no way to treat anybody."

Hallison's face had was nearly as red as his tomatoes. "What's your name?"

Ezra crossed his muscular arms on his chest, tilting his head back slightly. "Ezra Darson."

"Look, Darson." Hallison swallowed. "Maybe this *shouldn't* be an exception. Maybe you ought to just mind your own damned business. You think you can just waltz in here with your shabby little army situation and tell me what to do? And that there piece of trash you just saw?" Hallison shook his head, fuming. "*Where'd you even think to get the likes, cracker?*"

His hands pounded onto the counter and he leaned across it, glaring at Ezra.

"I got the likes because I'm a man that don't like seein' a woman get-"

"She's my *property*. I can't afford to have a bunch of blundering klutzes workin' my fields and takin' care o' my crops. If you owned anything, you'd understand the same."

"Just 'cause she's a different color than you don't mean she ain't human." Ezra glared back.

Hallison leaned further towards Ezra. For a moment, he continued to glower. Then he smirked and broke into a sardonic laugh. "Oh, Darson, you really believe that? Good lawd. You really believe them people is... on equals with *us*? Where'd you even come from, anyway?"

Hallison chortled, slapping the counter. "It seems you're more radical than I naturally thought, boy. But anyway, it don't matter. You shore 'nuff sound like a piece of abolitionist s---just now, fella."

He smirked, reaching into one of his pant pockets and bringing out a small paper bag. He grabbed a handful of tobacco leaves from it, stuffed them inside a pipe, then struck a match and held it to the pipe.

"Oh, and," He blew out the match, sticking the pipe in his mouth. "...if you wanna keep your brains inside that abolitionist head of yours, you best head back to your camp and preach your little sermons to them fellow soldiers of yours instead. I don't have time to listen to any more of this bulls--- and if you stick your ignorant self around here much longer, I just might be liable to get violent." He gestured toward the open door.

Ten greenbacks says I could get a whole lot more violent.

Expletives ran through Ezra's mind and his flesh tugged on him, urging him to drag the man outside and beat him to a pulp. But he just stood there, his fists clenched, face hot and crimson-colored.

"Well? Ya heard me. I don't serve your kind here. Skee-daddle!" Hallison waved a chubby hand through the air.

Ezra swallowed and tried to extinguish the hate smothering his insides. He gritted his teeth.

"God's watchin', Hallison, don't you forget that."

With a final glower, Ezra turned and strode out of the store without looking back. He rubbed his hands on his pants, noticing how clammy they'd become.

Ezra's cheeks felt as if they were on fire. He dug his fingernails into his palms.

"Ezra? Ezra!"

Ezra looked up to see Harold standing over him.

Harold looked down at his younger brother. "What's ailin' you? I saw ya sit down over here 'bout an hour ago, and then I glanced over later and it looked like you'd fallen asleep. Now you're redder than a tomato." Harold walked back towards his and Ezra's tent.

"A tomato…" Ezra grimaced. He got up and paced quickly to catch up with his brother.

Harry's skin wrinkled around his eyes, and his shoulders slumped. The balding man stretched his arms and groaned. "I'm certainly not as young as *I* used to be."

"You're hangin' in there better than the lot of us."

Harold's eyes looked glazed and distant. "No brother, God knows I'm as weary as anyone else. If there's one thing we all need, it's some affirmation. It's about time somethin' happened in these parts. Somethin' other than a little tussle." He shook his head, his knees popping loudly as he sat down on the ground in front of the fire. "I fear the morale is worse than it's ever been."

Ezra's soul groaned as he seated himself. What could he say in response to such a grim statement?

His mind was too tired to formulate an answer, so he just stared silently into the flames.

Chapter Six

June 25th, 1863

ZEPHYR

THE LAST RAYS OF SUNSHINE slipped into the west, sinking below the treetops.

Clarence lit an oil lamp in the living room, while Mrs. Darson, Zephyr, and Lydia worked in the kitchen, preparing dinner.

Zephyr tapped her fingernails on the side of the woodstove, absentmindedly stirring a pot of boiling beans. Music overflowed from her soul, filling her mind. Her fingers itched to tickle a set of ivories.

She'd gotten hardly any practice at the piano all week, and desperately hoped to get a few minutes in before the evening meal. Even if she could play just *one* song. *Something.*

Her eyes darted restlessly around the small kitchen, as her mother chopped tomatoes and Lydia put away dishes.

"Zephyr, I need you to go see how the boys are faring. They need to be cleaning the main room."

Zephyr sighed a little but nodded, trying to be respectful. Maybe there would be a smidgen of extra time, if that was all she had to do.

"Then come back here and clean up the mess you made earlier fixing the mid-day meal, and then go check the animals' food and water."

"I thought it was Clarence's job to check the animals?" Zephyr's jaw tightened.

Ma's mouth had formed a straight line.

Zephyr bit her tongue to keep her mouth shut. Besides, maybe if she hurried, she could still manage a few phrases on the piano.

As soon as Ma had gone to take plates inside the house, Zephyr looked critically over at Lydia who was hunched in the corner, reading a book. What Ma would've said if she'd caught her reading on the job.

"Lydia!" She scorned, "what are you doing?"

Lydia didn't look up.

"That's just plain lazy, you know that?"

Lydia didn't answer. She was obviously enjoying her little novella a bit too much. *Fine.* Zephyr sighed. She didn't have the energy to try and control the troublesome girl.

Why couldn't there be just a little time away from the dishes, cleaning up messes and taking care of animals? Why couldn't that all be put aside for a minute? Oh, just to play one song. One song! Zephyr stared longingly at the old upright as she passed it, headed to find the twins and Lemuel.

She entered the bedroom only to find Rudy and Royce in a squabble.

"Royce, you're s'posed to do this pile over here! I'm not pickin' up your shoes."

"Well Ma said you had ta do this side too! You gotta pick up it all and I'm not doin' it!"

Zephyr interrupted the scene. "What's the matter here?"

Both twins piped up, yelling over each other.

"Wait!" Zephyr held up her hands. "Hold on. I can't hear anything when you both are talkin' at the same time. Now, Royce, you first."

The little boy looked up at his older sister, a determined look on his slender face. "Rudy's tryin to make me clean up his stuff, and Ma said ya only have to clean up whatcha got out, so I'm not cleanin up his stuff! Ma said I don't have ta!"

Rudy's eyes narrowed. "That's not true. Sh' said ta clean up a side a' the room each!"

Zephyr placed a hand on one hip. "Alright, listen. It sounds like Ma wanted you to pick up what's yours, and that should take care of everything. So Rudy, you clean up your stuff, and Royce, you do yours. I don't want to hear anythin' more about it."

Neither looked very happy, but oh well. That was just how things had to go.

It was now after six-thirty. Zephyr hurried to feed the animals and barely kept from slamming the front door as she ran back.

She sighed in relief, settling onto the wooden piano bench.

Finally. There can't possibly be anything else to do.

The girl looked over her shoulder to see where Ma was—probably still in the kitchen.

Zephyr picked up a thick Chopin book and flipped through its pages, eyeing each piece longingly. It was the only sheet music she owned, and she couldn't read a page of it. She was blessed to have a piano at all, really. Most folks around these parts didn't.

Zephyr set the book aside again and stared down at the keys in determination. She promised herself that one day, she would master this instrument, and use it to point people to the Creator. Already she could play many songs without sheet music. But if she could read that too...

A shiver flew down her spine. She'd heard that Chopin's works were phenomenal, but she'd only had the chance to hear one piece for herself. It was one of his many waltzes, and possibly the most brilliant music Zephyr had ever heard. The idea of getting to *play* something so rich and beautiful was exhilarating.

"Time to eat! Everyone head to the table!"

She brushed her fingers over the keys, preparing to play the first note of Jesu, Joy of Man's Desiring.

"Time to eat! Everyone head to the table!"

Zephyr's heart crashed down to the piano pedals.

Really.

She grumbled and got up from the bench, looking wistfully at the piano one last time. Shuffling over to the table, where most of the family was now, she tried not to display too much annoyance.

"Boy, you should have seen Darcy chasin' Winnie today." Lydia looked over at Clarence as she gave herself a generous serving of corn and beans. "My word, is he after that girl!"

Clarence looked up at his sister. "Whaddya mean? I thought he wasn't allowed."

"Well, Zephyr could tell you all about it, she was there too. Ain't that right, Zeph?"

Zephyr stuck a forkful of beans in her mouth and rolled her eyes.

"What were you tellin' Clarence about?"

Lydia tossed her head to one side, and cast a sideways glace at her sister. "Oh, just today's happenings, that's all. Which, by the way, you did see yourself."

Zephyr swallowed a gulp of water. "Quit confusin' me. I thought I heard ya talkin' about Winnie and Darcy."

"Zeph, can I have some mo' corn?"

Rudy stuck his plate in front of Zephyr's face.

"What! Rudy, don't you be telllin' me you're done already." The girl's eyes widened, then they rolled back into her head as she emitted a tired sigh. "How is that possible? You just started five minutes ago!"

The boy shrugged and looked up at her hopefully.

"No, I don't think so, Rudy. Just wait a little. Let your dinner go down before you put some more in, for goodness sakes!" Zephyr shook her head, pushing the plate away.

"Zeph-errr," Rudy protested, with a disapproving look in his blue-green eyes.

Footsteps echoed across the wooden floor, and all eyes flew up to see their mother approaching. Mrs. Darson looked around the table at her children, and finally her gaze rested on Zephyr.

"Is everyone served, Zephyr? Did you make sure everyone has what they need?"

Zephyr cast an icy stare at Rudy, who was just about to pipe up again about his want for more corn. "Yes, Ma, have you gotten yourself a plate yet?"

"Only just now, dear, been in the kitchen this whole time you know." Mrs. Darson fixed Zephyr with a look that said "You know very well one can't serve oneself when serving the others."

Zephyr's eyes fell to her plate and she ate quietly for a while after that. She was too steamed right now to socialize. Her previous frustration was festering by the minute, and now she was turning into a human tea kettle again.

Pipe down, Zephyr. Stop being dramatic.

It was childlike to hold it in like this, or even to posses the feeling at all.

She needed to stop thinking so much about herself and what *she* wanted. The more she focused on that and the things she didn't like in those around her, the tenser she felt. But that was the thing. She knew what she was supposed to do. She just didn't want to do it.

"Alright now, who'd like to tell me what happened today while y'all were out? I've been hearin' some tales going around and you have me wondering what's been going about in the world. Y'all went to the Faircloths again I know, and the McIntoshs' too, but that's just about all you girls told me about."

Mrs. Darson looked around the table at her children, and they in return met her glance as it fell on each of them.

"Zephyr, what's wrong? You look rather red. It's not every day that you're this quiet."

Zephyr shrugged. She pasted a blank expression across her visage...or at least attempted to do so. It wasn't really working. She was awful at poker-faces.

"Oh, it's nothin'. I suppose it was a pretty good day." She jabbed at a stray bean with her fork, biting her lip.

She could have answered a thousand different ways, but ironically, nothing seemed worth saying right then.

Besides, nobody was really listening anyways. The little boys chattered amongst themselves like crows, Clarence was telling Ma about the large catfish he'd sighted in the swamp, and Lydia was aimlessly poking her fork at the remains of her supper.

Zephyr exhaled, a wall going up in her mind- a tall, thick wall that separated her from the rest of the family. She didn't really want it there, but somehow the bricks had placed themselves and she made no effort to destroy them. She allowed her mind to drift away, in a mellow fog of blurred colors as she slowly tuned out the noise.

After supper, Mrs. Darson brought out an old hymnal and placed it open on the table. "I think we ought to sing something. Which song shall we do first?"

"Nearer my God to Thee!" Royce called out.

"The Battle Hymn of the Republic." Clarence advocated.

"No, Jesus Loves Me!" Rudy argued.

Lemuel piped up amongst the loud proposals, "Wut a fwend we have n' Jesus!"

Zephyr smiled. Even five-year-olds could have strong opinions when it came to hymns.

"No, no, I've got one," Lydia raised her hand, and all eyes turned to her. "Lorena! Why not *Lorena*?"

She snickered as a look of disapproval crossed the faces of Ma and Zephyr. Clarence tried to hold back a giggle, and the little boys, not knowing what their older sister was talking about, just stared at the girl.

"Lydia, that's a war tune for goodness sakes." Zephyr stared at her sister in disbelief.

Lydia shrugged. "Well, didn't Pa write about such things at one point? I thought he said some fellas were singing those kind a' songs. I don't see what's wrong with it, why, it's just a love song!"

"Love songs like that aren't praises to God." Zephyr shook her head.

"But I thought *God* was all about love?"

Mrs. Darson flipped through the hymnbook, seemingly unfazed by the argument. Then she looked up at Lydia soberly. "We're not gathered here to sing songs the soldiers sing. They are the songs of lonely men who'd rather turn to physical charm instead of grace and virtue, which is *true* beauty."

Lydia grumbled something inaudible, turning her gaze away with a huff.

"Anyways, if you want a true love song, plenty of these here hymns fit that category just perfectly, because they talk of the Lord's love. What better love can be spoken of than His?"

There were a few moments of silence, and then Ma concluded, "Well, now that that's settled, I think we'll do Lemuel's choice."

Zephyr enjoyed offering praise to her Creator and Savior. Singing together as a family somehow made her feel united and safe.

It was as if they were all holding hands in a big circle, tight and together even though the world raged and dashed itself to pieces— along with Zephyr's own heart and mind.

But all too soon it was over.

After cleaning the kitchen, Zephyr wrote a few words in her journal. It was the only place where she could vent whatever pressed on her soul.

Upon saying goodnight to her mother, she retired to the children's bedroom and felt her way to one of the boy's cots.

In the darkness, she made out the faces of her younger brothers. She leaned down and kissed Rudy on the cheek, then did the same with Royce, Lemuel and even Clarence—although he didn't enjoy it to say in the least.

Royce yawned. "Can you tell us a story?"

Every muscle in Zephyr's body ached, demanding rest. "Not tonight, Royce, I'm too tired. Maybe tomorrow?" She climbed into bed beside Lydia and slid her legs beneath the covers.

"Alright."

A disappointed answer reached Zephyr's ears, and guilt thickened in her gut.

Was she being selfish again? She knew the boys were growing up (as was she) and before long, they'd not be asking for any more stories. A knot twisted in her stomach, burdening her heart.

No. It's late, and Ma would want them to be settling down. They need their sleep, and so do I.

She reasoned until the guilty thoughts vanished gradually from her mind.

Outside, all was dark, nearly pitch black. Silence engulfed the muggy summer air, except for the occasional hooting of an owl, and the chorus of locusts singing.

The young woman squirmed about, trying to get her sweaty body comfortable. There wasn't really a need for any covers, but a thin cotton sheet helped keep the bugs out of one's face.

She felt a jab in her arm. Lydia was wriggling around, and every time she moved she shook the whole bed and elbowed Zephyr.

Zephyr huffed, annoyed but too exhausted to give it any thought. "Could you settle down already?" She mumbled.

Lydia rolled over on her side, shaking the bed once more.

Zephyr exhaled. She stared up at the dark ceiling, listening to the locusts' repetitive song.

A face appeared in her mind. Unexplainable feelings crept over her skin. She saw hands hovering above a beautiful piano – long, masculine fingers dancing above the keys. Chopin's music flowed from those hands, like waves on the ocean.

Those fingers were certainly not hers. But whose were they?

She swallowed, another bittersweet sensation pricking her heart.

Silas.

Somehow, she could picture him this way, as a masterful musician. She wondered if he was as masterful a lover, as well.

Would she dream about him again tonight? Him and his haunting brown eyes? Would he be playing the piano for her this time?

This is downright silly. My imagination is twenty shades too vivid. Still...

Zephyr closed her eyes, letting out a long breath. Mixed emotions filled her heart.

She wasn't sure if she wanted to dream of him or not.

Chapter Seven

June 30th, 1863

EZRA

A FIDDLE. *A REAL FIDDLE.*

It was one of the most elegant pieces of wood Ezra had ever seen. Furnished out of shiny, rich mahogany, the graceful instrument appeared so out of place in this grimy camp. The surface was so clean and the curved edges so articulate. It looked just foreign in general, the more Ezra studied it. He realized that this proved how long it'd been since he'd laid eyes on a real musical instrument.

"That thing's too pretty to be here. Where'd you get it, sawbones?" Hayden puffed on his pipe, staring at it with a look of mild awe.

"Don'tcha think this place could *use* somethin' pretty?" Ezra stroked his whiskered chin, never pulling his gaze away from the fiddle.

Pratchit took it from the black velvet case and gave Hayden a look of disgust, as he gently brushed off the instrument's already spotless surface.

"I bought it a few years after I married my wife." He looked down at the violin, his mouth barely forming a smile.

"And when was *that*?" Hayden rolled his eyes.

"Lily and I got hitched in forty-nine."

"I asked when'd ya get the stupid fiddle, not when ya got married. *Nob.*"

Ezra shook his head at Hayden, finally taking his gaze off the violin. "Hayden, your unsavory discourse never ceases to amaze me."

Hayden shrugged, blasé as ever.

"Do I give a s---? Let's hear some music already." He blew a smoke ring at Pratchit, who threw a less-than-cordial look back his way.

At least Pratchit possessed a higher level of maturity. He didn't say anything in response to Hayden, he simply lifted the violin to his chest, nestling it carefully against his upper body. He grazed the strings with his bow, producing a soft yet distinctive sound, warm and sweet; smooth like honey. Ezra smiled. He'd heard other fellows make a ruckus with make-shift instruments of their own, but this was something entirely different.

Ezra watched Pratchit as he played. The surgeon's eyes were closed, and his lips curled up ever so slightly in satisfaction. His face matched the music his hands produced: mellow and tranquil, along with hints of bliss. Ezra had never seen him look quite this way. It wasn't that the surgeon never smiled, for that he did; but for the first time, the smile on Pratchit's face seemed completely genuine. It was as if the man had been swept away in his own music and forgotten about the world. He was as captivated as his audience, if not more so. For the first time, Ezra saw some kind of peace in his demeanor.

The songs were unlike anything Ezra had heard before. They weren't fiddle tunes that you could dance to, or raunchy tavern songs that the drunkards sang. And they weren't hymns, either. The notes waxed and waned like the cycles of the moon, rising and swelling like waves on the distant ocean. Etched within the fluctuation of soft and loud, it seemed the tones were speaking a language of their own. Not a language of words, but of emotion. One moment, it was a surge of joyous proclamation, the next, woeful lamentation. And it didn't end there. For the next ten minutes, Ezra was swept into an assemblage of anger, hope, solitude and everything in between. It was as if the feelings and experiences of the human soul had been stripped away and integrated into the very instrument itself. With each note that Pratchit played, he painted a vibrant picture of the essence of humanity.

By the end, Ezra was dumbfounded. He wasn't a musical being, but he'd be a fool not to admit that Pratchit was skilled. He could barely find the words to express the beauty he'd just heard. And he was sure that whatever he did manage to say would do the songs miserable justice.

It was amazing, the power music held over the human body. Especially when it was from a person who knew how to do it right.

"Heck, that was *some* playin' there, doc." Hayden took his pipe from his mouth, his eyes glued to the violin as if it were suddenly the most interesting thing on the planet. For the moment, it truly was.

Pratchit looked at the redhead and grinned almost triumphantly. "Practice makes perfect, they say!" He gave the instrument an affectionate stroke and placed it back in its case.

"Well, you sure must've been practicin' then." Ezra found himself smiling broadly. It felt so good to hear–and behold—something beautiful and elegant for once. Such a bright contrast to most of everything else in this desolate camp.

Guess this'll give us a morale boost for a little bit.

Hayden just shook his head one more time and raised his eyebrows a little, before shrugging and shuffling away.

It was marvelously satisfying to see that man baffled for once.

The sun had passed nearly three-quarters of the way through the sky, and Ezra suddenly realized how hungry he'd become. He thanked Pratchit for the music, then headed back to his tent to fix a cup of coffee before supper.

But as he walked, a familiar burden fell upon his soul. It pricked him like a needle, a syringe injecting his being with guilt for something he couldn't even place. He realized it was the same feeling he'd experienced before, when Harry had preached.

God, what's this about? What did I do?

And then his eyes landed on a familiar someone. Tucked away, hidden behind a group of other soldiers, it was a wonder Ezra even noticed the lad. He was so small and insignificant, if one judged him by his size. But Ezra didn't judge people that way, and now he found himself heading in the boy's direction. Somehow, he didn't feel right walking on without at least saying hello again. Who knew if the kid had *anyone* in this camp to talk to?

It was Frances.

Just like last time, he was leaned against a tree; wrapped up in his little book, one hand vigorously etching away. The look on his face portrayed his intense powers of concentration. Not at all unlike Pratchit earlier, the boy seemed immersed in a world of his own creation.

"Hey kid!" Ezra gave him a warm smile.

Frances glanced up, suspicion manifest in his hazy eyes. After a moment, he managed a small grin. "Oh, hi."

Ezra nodded to the book, sticking his hands in his pockets casually. "Whatcha workin' on?"

Frances' eyes shot up, and he shut the book defensively.

"Nothin'." A bit of pink flushed across his cheeks.

Ezra raised an eyebrow slightly, curiosity filling him at the boy's reaction. He thought about trying to get a glimpse at what he was working on, but decided that the lad might not appreciate it. Instead, Ezra's lip curled up slightly on one side.

"If it's nothin', then why have you been over here by yourself, hunched over it every time I've seen ya?"

"I only recall seein' ya once before, mister."

Ezra's half-smile fell somewhat. He nodded, looking away a moment. "I guess that's true." He was surprised at the sudden curtness in the boy's words. What was in that book that he could he be so defensive about?

Frances' cheeks had turned a vivid crimson. He clutched the book tightly against his chest, as if guarding it with his life. The not-so-amiable look in his eyes told Ezra that he'd asked one too many questions. *Time to back off.*

"Alright, alright. I'm sorry for intrudin'." Ezra exhaled, his smile once again fading. He'd always known he was bad at small talk, but he hadn't thought he was *this* bad. Or perhaps this boy was just extremely reclusive. Either way, the current discourse wasn't improving the morale at all.

Ezra turned to make his escape from the awkwardness, but stopped. His shoulders rose as he inhaled tiredly. He cast a final gaze in Frances' direction.

"Look, if you ever need somebody to talk to or if ya get bored or somethin', we have a chaplain who does services every night. Also, we have decent coffee." He offered a grin, looking at the boy sincerely.

Suspicion clouded Frances' visage. "What's a chaplain?"

Ezra balked. *The kid doesn't even know what a chaplain is.* He swallowed, realizing that the ball was back in his court. He had to respond with something that would convince the boy chapel services were worth going to. And he had to do it with *tact.*

Whoo-boy.

"Well, it's…it's a fella that talks about God and the Bible. This fella, he happens to be my brother as it turns out." Ezra smiled, searching Frances' face for any signs, trying to read what he was thinking behind that stony mask.

Silence.

His smile faltered. *Alright then.* He couldn't expect the boy to be better at conversation than he was, or even to be interested in this conversation at all.

Clearing his throat, Ezra continued, watching the boy carefully. "Ever heard any Bible stories? There are some real exciting ones. I bet you haven't heard 'em."

Frances looked down at his book. "I've heard a few," He murmured.

"Well, you should come. That way, you can hear a bunch more." Ezra nodded subconsciously, almost as if to encourage himself that he was doing alright at this.

More silence.

Ezra chewed on the edge of his lip. So much for that idea.

Chapter Eight

July 4th, 1863

ZEPHYR

ZEPHYR DROWSILY PRIED OPEN ONE eyelid, then shut it and rolled over on her side. She groaned, still half-asleep.

The sheets were clingy against her skin. Clingy sheets were not a pleasant sensation.

Rolling over on her back again, she stared up at the tin ceiling and exhaled slowly.

I guess we made it another day.

Eighty-seven years prior to this day, back in the year 1776, America had declared its freedom from under the hand of King George. Zephyr remembered the things she'd read about that glorious event. A new page had been turned, and after all the wars and fighting between the colonies and Europe, a resolution was finally made. She wondered what it must have been like to grow up in that time and what it would be like to experience liberty from such an oppressive government.

Yet now America was, again, in the midst of war and fighting. Once again, a new page turned, but no one knew yet the results of its turning or what was written on the pages after.

Once again men were fighting for independence, and once again, they were fighting for freedom from their oppressors. The only difference was, the lines weren't so clearly drawn in this war.

Is it really Independence Day already?

Zephyr pulled her wandering mind away from politics and turned to look at Lydia, who was still deep in sleep.

What time is it anyway? She glanced at the solitary wash basin standing beside the bed. Reaching over clumsily, she grabbed her pocket watch and eyed its shiny face. She looked at her cousin and shook her head.

Incredible.

It was almost six and the earlybird still wasn't awake.

Lydia's lack of activity wasn't the only thing different. Why was it so quiet? Usually the boys were all running around at the crack of dawn, yelling, laughing and slamming doors. There was no need for a rooster to wake a body, not here!

But apparently even the boys must've been tuckered out.

Climbing out of bed, Zephyr shuffled over to the bureau she shared with Lydia and opened one of its drawers, getting out her stockings.

If she wasn't mistaken, today was a Sunday and there would be meeting with the Collatts and Lowells. No Independence Day festivities, though. There hadn't been any since when the war started.

Zephyr sighed, remembering how joyous those days before the war had been.

Now, everything was different.

Pa was gone. That was the worst of all. With him absent, Zephyr's life felt torn. She wanted so much to find a way for something better, but she couldn't figure out what that way was. She only knew that her heart was well-acquainted with grief and sorrow.

The girl inhaled, closing her eyes abruptly.

No. Stay out of my head.

Silas' eyes flashed across the walls of her mind. Zephyr clenched her fists, her eyes still shut fiercely.

Go away! I know it's all just an illusion. The real Silas doesn't love me. And…and…I don't love him. We don't know each other. It's impossible to love somebody you don't know.

"Gosh, what in the world are you doing?"

Suddenly, she was pulled out of her mind and in the real world. Lydia stood beside her, shaking her ginger head in amusement.

Zephyr looked down at her clenched fists. No wonder the fourteen-year-old was gawking.

She mustered a forced laugh. *Get a grip already, Zephyr. The day's not even an hour in and you can't control yourself.*

"I'm such a stupid creature, aren't I?"

Lydia smirked. "No joke!"

Zephyr cast a fake threatening look as Lydia opened a drawer, rummaging through its contents. After a moment, Zephyr heard a sigh. From the corner of her eye, she saw Lydia eying her trim figure in the little mirror on the side of the bureau.

"I wish I had somethin' to wear that was actually *fashionable*."

Not *this* again. Zephyr opened another bureau drawer and retrieved the only nicer dress she owned. Most of the time she wore her wash dress, and sometimes even men's clothes, because that was most practical. This dress was worn only on Sundays and rare formalities. It was a pretty coneflower-blue cotton, with bishop sleeves and armseyes that sat just off her shoulders. Small white and yellow flowers dotted the fabric. The bodice was form fitting; the fabric gathered in the waist, while the skirt flared out, swishing with its many yards of fabric. It was Zephyr's favorite piece of clothing, and possibly the only one that made her feel like a true lady, or even just a woman in general.

As she slipped on the dress, she heard Lydia sigh again.

"What is it?" Zephyr inquired, more out of annoyance with the sighing than genuine care.

Lydia pursed her lips, huffing as she tugged her own dress on.

"It's no fun being poor."

"We're not poor."

"Most girls would have something besides a lowly cotton dress and petticoats, Zephyr!" Lydia moaned, holding up her skirts in dissatisfaction. "And look at all this fabric. Completely useless and embarrassing without a hoop. It's not fair that I can't even have a hoopskirt."

Zephyr opened the bureau drawer again, bringing out her comb. "Cotton isn't lowly. It's economical. And, what would you do with that hoop? Wear it while feeding the chickens? It would be a waste of money."

"That's what everybody says," Lydia grumbled.

"Maybe because it's the truth?" Zephyr rolled her eyes. "Stop whinin'. You should be grateful for what you have. Just starch your petticoats a little bit heavier."

Lydia furrowed her brow and looked at the floor. "Everybody says that, too." Her tone was about as cheery as the smell of burning oatmeal.

Am I really stuck with this girl for the rest of my life? Is she really my adopted sister?

Zephyr closed her eyes for a moment, releasing a sigh of her own.

Being the only girl born to her parents, she figured she should have welcomed a sister since all she'd had for playmates and companions as a child were boys.

Besides her own little brothers, there had always been Anson. For nearly all her childhood he'd been one of her closest friends. They'd had a quarrel or two, but generally they got along famously. Maybe a bit too well, as the lad had once tried to kiss Zephyr on the cheek…much to her disgust.

But that was then. She didn't know him now. The two had nothing in common, having grown up and gone their separate ways. Besides, Zephyr had given up hope of Anson ever wanting to talk to her again. Apparently he didn't possess the character for it.

And then there was Peter Cooper, a boy she had known her whole life, literally.

He was a quieter soul, more of a listener than a talker, and the same age as Zephyr. She hadn't spoken to him in ages. She wondered what'd become of him.

Zephyr had enjoyed lots of childhood memories with Peter. In the end, he and Anson were two of the best friends she ever had.

Was it abnormal that her best friends had always been boys?

Oh well. Who cared really, anyhow? Zephyr would never know the meaning of normal. It was contrary to her entire existence.

She wrapped her mass of hair into a bun at the back of her head, fastening it there with some pins. She looked at herself in the mirror. In the sunlight, her tresses shimmered a coppery-auburn. Her pupils had decreased in size, displaying the color in her eyes brightly: milky aqua-blue with faint flecks of fern-green. Zephyr grinned at her reflection. She liked her eyes.

I should be thankful for Lydia. She's still my blood and kin. Whether she's a twit or not.

Lydia was like a puzzle. A very difficult puzzle, that was missing a number of pieces.

Zephyr knew that if she were going to understand the reason for having this girl in her life, she'd have to trust God to show her.

***

Chores were in full swing. Breakfast was finished, and preparations for the church meeting were underway.

However, getting to church was proving a difficult task.

As far as Zephyr knew, Lydia was supposed to be milking the cow and goats, and Clarence feeding the chickens and horses. Ma was preparing supper so that it would be all ready when they got back from church, but Zephyr had been left with getting the little boys rounded up and ready to go.

Thankfully, getting them rounded up wasn't really too hard. It was the "ready to go" part that was difficult.

She found them running aimlessly around the main room.

"Boys!" She called. "I can't believe y'all aren't dressed yet!"

Rudy giggled. Royce just looked at the floor, and Lemuel sighed. Shaking her head with impatience, Zephyr marched them down the hall to the bedroom, and straight went to their wardrobe.

"Goodness, where is that other sock?" She groped around in the lowest drawer of the boys' bureau.

After several moments of frustration, she still hadn't found Royce's other sock and was ready to give up on it—when the little boy himself came up to her, wearing the matching sock on his foot.

"Royce! Where did you get that?"

Royce shrugged, and looked at the other sock in Zephyr's hand.

"I need to get my othow sawk on."

Zephyr sighed, shaking her head. She gave the boy his sock and flicked out her pocket watch. Her countenance fell upon seeing the time. It was disastrously late, and they weren't ready to go in the least.

"Hurry up, Rudy!"

Zephyr couldn't help being annoyed even though she knew she should remember her brothers' ages and the fact that they were *boys*. Still, there was no reason that they leave the house looking like wild animals.

"However in the world do ya boys get your shoes so dirty?"

She groaned as they clomped back down the hall to the main room.

"Now, just sit here on the…"

The front door was open. It shouldn't have been. Zephyr squinted suspiciously as Lydia and Clarence disappeared into the dining room.

"Lydia Ruth! Clarence Harold! Come back here this instant and close that door!"

Rudy leaped off the sofa. His twin and Lemuel were soon to follow.

Zephyr flew around to face them in exasperation. "Stop jumpin' on the couch! Sit down and…"

Clarence and Lydia's voices were present again, and their giggling reached Zephyr's ears. The two passed by and were about to walk out the door when she stopped them gruffly. "Where do you think you're going?"

The two stopped, leaving the door wide open, and even more bugs to fly in. Zephyr sighed, waving at the door.

"*Please* shut the door."

Clarence grumbled something to Lydia and she shrugged back at him. Finally, he went over and closed it.

"Clarence, have you swept yet? And Lydia, please go…"

The door opened again. Zephyr wanted to scream. Her face reddened and she bit her lip, breathing in deeply. Ma stepped inside, and shut the door, to the girl's gratitude.

Mrs. Darson studied the exasperated look on her daughter's face, and then glanced at Clarence and Lydia, then the twins and Lemuel, who hadn't stopped bouncing on the sofa.

The blond, middle-aged woman's gaze rested on Zephyr. She smiled sympathetically.

"Well, it appears you have been busy. Now calm down and take a seat for a minute." She motioned toward the sofa.

"Clarence, have you swept in here yet?" She looked over at her eldest son who was now staring sheepishly at the floor.

He shook his head. "No, uh, not yet."

"Well, then, you know what you need to do next." Ma eyed him with an it's-not-the-time-to-be-fooling-around look. He sighed and nodded as he slumped out of the room to go fetch the broom and dustpan.

After he'd gone, Zephyr let out a long sigh and collapsed on the sofa. "I give up." She shook her head, sinking into the folds of the meager cushions. "I just… I just can't do this!"

"Zephyr, there's nothing to worry about. It's not the end of the world if we don't get out the door on time. That's not the most important thing. Anyway, I'm quite certain the Collatts won't mind us being late. They're probably still trying to tidy up over there, anyhow." Mrs. Darson's gentle eyes looked into Zephyr's. "So, dear, settle down and try to be patient with your siblings. You're the eldest and they look up to you. You're practically an adult. Be a good example."

Zephyr closed her eyes, gritting her teeth, trying to overcome the impatient thoughts within. She hated admitting it, but she knew Ma was right. She was getting herself all stressed over something that really didn't matter.

Finally she looked up at Mrs. Darson. "You're right. I got carried away."

Ma smiled. "It's good you understand. You'll have to learn patience sooner or later, you know. It's something you're going to need an awful lot in life."

Zephyr nodded, slowly standing up. "I know."

Mrs. Darson looked around the room at the rest of her children. "It's time we get heading to church! Have your shoes on?"

Rudy, Royce and Lemuel jumped off the sofa and stood at attention. "Yes!" they all replied in unison.

"Well, then, everyone out to the barn!"

The boys ran out the front door, with Zephyr following and then Lydia.

Clarence slunk out from the hallway. "So, I don't have to sweep?"

Mrs. Darson eyed the boy with a knowing look that required no words to make her point clear.

The drive to the Collatt farm took about half an hour. The little boys played in the back of the buggy, and Clarence and Lydia talked amongst themselves. Ma and Zephyr sat in the front, on the box seat, and Zephyr drove.

Zephyr smiled as they pulled into the Collatt property and drove through their woods a little ways to the house and stable. She had such fond memories at this place, with these people. She loved the Collatts like family.

The Collatt children stood in front of the house, waving and smiling eagerly as they pulled up.

Fourteen-year-old Prudence stood holding little Jed, who was three. Tall, dark-haired Addy stood beside her, smiling broadly. She was twelve. Azellah, a sandy-blond-haired girl of eleven years stood beside her older sisters, beaming like a ray of sunshine.

And then there was Ethan, who was the twins' age, and Lottie, a sweet little six-year-old, both beaming with joy to see their friends.

The little boys piled clumsily out of the wagon, after Zephyr climbed down and tied Daphne's picket line to a nearby tree. The boys suddenly looked shy and hesitant.

Clarence jumped down from the wagon. "Stop that! You ain't shy, you're just actin' silly! C'mon, let's go." He pulled Rudy's arm and grabbed Royce as well. "Come on!" He urged them forward until they finally cooperated.

Zephyr grabbed the family Bible and the food Ma had packed for them. She stopped a few feet from the wagon, waiting for Ma and Lydia, the latter of whom was looking withdrawn.

"Lydia, what's the matter? I thought you liked Sunday meetings?"

Lydia slumped, her face sullen. "I like them fine." Her words fell out of her mouth as flat as a piece of paper.

Zephyr managed to keep from frowning. She didn't have time to worry about her sister's troubles. Prudence, Addy and Zelle were all greeting her and holding out their arms for a hug.

"How've y'all been?"

"Busy, but wonderful!" Addy replied, her eyes shining.

Zelle clasped her hands together. "Won't you play some songs for us, Zephyr? Pleeaaase?" The blue-eyed girl looked hopefully up at Zephyr, who couldn't help but smile.

Of course she didn't mind playing for them. An eager audience was never unappreciated!

"What songs do ya want?"

The four walked up the steps to the front porch, and then into the house where everyone else was.

Mr. Collatt sat in an old rocker, smoking a pipe and watching the little ones play and chatter. "Hello, Zephyr!" He smiled through his bushy beard. She nodded back, returning the greeting as the girls crowded around the Collatts' old piano.

The large main room had a dinner table on one side, a woodstove on the other, and a couple of chairs in a semi-circle around the woodstove. Furthest from the front door, sat the piano and its little wooden stool, where Zephyr now seated herself.

A grin had pasted itself across her face. Her heart swelled in contentment as she played one of her compositions. Even though the instrument was greatly out of tune, and the keys stuck, it didn't bother her. The thought that her friends loved listening to her play made it all worth it.

Zephyr finished her song and the four girls walked out on the front porch just as the Lowells were coming in. Zephyr stood aside to let them pass. There was Mrs. Lowell, who walked into the house first, carrying a pot in her small hands.

Mrs. Lowell was a small-framed, dark-haired woman with tender brown eyes and a pale complexion. She was at least three or four inches shorter than Zephyr.

Behind Mrs. Lowell came little Jeremiah, a rambunctious six year old. He grinned when he saw Zephyr, waving energetically.

Twelve-year-old Martha Sue was next, a girl with a head of shoulder-length, bouncy brown curls. With her sparkling hazel eyes and delicate smile, she was beautiful. She greeted Zephyr as well, carrying baby Matthew.

Pretty Rhoda came skipping behind her. Rhoda, like Martha Sue, had lovely brown curls which cascaded over her shoulders. She had stunning blue eyes, which everyone complimented her on. She was a happy girl of nine.

Mr. Lowell was next. He nodded to Zephyr as he walked inside. A slender man with short red hair and a matching red beard, he was average in height.

And, then, last of the Lowell procession there was Malinda.

Malinda.

Zephyr's chest tightened and she set her jaw.

Malinda was Zephyr's age, definitely shorter than she by several inches but similar in body type. Only, her face was rounder, and her nose smaller, narrower. Her curly brown hair was pulled back into a bun at the nape of her neck and several messy ringlets hung over her ears.

Harsh blue eyes gored into Zephyr's, in the way that they always did.

At best, it was a look lacking emotion. At worst, a look brimming over with hostility.

Zephyr tried to loosen her jaw.

"Hi, Malinda." She smiled politely.

Malinda didn't return the grin.

"Hello." The young woman's voice was cool and emotionless. She lingered a couple seconds longer, and then continued inside, leaving Zephyr perplexed and alone.

What was with that girl? Where were her manners?

Why does she always look at me like that?

Zephyr sighed.

The one girl I know that's my age. And she has to be an ice-block.

The entire group was present. Zephyr turned and walked slowly back into the main room. The young people seated themselves on the floor, and the adults in the few chairs that were present.

After a prayer and a unison of "amens" which followed, Mr. Collatt looked at the group, smiling. "Well, how about some singin'?"

A chorus of approval filled the air and he smiled broadly. "I thought so. What's a good hymn someone would like to recommend?"

Mr. Collatt scanned over the kids sticking their hands up eagerly. His gaze rested on Jeremiah. "Yes, Jeremiah, what would you like to sing?"

"Trust and Obey!"

"That's a very good one! Who remembers how it goes? Zephyr, since you're the musician, how 'bout you lead us?"

Zephyr stood up. "Yes sir, I'd be glad to. Shall everyone stand?"

The group rose to their feet, and music filled the air.

Zephyr liked being in charge of the music. She enjoyed trying to teach the rather musically-ignorant group how to improve their singing. Sometimes certain people tended to go quite off-tune, and that fact was painfully noticeable.

Still, it wasn't about sounding good. God didn't care about whether they were off tune or not anyway. It was just the fact that they were praising Him. That was what mattered.

At the same time, she also believed that when singing—especially singing to God—she should try and do the very best she could.

It was marvelous, just to harmonize with others. To contribute to a rich fold of varying vocal parts that all weaved together. The soprano parts, the altos, and mezzo-sopranos. The bass, and tenors, and contra-altos. She loved it all.

Zephyr sighed, letting her mind be swept away in another of her many daydreams. *Just to sing in a real choir with skilled musicians. Perhaps one of those large, city ones where the choir members all wore those fancy robes.*

Well, it sure ain't gonna happen here.

The group sang another several hymns, and then seated themselves again. Mr. Collatt was going to lead today. He and Mr. Lowell took turns every week presenting the lesson.

If Pa were here, he could be the one leading. He certainly could do it well.

Zephyr fidgeted on the wood floor, trying to position her legs in a lady-like yet comfortable manner.

Mr. Collatt opened his big, black Bible and flipped through the pages. Putting on his spectacles, he looked up at the group. "Let's turn to first John."

Zephyr listened as Mr. Collatt read some verses aloud and requested Mr. Lowell to read a passage. The lesson was about brotherly love among the body. It lasted three hours.

The group sang a few more hymns, while Zephyr accompanied them on the piano. And then everyone bowed their heads. Zephyr heard Mrs. Collatt whisper a few "Yes, Lord"s during the prayer. One of the boys sneezed.

Zephyr tried to focus on the words, repeating them in her mind as they were spoken.

A yawn escaped her lungs. This always seemed to occur during the church services, and it had nothing to do with whether she was enjoying the study or not. It just happened out of the blue for no apparent reason. And every time she yawned, her eyes got watery and she worried it would look like she was crying. So she immediately dried her eyes before the prayer was over and everyone saw the wet on her cheeks.

"...in Jesus' Name, amen."

Zephyr stretched her arms and looked around at everyone. She glanced at Malinda, who was standing across from her a ways, having just gotten up off the floor where she was sitting. Malinda caught her glance, but Zephyr broke eye contact as something touched her sleeve, causing her to turn. She smiled when she saw it was only Zelle.

"We're gonna go outside and play tag. Wanna come?" Zelle's bright eyes danced with energy.

Zephyr smiled. With the Collatts, she didn't have to worry about acting like an adult all the time. With Prudence, Addy and Zelle, you could run around like a wild animal and they would love every second of it. Nobody would judge you wrongly here.

Zephyr loved that. She loved how comfortable she felt around these people. They were like family, and even closer. They'd had their share of disagreements and bumps along the path, but that had only drawn them together all the more.

She loved them, they loved her, and it sure was a nice thing to know that fact.

"Sure thing, let's go!" Zephyr grinned youthfully and followed Azellah to the front door.

Time flew. The older children played tag and capture-the-flag, and then a game of pretend medieval times with the little kids.

Before she knew it, Zephyr heard Ma calling everyone in to dinner.

It was funny to Zephyr how sometimes the minutes ticked away so slowly, barely progressing at all. And then there were times like these, where whole hours fled away quicker than a snap of the fingers.

Dinner was a fine smorgasbord of black eyed peas from the Darsons, freshly baked brown bread from the Collatts, and some smoked ham from the Lowells.

After everyone had been served, the adults sat down at the Collatts' dining table along with the little kids.

The older ones all went out to the front porch and sat around the steps and on the wooden floor boards against the front wall.

After a short prayer, Zephyr dug into her meal. She loved black-eyed peas, and the brown bread and ham tasted pretty good as well. Especially since the ham was something of a treat: the Darsons didn't have it very often.

There wasn't any talking for a couple moments, since everyone was eating, but then Addy broke the silence.

"Hey Clarence, could you tell us another of your critter stories?"

Her eyes seemed to laugh. Addy was a girl who delighted in whimsical tales and storytelling.

Clarence grinned a little, sticking a forkful of ham in his mouth. "Sure, if you want."

"Yes, yes, please!" Addy clapped her hands together.

"Alright, then," Clarence replied, setting down his plate and swallowing his mouthful.

"Did I ever tell you about the stink bugs that sprayed Zeph a couple years ago?"

Zephyr made a face.

What a horrid memory! The nasty little insects had targeted her right in the face. Their spray felt like acid in her eyes, and oh, did that stuff smell! Zephyr grimaced at the fowl reminiscence.

By now, everyone had turned to see what her reaction would be. She made a face again in disgust.

"Oh those things were awful alright!"

"They're not *that* terrible," Malinda said simply as if the whole thing wasn't even worthy of discussion.

"Well, then you try seeing what it's like to have one spray you in the face!" Zephyr raised a brow and ripped off another bite of bread.

Addy looked over at Clarence again, leaning forward. "Alright, tell us about it, Clarence!"

The boy grinned, standing up and bowing, as if he were giving a speech. "Well, now, it happened like this..."

***

Soon it was time to go home.

Zephyr hugged her friends and said goodbye to the Lowells.

Since it was Sunday, there weren't many chores to be done back on the farm. After they had all changed back into their work clothes, Ma allowed the boys to play outside and do whatever they wished for a little while.

However, the animals couldn't be ignored simply because it was a day of rest. Clarence had to feed the chickens, and it was Zephyr's turn to milk the cow. Lydia would've had to muck out the stalls, but it was Sunday, so she was relieved from the duty. She was likely off someplace, reading a book again.

Zephyr tied Amelia's picket line to a post inside the barn. She put a slab of hay into her manger and pulled a short stool up besides the cow's big, round body. Then she aligned the milk pan under Amelia's udders.

Squeeeeeze, drip, squeeeeeeze. Drip, drip, drip, squeeeeze.

Zephyr's mind wandered as her hands worked. She mused whether or not Silas had gone to church in Micanopy–it was the closest official church for miles. Was he a church-going type? Was he a Christian at all?

Her heart sank. How she wished she knew more. It was pretty ridiculous, after all, how she'd allowed herself to become so fond of a fellow who might not even be on the same page spiritually.

How she wished she could talk to him in depth, about so many different topics.

But having a nice long discussion with him just wasn't going to happen. Not with Silas being such a shy fellow and her clamming up every time she was around him.

How it dismayed her though, knowing this. She was a realist, and while she continued to dream that someday her hopes would be fulfilled, she'd always return to the apparent reality that those dreams weren't going anywhere. Slowly and dejectedly, she exhaled.

What was she doing, wasting so much mental and emotional energy on Silas? Who said he was even worth it?

I could slap myself.

What could there be about him that would draw her so much? He was certainly easy on the eyes, and that was a fact. But there was more to people than just their looks.

Squeeze, drip, drip, drip, squeeeeeeze.

Lord, why do I feel this way? Why can't I get rid of these feelings?

The girl sighed again. Life here was wonderful, in comparison to all that was happening in the world. But at the same time, it felt empty when she stopped to truly think on it all.

Everything was fine—until she realized, as she did so frequently, how fast time passed. As it scurried into the horizon, she felt more and more failures heaped upon her shoulders. Failure to control her feelings. Failure to live up to her family's expectations. And most importantly, failure to understand God's will and act accordingly.

This haunted her. In this battle, she was sorely outmatched. Time was far too great an adversary, almost as unconquerable as her own self, which was the worst enemy of all.

She felt like she was swimming against the current, fighting a battle which could never be won.

Who of the human race could master time, tame and conquer it? How could one chase a thing and overtake it, when it is retreating at a pace far quicker than one's own?

Zephyr knew the answers too well.

Only God had power over the silent beast of time. Only the Author of time could conquer and subdue the great unknown, unseen, axiomatic thing. But, of course He could—after all, He was the One who created it!

Zephyr puzzled herself thinking on these things. How did time exist, what did it consist of? Was it a physical substance, like air, which one cannot see, but certainly feels and knows that it exists, or was it simply a law of science, like gravity?

All she knew was that it was slipping away from her. It would never allow her to do all that she wished and needed to do.

Why does my heart ache so? What's the missing piece in this puzzle, Lord?

Something just wasn't right. Doubts filled the young woman's mind. Painful questions.

Am I truly saved? Am I being punished for something? Where is the peace and joy that You promise your children?

A lump formed in Zephyr's throat. She swallowed, closing her eyes. She was tired of hurting inside and not being able to identify the hurt.

She wished there was a way to find the answers.

"What's happenin'?"

Pulled from the morass of questions, doubts, and confusion whirling in her head, she looked over to see Clarence climb over the stall fence.

The boy smiled at his older sister and leaned against the barn wall.

Zephyr wrapped up her mental debate with a concluding prayer, which brought a little bit of comfort to her soul.

Later, I'll get the Bible out and do some reading. I need to hear what Your Word says. I'm confused. I don't know what to do. I don't know what is wrong with my soul but I know there is something wrong. Lord, please help me to know what it is.

She glanced up, making a miserable attempt at a poker face.

"Not much."

Clarence tilted his head and yawned.

"Well, you sure been quiet, that's for sure."

Zephyr's brow furrowed. "What's that supposed to mean?"

"You used to sing when you milked." Clarence shrugged. "I walked up and saw you sittin' there with a mighty solemn look on your face... like you're thinkin' really hard 'bout somethin'."

"You wouldn't understand." Zephyr shook her head. "I can't even understand myself. It's a mess. You don't know how to fix broken hearts, confused minds and fill in empty souls, do ya?"

Clarence eyed her. "I don't see why you're so upset. You've got a great life. You just got to visit today with your friends, and you've got us all the time besides. What's the matter?"

Zephyr looked into her brother's eyes, wishing he could understand this torture. For a few seconds, their eyes locked in contact, Zephyr's penetrating his, searching them for any signs of recognition.

"I don't know how to say it. I don't know what's wrong. I just know something is."

The girl released the air from her lungs slowly. She wished she could explain things to her brother. She hated keeping it all locked within, like a prison. But who would understand? Clarence certainly wasn't going through the kind of warfare Zephyr was. He had his own battles, yes, but he was a boy, she was a girl, and she'd been on this planet three years longer than he. How could one not expect their battles to be different?

"Well, that's obvious." He shook his head, still eyeing her perplexed. "But I can't say I know what you're talkin' about. I mean, I always know what's wrong, when somethin's wrong. But that's just me. I guess we're all different. Some of us know stuff and others don't." He shrugged.

"Thanks for that word of encouragement." Zephyr murmured sarcastically, turning back to watch her hands as they squeezed Amelia's warm, wet udders. She looked forward to being done with this job.

She didn't know what else to say to Clarence. Perhaps there were some things he just wouldn't be able to get, not right now. Zephyr hated being reclusive about these strange feelings she was experiencing, but obviously the thirteen-year-old just didn't grasp what was going on.

And quite honestly, neither did she.

***

The house was dark, but for the lamp lit in the main room where Ma was sitting.

Shadows flickered across the meager living space, and the lamp's flames barely illuminated her as Zephyr padded softly into the room and looked down at her mother.

Don't cry. Don't show her watery eyes. Zephyr's throat tightened. Realizing her daughter's presence, Mrs. Darson looked up from her reading and smiled at the girl. Zephyr returned the smile, but hers was a tense, forced one. She felt terrible, inches from breaking into tears at any moment.

"Good night, Ma." Setting her jaw, she tried to avoid looking in her mother's eyes, for fear that they would see the pain inside.

"Good-night, Zephyr." Mrs. Darson's voice was soft as rye grass.

Zephyr stood there for a moment or two longer. Finally she smiled a little, as if to push aside her feelings. Half of her wanted to talk to Ma about those feelings; half of her didn't.

While she felt a need to vent the chaos tearing apart the depths of her mind, she also felt embarrassed to bring it up. It seemed so foolish for someone her age. Even though she knew Ma would listen carefully and try to encourage her, she didn't want to break down into tears in front of her mother. She wanted to be strong, or at least pretend to be strong, even if she wasn't. It was an effort in vain, but she *had* to try. For Ma. That woman took everything; she deserved to get a break from the fight. She didn't need to see her grown daughter babbling in front of her.

Ma needed all the encouragement she could get, herself.

I can't burden Ma with this. She already has enough on her plate without it.

Zephyr sucked in a breath and decided that she was merely being melodramatic. She couldn't even figure out why she wanted to cry.

She swallowed and leaned over to give Mrs. Darson a hug.

"I love you, Ma. You are the best mother there could be."

She smiled, full of love for the woman who brought her forth into this world. It pained her that she couldn't vent her thoughts to her, but it was for the best.

"I love you too, Zephyr. You are a precious daughter. Do you want me to pray for you before you go to bed?"

Zephyr hesitated, wanting desperately to leave before the tears escaped. She bit her lip. "Yes, please... I would like that."

Mrs. Darson laid her hand on Zephyr's shoulder and murmured a short, meaningful prayer.

The young woman returned to the dark bedroom. The boys and Lydia were out like a light, leaving the room as silent as it was pitch black.

It was too quiet. The silence filled Zephyr's ears. Throbbing silence. Zephyr stopped, listening to her own heartbeat.

Silence was a fearsome thing—even though it shouldn't have been. Because the longer Zephyr was exposed to it, the more likely she would be to hear words and whispers in the shadows. And it wasn't so much that these sounds would become apparent, because they always did; but more concerning were the questions that followed. Was that a real person talking to her? Whose voice did that belong to? Why was it there to begin with?

It wouldn't be long before the buzz and hum of those alien thoughts filled every crevice of her mind.

God, I'm so fed up with myself.

All Zephyr wanted to do was run outside and sleep under the stars, away from everyone else. Away from the rest of the world. Away from her own self. Her heart felt like it would explode with all the emotions boiling therein.

The girl couldn't stop her eyes from welling up. Her vision blurred with tears as she climbed into bed and mashed her face into the pillow, a sob working its way up her throat.

I'm so tired of being me.

Chapter Nine

July 10th, 1863

EZRA

THE SOUND OF HEAVY RAIN beating against the tent woke Ezra.

Lying flat on the ground, with only a thin blanket between him and the hard earthen floor, he gazed up wearily at the canvas roof as the rain pelted it.

It was a mighty good thing that this militia possessed some tents. Even if there weren't very many of them.

This particular one, which Ezra shared with Harold and four others, was a small A-frame - also known as a "wedge tent". Originally it had been designed to accommodate four men, but even four alone would've been a very snug fit.

Ezra went to sleep with two filthy, sweaty bodies crammed next to him and woke up to the same conditions. It could be hard to sleep at all sometimes, between the elements and the sharp, jabbing elbows poking into his ribs on either side of him. Yet he'd learned to tolerate it.

The thing was, he was truly well off concerning this tent. At least, compared to seventy percent of everyone else. Most of the other soldiers had nothing but *shebangs*, which weren't tents at all. They were shelters made with just about anything that could be found. Ash tree branches, small loblolly or Virginia pines, anything that could provide even a little bit of shelter. Back in Florida, they used palmetto branches, and those seemed to work a lot better than most foliage up in these parts.

A handful of the men had tiny shelter-halves, or "dog tents", which barely covered one man, let alone two. But at least they were actual, canvas tents.

That was one thing about camp life. Whether the men lived in an A-frame, shebang, or dog tent, they'd learned to make even the lousiest of shelters work decent enough to protect them from the elements. Decent enough. It barely cut, but it was sufficient, most of the time.

And that was all that was necessary.

Well, this is going to be an amiable day.

Ezra sighed, looking at the puddles forming on the ground beside him and the other bodies.

Rainy days were always hard to work with. While they seemed to purify the stench-filled air(to a degree), they were the prime times for overflows to occur down at the sinks.

Oh please. Not that today. I'm sure as heck not gonna wade through sewage to get to the well or to the wood pile. And I sure ain't going out there and shoveling up the crap, either.

Ezra let out a long sigh, sitting up slowly. He could feel the heat from the other men's' bodies. It wasn't a pleasant sensation. Neither were the unsavory body odors that filled his nostrils.

A couple of the men were already awake, but most in this tent were still trying to sleep while they could. They'd sure need it.

Ezra glanced about the wet, fetid living space and noticed his brother in the corner of the tent, sitting Indian-style on the ground. Harold's blanket was neatly rolled up and placed in the corner, as usual.

And once again, as he did every morning, the middle-aged man sat with his old leather Bible in his hands, reading intently.

Ezra smiled a little, watching the bearded fellow. Harry had always been the good example, the role model, and the natural leader. Of course he had many flaws and imperfections, just like anyone, but Ezra envied the man's resilience.

If anyone had learned to cope with this living hell on earth, it was Harold Darson. He had grit. True grit.

Ezra had had enough of the cramped conditions in the musty old tent. He'd had enough of being nestled in with almost a dozen other men, in a battered piece of canvas where lack of ventilation made breathing difficult.

Lying on a wet floor of cold, hard earth only made it worse. He stood, but had to hunch over or else hit the flimsy roof. Groaning, he wiped the smeared mud off his trousers.

"Where you off to, Darson?" Pratchit mumbled, sitting up.

Opening the tent's curtain 'door' and peering out into the dreary rain, Ezra exhaled.

The world outside was indeed a grey, bleak place. The sky was dark and overcast and you'd have no clue the sun was even out.

The grassy ground all around the camp had turned to mud, and pools of water were scattered all around. Ezra shook his head. This wasn't going to be pleasant.

"Nowhere."

Was it even worth it to carry on with drills in such a mucky swampland of an environment?

Lord, either make it stop raining or give Colonel Trigg the sense to call off drills.

Absentmindedly, the lanky man stepped away from the tent entrance and sat down on the ground next to his brother, who was still immersed in the Bible he held.

"Psalm 139," Ezra murmured, reading aloud the top of the page.

Harold nodded. He pointed to a verse a ways down the page. "This verse. It's one of my favorites."

"Psalm 139:14?"

Ezra read the lines beneath his brother's extended finger.

"I will praise Thee, for I am fearfully and wonderfully made. Marvelous are your works and that my soul knoweth right well."

A small smile formed on his mouth, as he pondered the words.

"Indeed, it's a good one."

Harry looked over at the grizzled man solemnly. "And yet most of the men in this camp don't believe one word of it..." He motioned to the Bible, his eyes lost in a cloud of sadness. "...or the rest of this, for that matter."

Ezra nodded, looking around at the others in the tent. A sad truth this was.

Harold's blue-green eyes were full of unspoken words. They were heavy, lost in thought.

"You're not gettin' enough sleep." Ezra noted the bags beneath Harry's sunken orbs.

"Neither are you." Harold raised a brow nonchalantly, peering at Ezra beneath his glasses.

Ezra filled his lungs slowly, looking down at his boots. Nothing could be said further about sleep. Insomnia was a normal part of the routine these days.

"Guess you've already figured out your sermon for tonight."

"I wouldn't call it a sermon, exactly."

"What else would you call it?"

Harry looked into Ezra's eyes with a serious expression written on his wrinkled, weathered face.

"Planting seeds, brother. Planting seeds."

Ezra watched Pratchit roll up his blanket. "Planting seeds," Ezra repeated, mulling the words over in his mind.

"What's the plan today with this deluge?" Pratchit's voice was groggy as he buttoned his dirty greatcoat.

"If and when it finally does stop, Triggs will surely get us on drills." Harold's voice reflected the tired expression on his face, but his tone was even and cool.

"And if it doesn't stop raining?" Ezra asked, his heart sinking.

"We'll just have to get out there, grin and bear it anyway. If we're truly men, we need to act like it. A little rain ain't gonna kill any of us—that's a fact."

There were noticeable bags under Pratchit's eyes.

"With this Noah-rain, the sinks are shores gonna flow over."

Ezra massaged his temples, trying not to think about that possibility. He wiped the sweat from his brow, and ran his hand through his greasy hair.

The sink trench was already a pathetic, horrific excuse for an outhouse. It was just a long gorge, cut about five feet deep, that the men did their business over. It reeked so badly that there was literally no comparison to its vile stench. Even the rodents were fearful to venture near it.

"I keep expectin' somebody to keel over just from the darned fumes." Hayden groaned, tugging his wet shirt off and wringing the moisture out.

Harold cracked his knuckles and pushed his spectacles up on the bridge of his nose. "Nobody died yet of smelling the sinks. What are y'all, a bunch of deadbeats?"

"No, but shovelin' five tons of shit ain't exactly my idea of a fun day." Hayden continued to wring out his shirt, then threw it on the ground beside him in annoyance. His ribs protruded as he leaned forward and pulled off his shoes.

Ezra sighed and rolled his shoulders back, trying to ignore Pratchit as he fell into one of his coughing fits. "Who said this whole affair was supposed to be fun?"

Hayden grumbled something unintelligible, not looking up.

The rain continued to pelt down on the tent's roof, making loud patter-patter sounds as each drop hit. It created quite a din, but the men had learned to tune it out by now.

Ezra willed his lungs to fill with oxygen, but it was a chore. The air was stifling. His stomach gurgled, pangs of hunger gripping him. It was too wet to start a fire, and hardtack sounded utterly despicable right now. There was nothing to do but wait till things dried up before he could fetch some grub.

The man sighed, standing up. "I'm going for a walk."

He ducked beneath the tent flap door before anyone could comment.

God, please clear my mind before I lose it.

What used to be mere puddles had turned into small lakes. It wasn't an encouraging sight when this would likely mean a long day of cleaning up overflowed sinks after the rain had ceased.

Ezra rubbed his stiff, achy biceps, as he trudged through the deluge. He didn't care that his clothes were drenched—or that his hair was matted, hanging in loose, wet clumps down over his eyes.

He hardly even felt the wetness of the rain pelting against his skin.

You can't expect me to be like my brother, God. I can't ever be another Harry. He's a natural leader. I'm a natural failure.

Harold's life was full of blessing and success. He had a wife and children. A large farm. He was skilled in speaking to people. He worked hard and took responsibility for himself and his mistakes. His fellowship with the Creator seemed strong.

Ezra's life hardly mirrored his brother's. He'd never married. Never had much success with womenfolk, really. Before the war, he'd barely been able to provide for himself, let alone other people–a household. He couldn't talk to people worth beans, and he ran from the face of potential failure. He didn't even know if he possessed a true fellowship with the Savior. What he had felt so mediocre. Sometimes it didn't even seem there was much of a difference between him and Pratchit or Hayden.

Maybe he wasn't putting enough into it. Maybe his faith was dwindling and that was keeping him from a true connection with the Lord.

And amid this doubt, there was that burden lingering in his heart. A task unfinished. A task *he* was expected to complete.

Lord, I'm as clueless as anyone. You have to make known this stuff to me.

Harold always looked so certain and unashamed, almost fearless, when he engaged in spreading the word of God. He could quote Scripture effortlessly and he did so liberally.

Ezra? He'd always been a wall-flower as a boy, and not much changed as he'd entered adulthood. As to Scripture memorization, he'd barely even read the book of Genesis. "Erudite in the ways of God's Word" was not something that he would have used to described himself.

What worried him was that he might not communicate the gospel properly if he tried, and in result, accidentally turn somebody away from wanting to follow God. He just didn't know quite what to say.

Maybe he was just making up excuses. Not owning up to his job. Not taking responsibility. Not being the man God intended him to be.

Ezra pushed his hair out of his eyes, looking at his weathered palms.

How can somebody as inadequate as me be used for the kingdom of God?

***

Ezra was hauling buckets of sink-waste when he spotted Frances. The freckle-faced kid was lugging an armful of wet firewood in one arm and a bucket of water in the other. Ezra watched the small boy as he hauled the stuff to one of the fire pits within the camp.

On his way back from dumping the fetid slop of excrement, he saw the boy again. This time, he happened to look over just as the boy's gaze met his.

Ezra found himself smiling at the kid, who only stared back, a blank expression pasted on his face. His small mouth was in a straight line, and his whole being looked tense and uneasy. It was as if he was a distrusting, stray dog, stiffening at being petted.

That sharp, speckled little face haunted Ezra for the rest of the day. He mused and pondered on the boys' many different possible stories of origins: where he had really come from, why he had run away and enlisted, who his parents were, what he was keeping secret in that little book…detail upon detail that lay enshrouded in mystery.

At least Ezra had something to think upon. It helped with the boredom he had to deal with, doing the terribly mundane and monotonous humdrum every day for week upon week.

The hours passed sluggishly, unhurried, the day trickling away at a pace slower than molasses. Ezra was greatly thankful for evening when it arrived. His back ached from that long, sickening spell of sewage shoveling, and he found himself suffering from a severe headache.

Attempting to talk to Frances again would have to wait for another day. Tonight, he was far too tired and he hoped to hit the sack early.

Supper was meager, as usual. The air was still heavy and damp, and the smell of precipitation hung in the air. Sweat trickled down Ezra's forehead as he devoured the bit of baked beans on his plate, and little piece of brown bread. There wasn't any meat tonight.

He sighed. A little bacon would have been nice right about now.

As he headed back to the camp after he had gone and relieved himself, his ears picked up the sound of footsteps behind him, rustling the grass and crunching on leaves.

He spun around, scanning the moonlit landscape.

Before long, his eyes caught sight of three figures, heading into the shadows of the woods which stretched yonder. He squinted, trying to discern who the dark figures were.

Soft, blue moonbeams fell across the tree tops, which cast their black shadows down on earth, concealing the mysterious outlines sneaking away before him. He decided to investigate the trio and what they were up to at this time of night. It wasn't permitted to leave camp without a pass.

He proceeded after them cautiously. His eyes were watchful in the moon-bathed terrain, and he walked faster, trying to catch up to the figures.

Momentarily forgetting his sore back and aching muscles, Ezra followed the small company until they came to the road heading to the trading post.

Dade?

Ezra squinted as he glimpsed a familiar face.

Hayden?

He narrowed his eyes, squinting further. *What in blazes?*

"What are you madcaps doin' out here this time of day?" He called out, jogging up to the men, all of whom swung their heads around to look at him.

"Darson! What the devil?" Hayden stared at Ezra with a mixture of annoyance and suspicion.

"What's going on?" Ezra eyed the redhead and his partners in crime, wiping sweat from his brow and swatting at a couple of mosquitoes buzzing about his ears.

Hayden's mouth curled into a humored smile, exposing his crooked teeth.

"Wasn't expecting *you* to join us."

"I just happened to be taking a spell to alleviate myself and saw y'all heading out." Ezra replied, a bit deprecatingly.

"Nobody's getting hurt by leaving for a couple hours."

"Where you going?" Ezra crossed his arms on his chest, his tone no less suspicious.

William grinned impishly, a not-so-innocent look in his youthful, blue eyes. "There's a fancy girl in town."

Ezra's stomach gurgled. He coughed, hoping he'd heard wrong. "A *what?*"

"A fancy girl! Forgot they even existed anymore, did ya?" The other man's cracked lips formed a sardonic grin.

Ezra swallowed, anger sweltering under his skin. *A prostitute? That's why they were out here? Well, beat the dutch* - if that didn't beat all.

He looked over at Hayden, who was grinning, apparently amused at his reaction to the announcement.

Ezra raised an eyebrow coldly. "Well, bully for you." He set his jaw. "Where is she?"

"Cool it, cracker." Hayden's eyes sparkled roguishly in the moonlight. "We set it to meet her up yonder in the house a couple oft from the trading post."

Ezra frowned, his dark brows knitting together.

"You're welcome to join us if you have some money to throw in the pot." Hayden continued, examining his scarred palms nonchalantly.

Ezra tried to keep an emotionless, unflappable expression pasted on his profile.

"I don't think so."

William snickered. "Wet rag. Not even down for some horizontal refreshments."

Ezra exhaled. His insides boiled at the wickedness and irresponsibility of these three individuals. Scores of insults flashed through his mind, but nothing came to his mouth. He found himself clenching his fists unconsciously.

Hayden grinned in dark amusement. "Sure you don't wanna come? You'll be missing out on…" He paused a moment, raising his eyebrows and grinning broader for emphasis. "…A hell of a lot of fun."

Her feet go down to death; and her feet take hold on hell.

Ezra shook his head, recalling a verse from Proverbs that Harry had recited last week. "Not a chance. I…well, you see…it's…"

Frustration caused the man's face to turn red. He stuttered, unable to find the adequate words. "It's just not right…real men don't resort to this crap."

"*Crap?*" Hayden raised a brow and laughed dryly. "Well, *somebody's* set in his ways."

"Or maybe he's n'er touched a woman in his life and don't know what to do with one." The other fellow chimed in crassly.

Ezra's jaw stiffened. His eyes shot darts at the man who'd just spoken, bile seeping up the back of his throat.

"Somebody needs to take a cow-whip to your nasty, perverted hides."

Hayden turned slightly, his eyes snapping back at Ezra. "If it's such a wickedness to you, why don't ya just get away from our filthy swath of ungodliness? Where's yer soapbox? Are you gonna preach at us like your brother? I thought you were better than that, Darson. Thought you might be a decent fella. I thought there was hope for you." Hayden penetrated Ezra's eyes with his own.

"You must have a different definition of hope. One I don't know."

Ezra glared at Hayden and stormed away before anyone had a chance to say anything else.

Inside, he fumed. Partly because he didn't know how to react to Hayden's parting remarks, and partly because he'd made himself look like a self-righteous fool.

His cheeks burned, and his fists remain clenched. He looked up to the starry heavens in discouragement and frustration.

Lord....just why. Why'd you put me in with such a sorry case of losers?

Sighing, he shook his head in despondency.

God, You have to help me here. How can I speak truth when no words come to my lips?

Chapter Ten

July 20th, 1863

ZEPHYR

ZEPHYR KNELT DOWN BESIDE THE bed, forcing her mind to focus. She sighed, closing her eyes wearily.

How out of touch she felt with her Creator. How distant her heart seemed to have strayed from His presence, and how the ever-present knowledge of this pained her.

She groaned. Her head swam in a morass of thought and emotion. She longed for the chaos within her to cease, even for just a moment, so that she might hear a word from the Lord.

Anything.

Three years ago, she had knelt beside her bed, just as she was doing now. Her thirteen-year-old self had cried out in earnest to God and spent nearly two hours that evening in prayer.

Zephyr swallowed, cherishing those blessed moments of yesteryear. She missed them. That evening was perhaps the first time she had ever heard the Holy Ghost distinctly talk to her.

Oh yes, it had been an audible voice, Zephyr heard it plain as day. Maybe it wasn't audible in the sense that anyone else could hear it, but regardless, it was real. It….she couldn't exactly explain how it sounded, for it was something that you had to experience for yourself. The fact of the matter was, she heard a voice. And it wasn't like the ones she typically heard.

At first she had wondered if it was merely her own mind, babbling as it always did, going from one topic to another in split seconds.

But somehow, she knew it wasn't her own thought. It had to be the Spirit. It just had to be.

She had been complaining to Him about how imperfect she was...how dirty, sinful, flawed.

"No, you are made perfect in Me." His reply had been soft but ever so clear. The words never left her mind. She cherished them more than anything.

Radiant sunbeams fell through the curtained window, as they always did this time of morning. Zephyr felt the warmth of their rays on her back, which contrasted sharply with the memory of that cool, dark evening in which she had heard the Lord speak.

Her pine-colored hair glowed with copper highlights, as the sun touched the tresses.

Lord Jesus, I can't begin to say how unworthy I am of Your grace and love...Your provision. I don't deserve any of it. I don't understand why you've blessed me so greatly when I've only brought you disappointment and grief.

Caught in an immense sea of gratitude for her Savior, the girl buried her head in her arms against the bedside.

Thank you for giving me this family that I can be a part of; and thank you that we still have the freedom to live in the manner we do. Please be with dear Pa; place a hedge of protection around him.

Zephyr opened her eyes slowly, lifting her head from her arms.

You can take care of him, I know you can. But can you please bring him home soon, Lord, real soon?

Hearing a stampede of footsteps in the hallway, Zephyr remembered she had a full day of work and responsibilities ahead, as usual. She needed to go make breakfast, for one thing. Muffins.

She stood up, her knees popping in protest.

Well, Lord, thank you for letting me be alive another day. Please let it be a productive one.

Entering the hallway, the girl was nearly barreled over by her three youngest brothers as they thundered past.

"Boys!" she hissed. Her eyes followed them as they plummeted out the back door without paying an ounce of heed to her admonishing.

Patience, Zephyr. She let out a short sigh, trying to shake her head of the frustration she was already feeling towards her brothers. It was too early in the morning to be getting upset with them. She needed to focus on doing what she needed to do...focus on honoring the Lord and focus on setting a good example.

Focus.

"Good morning Zephyr!"

Mrs. Darson's gentle voice greeted Zephyr as she swung open the kitchen's screen door and stepped inside the small edifice.

Zephyr forced a small smile. "'Morning." She quickly set to looking for the ingredients for breakfast.

"You're late coming in this morning, yet again." Ma's tone was moderate, but her words stung like rubbing alcohol in a wound.

Zephyr flitted about the kitchen trying to finish the task before her as quickly as possible. Baking soda, where was the baking soda?

"I know, I should've gotten up earlier," she admitted. "Where'd you last put the baking soda?"

Mrs. Darson nodded toward an array of jars and containers on the counter.

"In its usual place, Zephyr. Where I *always* put it."

Zephyr paused, forcing herself to look carefully and precisely, instead of lazily glancing over it all.

Aha.

Mrs. Darson was busy blanching okra on the woodstove. "I'm going to head up to Micanopy today and see how Grandma's doing, so I need you to make sure everyone gets their work done. Try to give the little boys their school lessons, too."

Zephyr nodded absentmindedly. "You wanted me to make biscuits, right?"

"No, Zephyr. *Muffins.*" Mrs. Darson replied, in a mildly chiding manner.

The sixteen year old bit her lip. "Oh. Guess I forgot already."

She tossed teaspoons and tablespoons of the different condiments into the mixing bowl.

"How long will ya be gone?" She bent down and scooped a tin cup of wheat berries from their sack, then dumped the berries into the small grain-mill's hopper.

"Several hours. Not too long. It's been a little while since I've talked with her and I felt I should go see how she's fairing today." Mrs. Darson put a lid on the pot and wiped her hands on a dishtowel. She looked up at Zephyr soberly. "I can't believe it's been three years."

Was it really that time of year again? The anniversary of her grandfather's passing? Zephyr swallowed. Of course it was. How could she have forgotten?

"Make sure you clean up any messes you make." Mrs. Darson reminded, turning down the heat on the stove. "I'm heading out to the barn. Remember, the boys' lessons."

Zephyr let out a very subtle sigh, careful not to let her mother notice.

It's not like I'm a child, Ma. You don't have to tell me things I already know.

"I will." She answered, turning the handle on the mill to grind the wheat berries into flour.

As her arm pumped back and forth, cranking the mill's handle, she let her mind wander. The kitchen was so quiet without anyone else to accompany her.

Ten minutes passed.

And then the dogs started barking. And barking. And *barking.*

Ma can't be back that quickly.

The persistent yapping continued. Zephyr huffed and dropped her work with the flour, stepping outside to see what was happening.

"Grizzly! Nina! Hush!" she yelled, barely out of the kitchen door.

That was when her heart stopped. She gasped, staring at the wagon parked alongside the road. It was a simple Conestoga frame, without the tarp roof attached. But the wagon itself was not what stopped Zephyr in her tracks. It was the figure walking toward the front door.

What on earth…

Zephyr felt herself breaking into a nervous sweat as she stared at the wagon like a smitten fool.

"Zephyr!" Rudy's voice echoed across the yard. "It's Silas! Silas is here!"

Zephyr's mouth went strangely dry and her heart pounded.

Leave it to little brothers to announce everything smoothly.

The young woman sighed loudly in embarrassment.

What am I supposed to do now?

She felt her cheeks flushing. *Stupid girl, you can't just leave him standing there…*

Without a second thought, Zephyr ran to the back door, letting it slam behind her as she bolted down the hall and through the house to the front door.

As she reached it, she came to an abrupt halt, quickly trying to rearrange her hair and wipe any flour off her clothes. Her *clothes.*

Zephyr groaned, staring down at her trousers. Why did she have to pick today of all days to wear *trousers?*

Fine. So I look utterly beastly. It doesn't matter. She bit her lip, trying to find her resolve again.

With her heart pounding and her hands jittery, she opened the door.

"Good morning, Zephyr." A husky, magical male voice greeted her ears.

Zephyr's eyes widened. There he stood, the one person that tugged on her heartstrings and perplexed her to no end. She chewed on her inner lip, quickly taking in his handsome dark hair and slender, muscular arms. "H-hullo, Silas," she stammered, staring into his eyes.

"You're... probably wondering what I'm doing here, I suppose." Fortunately, the young man didn't seem to be any less nervous than Zephyr was. His eyes penetrated into hers for a moment that felt like an eternity, and then they dropped, flitting away.

Zephyr studied his shy, boyish face for a moment while he was still looking away. She loved the way his long nose sloped, the dark bushiness of his eyebrows, and the sharp contours of his jaw. If ever there was a good-looking male, he was it.

"Uh, yeah, actually..." She cleared her throat awkwardly.

He seemed to have fixed his gaze on the front step.

"Well, Maw said to stop making y'all come over to our place to drop off the milk...she thought it wasn't polite of us. So here I am."

His eyes didn't move, hinting that he also was caught up in the intimidation of being in the presence of the opposite gender. Zephyr wondered if he was like this with all other girls he knew. Or could it possibly be just her? For a split second the prospect wandered into her mind that maybe he felt the same way towards her that she did towards him.

No...no, that would be too good to be true. It just couldn't be.

"Uh, I was uh...wondering..."

Zephyr pulled herself back to reality, glancing up at him as his gaze locked on something behind her. She stared at the young man, waiting for him to continue.

His Adam's apple bobbed as he scratched his forearm, his gaze glued on the wall. "Never mind. It's two gallons as usual."

"Alright. I'll be back in a minute." Zephyr tried to decipher the look in his eyes for a brief second longer before she turned to exit.

Once she was out of sight, she ran back down the hallway and out to the kitchen again.

Breathlessly, she burst through the small building's screen door. She had to clear her head before she could go back in that room. Everything inside her was exploding. Her whole body was going haywire.

Clarence was poking a fork around in the okra on the stove.

"They came for their milk." Zephyr let out a long sigh, opening the cellar door and retrieving two gallons. "I mean…he did…*ugh*. I sound like such an idiot."

The boy smirked, raising an eyebrow slightly. "Oh yeah, I saw Silas out there. Don't act too infatuated."

Zephyr growled as she headed back out the door again.

She grinned self-consciously as she entered the main room again. "Here you go. Sorry I'm all out of sorts. I wasn't expecting anyone to drop in and…"

The girl stopped, speechless. Music reached her ears. Piano music.

Her eyes widened as a lump formed in her throat. Her heart pounded against her chest with a newfound violence, and she had to blink, wondering if this was all a dream.

Silas was playing the piano.

Silas was playing the piano in *her* house.

Silas was playing the piano!

Zephyr stared as his long fingers danced over the keys. His eyes were closed. Zephyr didn't utter a word. She didn't want to ruin the perplexing beauty of this moment.

Elated emotions flooded her soul. Tears pricked at her eyes. *I must be dreaming again.*

And then it was over. Quick as it had begun, the magic was no more. Disappointment filled Zephyr's being as she exhaled quietly. Silas opened his eyes quickly, almost as if snapping awake. He stood again quickly; blushing and moving a few steps back toward the door.

"I'm…I'm sorry. I shouldn't have done that." He lowered his voice, red creeping across his face. "I…I just haven't seen a piano in so long." He shook his head, frowning as if he'd done a shameful thing. "I'm sorry."

"No...don't be." Zephyr swallowed. She realized she was smiling. "That...was beautiful."

Silas' eyes met hers, and for a moment they stayed there. "Th-thanks," he murmured, dropping his gaze again.

Zephyr smiled, still lost in the euphoria of his music. And then she realized she had the milk jars in a death grip. She swallowed again, her face flushed. "Oh, sorry...h-here." She tried not to be inelegant as she handed him the clanking bottles.

He took them from her cold, sweaty hands, his fingers briefly touching hers. Zephyr shivered as a bolt of electricity flew down her spine at the feeling of his skin against her fingers.

Wow.

She looked up at him, just as his glance happened to meet hers. Their eyes locked for an ever-so-brief instant, and his gaze penetrated into her soul as it always did.

She couldn't escape his gaze. Her eyes were locked in the elegant richness of deep umber.

Haunting brown eyes.

Zephyr swallowed, trying to keep her mind from flying away in the clouds. She was utterly mesmerized and helpless to stop it.

Finally, who knows *how*, she managed to pull her gaze away from him.

"That'll be...that'll be twenty-five cents, please," she stuttered, staring at the ground like a dunce. He knew how much the milk cost, but she felt the need to say *something* to break the awkward silence engulfing them. Even if what she said was an obvious, unnecessary statement.

Silas reached into his pocket, retrieving a couple of coins. Zephyr's eyes drifted back up to him, as he dropped the nickels and pennies into her hand.

"Thank you," he mumbled, his gaze brushed hers once more, before he lowered it diffidently.

"No...thank *you*. For the music, I mean." The words came gawkily, as Zephyr tried to return a suitable response. "You're an excellent pianist." She smiled broadly.

"Not really." The fellow shook his head. "But I'm glad you liked it. I- I guess I should go now."

Zephyr swallowed, realizing she'd been fidgeting with her hands the entire time as usual. "Take care."

Nodding a simple farewell, the young man started to walk back to his father's wagon.

He didn't look back.

Lost in a fog of emotion, Zephyr reentered the house, shutting the door behind her as if to shut out the consuming, eternal memory of Silas. A stranger she was now utterly infatuated with.

Chapter Eleven

ZEPHYR

THE YOUNG WOMAN LET OUT a melancholic sigh and shuffled back through the house to finish fixing breakfast. An unexplainable feeling had embedded itself in her heart, and she felt as if she had been hit by a herd of cattle and trampled ten times over.

The sensation of looking into Silas' eyes had been exhilarating. But the remembrance that he had only come to collect milk for his father was not. The recollection that he was far too shy to ever talk in any depth to Zephyr made her insides tie up in knots. Still, she'd felt his eyes on her. She'd felt that sense of longing in them. Was it too much to hope...hope that maybe...

Zephyr sighed again and flew out the back door, slamming it behind her. *No.* The whole notion was ridiculous, and she knew better than to let her imagination go hog-wild.

He actually plays the piano. Just...just like I dreamed.

Opening the kitchen's screen door again, she set the milk money on the counter and returned to grinding flour.

Why, God? Why am I so drawn to Silas? He's torturing my soul and driving me to insanity. Lord, why did I have to fall for him? Why does he have to be so shy, and why do I have to be so... so bungling?

Zephyr exhaled, venting to God her quandaries.

Help me control my feelings, Lord. Clear my mind and help me to think straight. I can't let myself think of that boy like this. I ought to be thinking of more important things.

Aware that breakfast needed to be done soon and that she was already late enough with it, Zephyr worked faster, combining ingredients and whisking together a thick batter, which she poured into the muffin tins she had set out.

Finally, the muffins were in the woodstove oven baking. Zephyr wiped the countertop clean, and put away the remaining ingredients. Then she scampered out the screen door and into the house. There was schoolwork of her own to do next, while she waited for the muffins to bake.

She padded through the house to the parlor.

Algebra. Oh joy.

A little sigh slipped out as she bent to retrieve a thick volume from the bookshelf. Maybe she could forget about Silas by immersing herself in the unpleasantness of its complexities and enigmatic equations.

Collecting the heavy, drab book and a small slate, she shuffled to the bedroom and flopped inelegantly on her and Lydia's bed.

Turning to lie on her stomach, she sprawled her long legs out behind her on the bed, in a fashion she'd done as a little girl.

Zephyr grinned slightly, almost mischievously. Nobody else was in the house, so for the moment she had nothing to worry about. For the moment, since no one was there to see, it didn't matter if her body was positioned in a rather unladylike manner. She highly doubted that God would mind.

The last thing she wanted was to cause a brother in Christ to stumble because of her own carelessness. It was bad enough that she already had a flirtatious side left over from her more reckless childhood. Bad enough, that as a rebellious twelve year old, a birthday party resulted in havoc because of her foolish, naïve ways. Bad enough, that as a young teen, she let Anson kiss her on the cheek, play with her hair, and try to entice her into his bed. Sure, she might have smacked him when he first reached over to plant that kiss, but beyond a few scolds, she let him go easy. He was, after all, her best friend.

Zephyr rolled her eyes. Well, there weren't any young men around and he *certainly* wasn't there, so she could sit however she wanted.

Drat. I've already let my mind wander again. Guess I'm pretty excellent at doing that. If I got paid for every daydream or idle thought I'd be a millionaire by now. Why'd I have to waste five minutes thinking about Anson Whistler of all people?

Zephyr huffed, forcing her mind back to the pages before her. Her scatterbrained train of thought often annoyed her with the places it traveled. She didn't have time for this. The muffins would be done soon and she'd miss her opportunity to get any of this algebra done.

Not ten minutes into her studies, a voice echoed out across the hallway.

"Zephhhhyrrrrrrr, the muffins!"

It was Lydia.

With a hint of annoyance, Zephyr sat up and stretched her arms briefly.

That's what I get for letting my mind choose in what direction it flies.

Zephyr pursed her lips, trying to compose herself as she jogged back through the empty house and out to the kitchen again.

The smell of muffins cooking met her as she threw open the screen door. It was a pleasant, welcoming smell, and Zephyr inhaled it with a sense of satisfaction.

Mmmm.

"Are they done?" Lydia was washing dishes in a basin nearby. *For once...she's doing something to help?*

Zephyr leaned down and swung open the little woodstove's front door, feeling her eyes water as a blast of heat sweltered out on her face.

"Nope, not yet." Carelessly, she slammed the door closed again and turned to stampede back into the house.

"Burned muffins taste horrible." Lydia wrinkled her nose.

"They're *not* burning." Zephyr rolled her eyes. "I say give 'em another five minutes."

Five minutes passed - as quick as lightning, and quicker. Soon, fifteen minutes had flitted away, and Zephyr was still in the bedroom, attempting to study.

Her mind was immersed in the paradoxes of the algebraic world, when she suddenly noticed a horrible, dreaded smell.

Oh no...

Zephyr's eye widened. Suddenly, she remembered.

Five minutes. Five minutes had passed. How long had it been, now?

She sprung off the bed like a hyper calf.

The muffins.

They were burning. Ma would have a fit. Breakfast would be ruined, and she'd have to start over…which would wreck the entire day's schedule.

Nobody liked to eat burned muffins.

She raced through the house and out the back door as if her life depended on it.

Breathlessly, she threw open the kitchen screen door only to find Clarence, standing by the stove, a reproving expression written across his face. "I should've seen it coming." He shook his head.

Stopping a second to catch her breath, Zephyr swallowed, taking in the situation. A light puff of smoke was spewing from the woodstove, and the smell of burned food lingered in the humid air.

"Why didn't you take them out?" She asked her brother in agitation.

Clarence frowned. "It's not my job."

Zephyr huffed and yanked open the woodstove door. Still lost in a blur of aggravation and impulsiveness, she grabbed a dishtowel from the counter and reached into the stove to retrieve the muffins from its smoldering belly.

A vehement, abrupt wave of pain hit her as the hot pan touched one of her fingers.

"*Stupid pan!*" Zephyr screeched.

She found herself hurtling the entire thing to the floor, sending its contents airborne.

"*What in blazes, Zephyr?* Have you gone raving mad?" Lydia's voice reached her ears and she realized that several pairs of eyes were staring at her.

Her thumb now had a large blister where the skin had been burned. It throbbed and seemed to swell by the second.

The anger and impatience which Zephyr had harbored hadn't left. Her face was red again, but this time it wasn't from shyness or the presence of a boy.

Tears were trickling down her cheeks. *Oh blast. Why? Just why?*

"You just don't know! *You just don't know at all!*" She heard herself shout.

Flinging open the screen door and stampeding outside, she determined to get as far away from any form of human life as possible.

Clarence and Lydia's questioning voices echoed out behind her.

Zephyr let out a long sigh, tears stinging her eyes. What had just happened? Why had she lost it so bad right then? What was wrong with her?

She stared up at the blue, cloudless summer sky, her vision blurred by the excess water trickling from her eyes.

Absentmindedly, and quite morosely, she began pacing into the woods. She had to get away. Get away, and sort things out in her mind. She had to compose herself again.

There was no possibility of going back to the kitchen in this current state. She'd already humiliated herself enough.

Zephyr let the tears dry on her face. She breathed deep, her eyes still smarting.

Lydia would have even less respect for her now. And Clarence would be taunting her for the rest of the week. Both would see her as even more of a freak. A weakling.

Splendid.

The woods glowed in shades of lush, rich green. Zephyr realized one benefit to the hot summer months—the trees and grass all thrived in this season. They were so beautiful right now, a sharp contrast to her mind and soul.

Zephyr closed her eyes and tried to swallow. Her throat was painfully dry, and the throbbing in her finger hadn't gone away. She looked down at it and sighed.

The pain in her heart hadn't gone away, either.

And the worst thing about it was, she didn't even know why that pain existed. Why was she so angry? Why did she feel this oppressive spirit weighing her heart down?

Was she just being overly emotional?

Maybe Zephyr was just plain out of it, completely. Maybe hysteria was what drove her to such ridiculous ends. Perhaps something was wrong with her brain. What if she had been dropped on her head as a baby, and neither Ma nor Pa had ever told her?

No. She wouldn't allow herself to think such dooming thoughts.

Vacantly, she found herself kicking at the pine-needle covered ground.

A myriad of thoughts and emotions swirled through her, and hard as she tried, she couldn't separate one from the other. They all screamed in her mind, creating a deafening drone which only made her all the more provoked.

It was as if a storm had taken residence in her head. And like a ship stranded in the midst of an angry sea, so her soul was, tossed about on the raging gulf of her thoughts and emotions. Swirling endlessly into pandemonium. Utter chaos.

She couldn't figure out why this anger had set in so strongly, or where it had come from to begin with. Who was she angry with? God? Silas? Her family members? Herself?

Her mind seemed to cloud all the more as she tried to figure out the root of her problems. She rubbed the palms of her hands into her forehead as if warding off a headache.

She had no reason to be angry at God. This was plain as day.

Was Silas the cause of the turmoil in her mind? Maybe. He had a tendency to do strange things to her heart.

At the moment, she was filled with more resentment towards the young man than admiration. It would be so much easier if she had never even met him. What was the point of their being acquaintances? How was it, in any way, productive or meaningful?

Zephyr was tired of trying to figure out the perplexing nature of Silas. Most of all, she was tired of her heart breaking again and again, all because of him.

He had caused her more pain than pleasure. Really, the whole ordeal seemed stupid and ridiculous when aligned with the fact that he was still little more than a complete stranger.

Zephyr threw herself down on the ground and buried her head in her arms.

This was not how today was supposed to be going. Already she'd made such a mess of it—oh, if she could only go back to bed and start it all over!

She sobbed miserably. She didn't try to stop herself or look around to see if anyone was watching. At the moment, she didn't care. These were tears she'd been storing up and hiding for what felt like eons. Now it was time for them to leave her. To escape. It was time for her to be cleansed.

For several minutes, in this state of relative impassiveness, the young woman allowed her mind to drift aimlessly. To Silas and his beautiful, yet painfully enigmatic eyes. To the chiding quips of Clarence. To Lydia's icy little sneers, which reminded her of a venomous snake, always threatening to strike. And then, she let her thoughts drift to her father, hundreds of miles away, in a world stained by the corruption and filth of war.

She didn't try to dictate the direction of her thoughts. It was as if she had released control of her mind and let somebody else take the wheel for a little bit. It was a clamorous ride…yet, almost peaceful. For the first time this morning, she felt what seemed to be a smidgen of serenity.

How peculiar, Zephyr mused sedately. Quiet waters in the midst of a raging ocean. It didn't make sense at all.

For a moment, she lay there on the earthen floor, her eyes closed in surrender and submission.

"God, I don't know what's wrong with me. But I need you to cure whatever the disease is."

She found herself murmuring a short prayer, her eyes still shut, dried tears staining the sides of her face.

Go back, Zephyr.

A sinking feeling hit the young woman's stomach. Go back? That would be difficult. With her pride already so wounded, could she bear to take another blow?

Zephyr closed her eyes again, letting the remaining fire and emotion drain from her body. It was hard, but she had to release it or things would never be fixed. She exhaled, her soul crying out for direction and guidance.

Whatever she was holding on to that was causing her to feel this way, she must let it go.

Go back, Zephyr.

The young woman rose to her feet. Voices echoed across the landscape, and she forced her eyes open.

Unfamiliar tones.

Zephyr's feet began moving toward the house. Something was amiss.

Before she knew it, the girl had increased her pace. Soon she was running out of the woods and into the open, her heart pounding with fear of the unknown.

Something's wrong. Anxiety crippled her mind.

Zephyr stopped just outside of the garden as she glimpsed what lay beyond the front lawn. Her stomach churned.

Ten or so mounted horses were gathered at the road. At least two dozen men total. Two with military-looking uniforms were dismounting.

Zephyr's heart rate increased as she slowed her pace and cautiously crept around the garden to the back door of the house. This didn't look good. Something felt off about the whole congregation. These men didn't belong here.

Where are the little boys? Clar and Lyd? The young woman gulped as she entered her parents' bedroom quietly. She glanced around herself, her entire system tense.

Her eyes searched until they found what she was looking for. The large, double-barrel shotgun was tucked in a corner behind the wardrobe. It had been untouched for who knew how long.

Zephyr swallowed as she took the firearm in her arms. The metal barrel was cold and clammy against her skin. She checked to see if it was loaded. It was.

God, help me, she murmured quietly, grabbing a handful of cartridges from the box of ammunition sitting atop of the wardrobe.

Shoving these in her trouser pocket, she made her way back outside through the back door. She didn't like the idea of greeting this company in a predictable manner.

Nina and Grizzly's barking continued, only adding to the ominous tension in the air. Zephyr took a deep breath and walked slowly alongside the exterior wall of the house toward the front yard. Forcing herself to remain calm and undaunted, she tilted her chin up and propped the gun against her shoulder in a defensive yet still-unthreatened manner.

Where are those kids? She continued to scan the premises for her siblings. If this was trouble, she didn't want them anywhere that they could get pulled into it.

One of the men approached her, walking away from his group by the road. She tensed. His colors were blue and he had a large, US belt buckle.

Her heart pounded as memories flooded her mind. Memories of when Pa talked about the CS recruiters riding up and demanding he join them or suffer the consequences. She eyed the man and then the crowd a ways behind him. She didn't like this at all. It couldn't be good.

He raised a hand in the air, eyeing the large shotgun.

"Excuse me ma'am, I'm Phil Carson with the Federal army."

Zephyr's jaw tightened as did every other muscle in her body. Where had these northerners come from? She'd never seen a Union soldier in her life.

"What do you want?" She continued to watch the man suspiciously, her lips pressing together.

"We're recruitin' able-bodied men and boys to help rustle cows to take to the soldiers up north."

Zephyr's stomach dropped. Her fingers trembled, instinctively moving closer to the trigger.

"Y-you won't find anybody here."

The man tilted his head and looked at Zephyr, his eyes communicating distrust. He nodded toward the large garden plots on the western side of the house.

"You keep this all up yourself?"

Zephyr tried to steady her shaky hands. She looked into the Fed's eyes, mustering a steely expression.

"I'm capable of a lot more than you think." She glanced nervously to the side, hoping that wherever her siblings were, they'd stay put.

The soldier's eyes flitted back to Zephyr and his gaze dragged over her body, resting on her full, womanly curves. He raised an eyebrow. "You're a solid piece of work indeed, but I ain't buyin' that you're here all alone. Where's your man at?"

"I don't have one." Zephyr lifted her chin ever so slightly. She exhaled, forcing air out of her lungs and gripping the gun barrel tighter.

The man moved closer, paralleling Zephyr. In contrast to her tight-lipped, apprehensive appearance, he looked composed and unruffled. Too much for Zephyr's liking. She wanted him as on edge as she was, not cool as a cucumber.

"Oh come on, now. A fetchin' girl like you? You're certainly old enough. You ain't got *anybody*?" A small chuckle came from the man's lips. "You're a poor liar."

Zephyr felt her face flushing. "I'm no liar."

He took a step closer, still watching her. A small smile twisted at his mouth, making Zephyr even more uneasy. She didn't like the hungry way he was looking at her. His eyes kept drifting to places they shouldn't.

"Young lady, if you'll just be honest, I can tell my men to move on to the next homestead. I'll be out of your hair for good."

That's highly doubtful.

"Wh-who says I should trust you?" Zephyr stammered, her finger hovering above the trigger. She lifted the barrel so that it aligned with his chest. "Who says you're not just some band of deserters tryin' to act all high and mighty?"

The man smirked. "Calm down. I can show you my US government papers if you so desire."

Zephyr swallowed and continued to look him in the eye. "You'll find nobody of use here. My father's already in the army."

"Is that so? What unit?"

"Florida 7th. And I ain't ashamed to tell you. Also, I ain't afraid to say that I already hate your kind." Zephyr's arms stiffened. "Now, if you would, I'm growin' weary of this jawin'. Would you kindly escort your posy off my land?"

The man frowned and glanced toward the barn. "Such an adamant girl! So you're for the enemy, then. Well, your loss. You had a chance, miss. You may be supporting rebel scum, but that don't mean you ain't got things my unit can use. Oh, and you might be of some use yourself, now that I've thought about it." His gaze moved up and down her body again and he grinned coyly.

Zephyr's throat tightened, as did her grip on the gun— if that was possible at all.

"*Leave.* You have no right to anything here."

His eyes penetrated hers, and he raised a brow subtly, as if in amusement.

"As far as I'm concerned, I have all the right in the world. Save your breath."

He turned and waved to his group.

"Search the house and barn! Take the animals and anything else of use that you can find!"

Zephyr's eyes widened and her mouth fell open.

"And you go around recruitin' men for your cause...what was that cause for again? 'Freedom?'" She spat out vehemently, her heart racing. "F-freedom. Freedom to what – steal and plunder?" She leveled the gun at him, preparing to shoot. "You let your men go any further and this thing'll blow your cussed arm off. Or, maybe someplace else." She dipped the barrel lower, pointing it at his crotch momentarily.

The words she heard herself speaking surprised her. She'd never threatened to shoot a person before, let alone actually done it. Her fingers shook so much she wondered if she could actually pull it off.

But there was no way she was letting these men into the house or barn. She knew plain as day they'd take Clarence if they saw him. He wasn't a man by any means, but he was big for his age and strong as an ox.

Zephyr Darson had already lost one family member to this cursed war effort. She wasn't losing another.

Oh Lord, please keep the children hidden. Keep Clarence hidden.

The young woman hoped they'd noticed that something was wrong and had gone to find a decent hiding spot. The youngsters were so good at hide and seek. If only they'd put that skill to use at a time when it was actually needed.

A small swarm of men barged through the front door. Another group headed out to the barn. Nobody paid any heed to Zephyr's warning. The girl's knees buckled as she stared around in horror.

"Listen, miss. Consider this a repayment. If you ain't got any men here, we'll have to improvise. Make up for the time that was lost, ya know?" The man started to head past her, unfazed by her threat. "Now, don't try and run off anywhere yet. I'll be back." He threw in a subtle wink that made her stomach turn.

Zephyr didn't know what to do. The thought of shooting somebody terrified her, but the thought of her brother being discovered was even worse. She couldn't stop them if they found Clarence. And then there was the idea of that man taking her… that slimy federal…

Lord, give me strength.

A distraction. She needed a distraction. There were ten horses just idling out there by the road…what if…

"Zephyr!"

Lydia?

Zephyr spun around. A skinny ginger raced across the yard from the other side of the house, her face red and eyes wide.

Lydia nearly flew into Zephyr. "What on earth is happenin'?" She panted, fear making her voice crack.

Zephyr swallowed. Her entire body quivered and she'd broken into a cold sweat.

"I...I don't know." She couldn't speak. Her own voice sounded alien. Everywhere she looked, there were men rushing around. Some were in the garden, their arms loaded with okra and cucumbers.

"Zephyr..." Lydia squeaked, elbowing her as somebody led Amelia away on a rope.

"Wh-where are the boys?" Zephyr stammered. Her gaze locked on the men emerging from the house. Some carried things in their hands, but Zephyr's vision had blurred too much for her to know what they were taking.

Lydia's green eyes were as big as saucers. "I don't know." She watched as the goats were corralled out of the barn. "What are we gonna do?" she whispered, her voice shrill.

Zephyr started walking toward the road. It was as if her feet were just moving themselves without her knowledge. "Come on." She croaked, still gripping the shotgun as tightly as ever.

"Where did you last see Clar?" She asked. For once, her voice carried no tone or emotion. Blankly, she stared straight ahead.

"Uh...in the kitchen?" Lydia caught up with the older girl, looking around skittishly. "What...what are you doing?" Her voice had become two notches higher than normal.

Zephyr exhaled slowly, her eyes smarting. Her throat constricted and she pressed her lips together, trying to overcome the tremors twisting through her body.

"I'm not gonna let this happen. They can't do this—"

"Zephyr...*what are you doing?*" Lydia's voice rose louder, shriller. She sounded like a shrieking witch.

What am I doing?

The young woman set her jaw. Breathing had become scarily difficult. It was as if all sound had been canceled out. The throbbing of her heart was torturous and unending, rollicking her brain like a giant drum. Every breath she took seemed to take a lifetime. She moved in slow motion, cocking the large firearm almost subconsciously.

Her finger encircled the trigger.

"Alright men, get back to your horses! The Captain wants us to hit a few more places before it gets dark."

Zephyr blinked, trying to focus her vision. Everything was blurry. She saw movement in front of her, but it wouldn't register. Blackness swallowed her little by little, creeping in around the sides of her eyes. She felt lightheaded, disoriented. She tried to steady herself, but everything spun in front of her.

Thunderous sounds reverberated through the air. Muddled noises – horses whinnying, and hoof beat against the road. Aggravated shouts. More whinnies, and the scuffling of footsteps running past her.

Zephyr's knees turned to jelly, and that was the end of it. All sensory awareness closed down.

She was losing control.

Blackness.

Blackness.

Nothing.

***

"Zephyr!" Lydia's muffled shriek reached Zephyr's ears but it was if she hadn't heard it. The sound waves bounced and echoed against her eardrums. No feeling came to her limbs. The scene before her was like looking into a muddy pond – murky and gray.

Nothing made sense. Was she dreaming? Surely this wasn't reality.

Gradually, her sight came back, and the darkness receded.

What…what happened?

It didn't feel legitimate – it didn't seem *real*. None of this did.

Zephyr felt her arms being gripped by something…someone. She blinked and tried to make out her surroundings. Her head swam and a dull throbbing had taken up residence behind her temples.

"Zephyr! What'd you do to yourself?"

Lydia's face was inches from hers, her hot breath blowing in Zephyr's eyes.

The young woman tried to push herself up, without responding to Lydia's stunned words. It was in vain. She was too weak.

Something had gone awry. But what, *exactly*? She couldn't think straight. She wanted to speak but no words came. It was like her brain had been turned off.

All her memories had vanished and she couldn't remember a thing to save her life.

I fainted.

Well, at least she could recall that much.

"What happened to her?" It was another voice, separate from Lydia's. *"What's going on?"* Definitely not feminine, but it sounded familiar. Something shot to life in Zephyr's brain, wailing like a warning signal. Her stomach twisted. She knew she had to do something—to get up and return to whatever had been happening before she passed out. But what could she do when trapped in a completely disoriented mind and unresponsive body?

Somebody was pulling her to her feet. Her head fell limp on one shoulder, and she stared expressionlessly at the new face. Curly blond hair. A slightly-round face. Blue eyes. A gray haze diluted everything and melded the colors together.

Clarence?

"Wh-what   is...wh-wh-where...uh....where...a-are...uh..." Zephyr tried desperately to articulate syllables. She summoned up all powers of concentration, but it was in vain. Her mouth was as detached as every other part of her. She felt like a stupid fool. A monkey blabbering gibberish.

"You need to sit down. Come on, Lyd, help me get her inside." Clarence commanded, holding Zephyr's arm firmly and ushering her forward. Lydia took her other arm.

"My...my...le..." Zephyr babbled like a baby, stumbling over her numb heels. Her lip hung open, and the taste of blood greeted her tongue. Her head had only cleared a little. She was still helpless, completely reliant on her siblings to direct her.

"What happened?" She heard Clarence ask.

"Just when it looked like she was gonna shoot that dern thing, the Feds decided to up and leave." Lydia's voice was less shrill than earlier. "The rascals got over to the horses and our animals, then they all done scattered down the road. Took off like a bolt of lightin'. Well, I guess Zephyr was too shook up right about then because she passed out."

Zephyr's head bounced limply. Her eyelids were heavy and the throbbing in her forehead hadn't subsided. "Wha...where...where... th-they...go?" Finally. She'd managed to utter something faintly intelligible.

"I dunno. Maybe they'll forget 'bout us now. All I know is once they got their orders they were outta here. But as soon as that happened, *you* were out like a light." Excitement had replaced the former horror in Lydia's voice. "I still can't believe you actually *fainted,* Zeph."

"I...c-couldn't...couldn't...h-help..."

Ugh, forget about trying to say anything. At least they're gone.

It seemed like forever before her mind cleared completely.

Sunken against the couch's worn cushions, Zephyr remained silent. Numb. All she could do was wait for the storm to pass. For the cloudiness to dissolve and her brain to recover. Chills had taken her body and she shivered, despite the hundred-degree weather. Goosebumps pricked her arms.

Everything will be fine. It'll be over soon. Just hang in there.

Everyone had gathered in the dining room. Zephyr had plopped down on the sofa, while Clarence and Lydia jabbered endlessly about the soldiers. The little boys joined their older siblings, and soon, the room was buzzing with excited conversation.

"What're we gonna do 'bout Amelia?" Rudy scrunched his eyebrows together. "And the goats...and..."

"I just 'bout wanna hunt down those varmints myself." Clarence scowled, pacing erratically with his arms crossed on his chest.

Lydia looked as if she'd been sprayed in the face by a stinkbug. She too was standing, equally jumpy. "You're the whole reason they even came here, stupid."

Zephyr pushed herself up slightly on the sofa and groggily cleared her throat.

"We shouldn't be in here. We need to get out of the house. Hide. Just in case they come back."

Finally, her mouth had decided to cooperate with her brain. Fear lingered in her mind, but she made her legs stand. "This'll be the first place they look. We need to get out in the woods."

All eyes fell on her. For a moment, the children were quiet.

But only for a moment.

"Hide? For what? If those suckers come back, I'm sure as heck not gonna go cower in the woods." Clarence flashed his sister a look of contempt.

"Oh, yes, you are." Zephyr leaned against the sofa unsteadily, feeling returning to her limbs. "I don't care if you think it's cowardice. It's not. It's called being smart. We need to go *now*. Where's the gun?"

Lydia rolled her eyes and shook her head. "Wherever it is, you sure aren't getting a hold of it again. Not after all that. You could've shot yourself accidently when you fainted."

Zephyr exhaled impatiently. "I didn't ask for permission to handle it. *Where's the gun?*"

"I grabbed it," Clarence replied sternly. "Fine, we'll go to the woods. But it's overkill, I say. If they even come back at all, we could just shoot 'em down one by one from here."

Zephyr took Lemuel's hand in hers and headed for the back door. "*Forget it,* Clarence. Come on. Let's go."

They stole our animals and who knows what else. Clarence could've been taken. Ma's still gone...

The entire ordeal barely registered in Zephyr's mind. Her feelings had been numbed. Anxiety continued to rage on within, but it didn't feel as vivid as before. Previously sharp as a knife, now it was only a dulled, murky cloud floating over Zephyr's head.

For an hour, the little group camped out deep in the woods. Time crawled. Zephyr found herself wrapping her arms around Lemuel tightly. She didn't let go.

The girl stared vacantly into the green landscape she'd only just been sobbing in, earlier that morning.

This was not a dream. And yet it was far too frightening to feel like reality.

Chapter Twelve

ZEPHYR

Two DAYS HAD PASSED SINCE the raid. Two long, tedious days of waiting.

Mrs. Darson had returned safely, but Zephyr had insisted that everyone stay out in the woods far away from the house, just in case the soldiers returned. Going back and trying to clean up the mess they left wasn't worth potentially losing Clarence—or anyone else, for that matter.

In all honesty, Zephyr was terrified. The fear welling up in her stomach hadn't left since that horrible day. It still consumed her like a powerful acid, eating away at her bones and joints. She'd even lost her appetite, and had to force herself to eat.

The little boys didn't seem to take notice and had to keep being reminded not to venture out of the woods. Zephyr wished she could live the way they did, where she was too lost in play to be haunted by worry.

There's no place in my heart for fear. You tell us not to fear, Lord, I know that.

The only way she'd managed to keep a sane mind was by praying and trying to focus on the promises in Scripture. Amid the gnawing dread of the Federals' return and all that could go wrong if they did, at least there was the comfort of knowing that God was in control. It was a difficult thing to live with, but Zephyr knew there was a reason for everything, and all she could do was learn to accept whatever that reason might be.

"This is positively ridiculous. Don't you think they've moved on by now?" Lydia scoffed, sitting on the ground and flapping her skirts to fan herself.

Zephyr shot the girl an icy glare, partially because she was tired of her complaints, and also because the skirt-flapping was distasteful and unladylike. Silly girl should have known better, being fourteen and all.

"Well, it's not like we're the only folks out here. There are other farms to plunder." Lydia rolled her eyes in indifference.

Zephyr didn't respond. She stood up from her kneeling position, her eyebrows knitted together. She wasn't in the mood to argue over something so blatantly obvious. Honestly, she only wanted to retreat deeper into the woods and isolate herself from everyone. Part of her was still reeling from the entire experience—she needed time and separation to sort all the emotions apart. Of course, time and separation were rarely things she could get her hands on, so what was the point?

Zephyr's eyes scanned the sweet gums and pines, catching her youngest brothers up in the hammock like bear cubs.

Good. That means they'll be occupied for a while.

The bright green foliage swished and swayed as the boys clung to the upper trunks with ease. At least they weren't trying to run off into the clearing like earlier.

Clarence, however, was another matter. He paced angrily, yammering about all the ways this entire mess could've been avoided.

"If I had the gun, there wouldn't have been any Yanks left to flee." The boy threw a rock against a tree, his face crimson with frustration.

Nobody said anything. Not even Mrs. Darson commented on her son's outburst; she simply sat against an oak, cracking open acorns and harvesting the meat into a little wooden bowl. Nobody had done that for a while in the Darson home. Acorn meat was bitter, and had to be soaked to get the acids out. But it made a decent coffee substitute and even a flour replacement. Zephyr remembered its unique taste quite clearly.

Clarence balled his fists, glaring into the woods.

"Why do we stay out here and hide when we could easily set up a stakeout and attack them if they returned?"

"Would you shut up about it already?" Lydia snapped. "I've only heard that come outta your mouth a dozen times these past ten minutes."

If we stay out here too much longer, we'll probably drive each other mad.

Zephyr turned away, her face to the woods, exhaling quietly. With two days elapsed, wouldn't that have been enough time to be sure that the soldiers had moved on?

An unpleasantly loud rumble emerged from her gut. There was certainly cause for it: the last meal she'd eaten had been yesterday afternoon.

It surely must have been worse for Clarence, since he had the appetite of a cougar.

Why did food have such a big impact on everything, as trifling and menial as it was?

Zephyr groaned, debating the possibilities and risks of stealing back to the house. Finally, she turned around and faced the others conclusively.

"We might as well go see what's left."

All eyes fell on her.

Lydia jumped to her feet with a huff. "It's about time."

"Do you think it is wise at this point, Zephyr?" Mrs. Darson looked at Lydia and Clarence before shifting her gaze to Zephyr.

Zephyr took a deep breath, stretching her arms to relieve some of the pressure on her spin and muscles. "I think we could at least go and hustle up something to eat." She glanced at Clarence, seeing that he had stopped pacing. "I mean, there's no way to really tell if the soldiers will return. We might end up waiting out here for weeks and nothin' happens." She shrugged, her eyes meeting Ma's. "Lydia and I could go check, and y'all wait here, just in case."

"You and *Lydia*?" Clarence exploded. "Why not me? Neither of you would be able to protect yourselves if anybody was still around."

"Listen here." Blood rushed to Zephyr's temple, and her face burned in anger. "Unless you'd fancy to get taken away, you're stayin'. *And don't even tell me I couldn't protect myself if I had to.*" Zephyr growled, spearing her brother with a glare.

Clarence fired back a vehement glower. "I'm not a child, Zephyr. You can't tell me what to do."

Zephyr took a step forward, clenching her fists at her sides. "Can't you *see* the danger here? If you even show your face, and somebody's out there, it's over. Is that what you want? Are you *trying* to get taken? Would that make you feel more *manly*, or somethin'?"

"Both of you, calm your heads!" Mrs. Darson intervened, raising her voice above Zephyr's. She emitted a short sigh of thinly-veiled frustration. "The three of you can go. There is strength in numbers, and if something goes amiss, at least one of you could perchance run to get help."

Run to get help...*where?* Zephyr exhaled through her teeth. There was nowhere to get help from. Everyone they knew lived miles away, and she wouldn't want to put them at danger even if they did live closer.

There was no local government, and there were no police officers. As to the Confederate government, it certainly wasn't there to aid them in any capacity. It was too busy trying to break away from the Union to care about the people it claimed to represent.

It was what it was. Unless God intervened, they were on their own.

"Ma, are you *sure*...?"

"Yes, Zephyr. Don't question it." Mrs. Darson's voice was as firm as steel, thus silencing her daughter.

Zephyr tried to loosen the tension in her jaw as she sucked in a breath and turned to Lydia and Clarence. "Come on," she muttered under her breath.

It was such a perturbing sensation, having to walk back to your own house in dread of what you might find. The comfort and security of home had vanished, leaving in its wake a gaping hole, proving how easily the physical sanctuaries of earth could be violated and torn apart.

It didn't feel quite like home anymore. Now it seemed so vulnerable and open to the outside world. A shiver flitted down Zephyr's spine at this thought. She had always considered this place to be one of refuge, in which nothing bad would ever happen. She'd never dreamed that the war, miles away up north, could have such an impact on the isolated state of Florida.

She never dreamed the war would steal her father and plunder her family's home.

Clarence jogged ahead to the front lawn as the threesome neared the house. Zephyr's eyes scanned the area, the hairs on the back of her neck standing up. She couldn't shake the restless, uneasy sensation in her gut.

Still, all was quiet. No signs of any intruders, other than the wake of destruction they left behind. The okra, cucumber and tomato patches bore the scars of careless thievery, with their trampled plants and shredded foliage scattered abroad.

Zephyr stepped warily inside the kitchen, scanning over the inside. It had been ransacked. She closed her eyes in dread, wondering how much the soldiers could have possibly done in a mere ten minutes. She moved deeper into the little building.

Opening the cellar, she was relieved to find that the stores were untouched. Well, that was definitely a good thing.

Zephyr swallowed and left the kitchen, cautiously entering the house. Without the boys running around, the ambiance was eerily quiet. It was oppressive, abnormal.

A quick look in the bedrooms revealed clothes and other such items scattered over the floors. Apparently, the solders hadn't had a use for women's and children's attire.

Zephyr's eyes darted from the hallway walls to the floor to the ceiling and everywhere in between. Her skin crawled with the thought that someone could have been watching her this entire time. What if a soldier stayed behind when the others took off? What if more than one had lingered?

The girl had to force her mind off the idea. Her heart raced and she realized how sweaty her palms had become.

Clarity of mind. Clarity of mind, Zephyr whispered to herself, concentrating on her surroundings.

We'll survive. This isn't the end of the world.

***

Strands of loose hair falling from her bun, and sweat pouring off her body, Zephyr bounded down one of the Collatts' many wooded paths.

It was Sunday yet again, and the three families' little service hadended two hours before. The Sunday meal had already been eaten, and now commenced the pleasant hours of fellowship. Presently, the children were all outside, and the adults sat on the Collatts' front porch, watching the younger ones and talking.

With all the stress revolving around the past week's events, Zephyr had had difficulty making room for any sort of peace in her heart. However, running around with the kids had a way of helping her forget about it for a few hours.

"Zephhhhhyrrrrrr! Make haste and come tag me will ya?"

Waves of adrenaline hit Zephyr as she flew through the forest of shrub-like palmettos in search of her fellow teammates. Was that Addy's voice she'd just heard? Taking a side path, she cut to the right and slowed her pace to a jog.

It was only a game, but such a game with fifteen people involved was quite entertaining. Most everyone took it very seriously at this level.

Zephyr let her legs relax as she slowed further to a walking pace. Her eyes surveyed the landscape, and her ears strained for signs of activity.

She was getting close to the enemy camp. Soon there'd be swarms of scampering children to dodge and avoid.

She must be swift, and not a hint less of cunning. Rudy, Royce, Jeremiah, and Rhoda would swoop in as a pack. They may have been small, but a group of them could be trouble. Zephyr could likely outsmart the little pack by dodging about sporadically or running through the midst of them at her fastest speed.

But then there was Clarence, who everyone knew to be fast – quite easily, the fastest in the group. He'd be tricky to outrun. All she could hope was that he'd either not be in the vicinity or that he simply wouldn't take enough interest to chase after her.

Peeking through the palmettos' fan-shaped brush, she spotted Zelle, who'd been tagged immediately after the game had begun. Not too far from the edge of the wood, where Zephyr stood now, was Addy, whose flustered expression matched her earlier call for help.

Creeping along the edge of the woods, Zephyr's heart raced. She began devising a plan to release her fellow team members.

Oh-ho, looks as if I've forgotten an opponent. Zephyr's eyebrows rose as she spotted an unemotional Malinda, standing near Zelle.

Puppy-guarding.

Confidence flooded Zephyr's being and she smirked. She had outrun that girl before; she could certainly do it again.

She continued to scan the area cautiously.

Looks like now's my time.

Springing from her lowered position, she bounded towards Addy.

It didn't take long before she was noticed. Within seconds, Rhoda was screeching the news to every ear within a five-mile radius. Adrenaline flooded Zephyr's system; her pulse quickening as her bare feet pounded the earth.

"Zephyr - It's Zephyr over there, quick, catch her somebody!"

Zephyr heard a voice echo across the clearing, but was too focused on keeping her strides long and swift to tell who the voice belonged to.

Nearer and nearer she grew to Addy, who was now watching the tall girl approach in anticipation.

"Hurry Zephyr!" she called impatiently, reaching out for Zephyr to touch her hand.

Closer and closer, she moved in, and she was just about to tag the dark-haired girl when she noticed the inevitable—she'd been followed.

Malinda.

With a quick glance from the corner of her eye, Zephyr noted the eldest Lowell daughter loping after her.

Zephyr's heart pounded against her chest like a hammer as she quickened her pace and flew by her tagged teammate, slapping her hand against Addy's as she passed.

"On you go!" Zephyr grinned as much as she was able, her profile already pink from the rush of red blood cells to her face.

Addy articulated a brief thanks, but time permitted nothing more. As she bounded off in another direction, Zephyr didn't stop running. A sliver of pain hit her from where she'd stepped on stinging nettle, but she didn't let this hinder her ability to keep going.

She didn't know if she was still being followed or not. She changed directions and raced toward the woods again.

Zephyr had just begun to slow her pace when her ears picked up the crunch of footsteps, the sound of one in pursuit, running at nearly the same speed she was. Instinctively, her gaze swung around and her eyes widened in surprise.

Malinda was still on her tail, and gaining.

Zephyr pumped her legs harder.

She must evade Malinda. Being tagged this far out in the woods away from everybody else meant all chances of rescue would vanish completely.

And more importantly, Zephyr hated to be outrun.

Not gonna happen.

She sucked air in, sprinting at three-quarters of her peak speed. Malinda was still behind her.

Zephyr knew Malinda's fortitude had to be less than her own. And since the curly-headed girl was a few inches shorter, that alone should give Zephyr the upper hand, since she carried a longer stride.

These thoughts gave her hope as breathing became increasingly harder and her abdomen wrapped itself into knotted cramps. Malinda would have to quit soon.

The path had become a straightaway now, and Zephyr was flat-out running at top speed, since there were no obstacles to interfere with her footing. Pain shot up her insides as the muscle cramps worsened.

Come on, Mal.

She forced herself to breathe, and swallowed a mouthful of spit painfully. As she turned to glance at her opponent, her heart revived.

Finally. She let out a long exhalation in relief as her legs slowed, her abdominal muscles screaming in pain.

"Got wore out, did you Malinda?" Zephyr managed to yell, continuing forward at a moderate jog.

She couldn't help but grin a little to herself. Malinda stood stock-still in the midst of the path, panting heavily. Zephyr thought she saw a frown on the girl's flushed face.

Zephyr felt almost pleased with Malinda's expression. Maybe it wasn't very kind of her, but at the moment, she didn't care. With all the times she'd tried to reach out to Malinda and involve her in their activities, only for the girl to return with acidic remarks and toxic looks, somehow beating her at a minor children's game felt good.

Victory was hers.

Zephyr strode confidently out of the woods, wiping her sleeve across her sweaty face and neck. As she entered the clearing and approached the Collatts' house, she pondered where all the others had gone. There wasn't a soul to be seen, and Zephyr wondered if she'd lingered in the far edge of the woods a bit too long. She'd done it to be cautious, lest Malinda try and secretly come after her again, but now, she doubted the wisdom of that trivial decision.

Looking down at herself, a knot twisted in her throat. Any hope of appearing ladylike and proper had flown out the door, with all sense of dignity at that. Now she'd have to reappear before her family and friends looking like an unkempt street child.

Her favorite church clothes were soaked in perspiration, and part of her formally white petticoats had been soiled with dirt. And this was her mere clothing. Her large, unfeminine feet were swathed in dust and had turned an unpleasant dark grey.

She sighed. She could only imagine what her hair and face looked like.

Nonetheless, she couldn't stay out here forever if everyone else was inside. That would only make her seem impolite, as well as unkempt. Breaking into a trot, she headed up to the Collatts' front porch and jogged up the wooden steps.

Swinging the front door open, her eyes took a moment to readjust to the relative darkness of the parlor. The familiar drone of dozens of voices enveloped her, and she shut the door a bit louder than necessary.

"Oh, Zephyr, there you are!" Prudence came over and touched her shoulder. "Wherever have you been gone to? Didn't you hear us calling?"

Large white circles floated around in Zephyr's eyes from the exposure to the bright sunlight outdoors.

"No…I guess I was too far out too hear anything. I didn't know…" Zephyr squinted, trying to get those blasted spots out of her vision.

A frown crossed Prudence's face. "It's alright, but it's a good thing that you came back when you did."

Zephyr blinked, thankful that some of the spots had receded. "What is it?" Prudence's serious tone struck a chord of worry in her heart.

"Well, I know ya told us about the Feds comin' the other day and all." Prudence looked at Zephyr with heavy eyes. "We didn't see 'em. Guess they weren't headed this way. I still can't believe it happened."

Zephyr's heart rate increased. Traumatizing memories flooded her mind and she swallowed hard. She didn't want to think about that day. The day Clarence could've been taken. The day the Darsons' livelihood had been shattered. And that vile federal officer, with his vile, leering eyes. She wanted to forget about how stunned she'd been while the soldiers searched the house and barn. She wanted to forget it *all*.

"Zephyr?"

She hardly heard Prudence's query of concern. "I– I know," she stammered, swallowing. Foul tastes formed in the back of her throat.

Prudence's bright blue eyes dimmed. "Did you know anybody who got taken?"

Zephyr shook her head, searching her friend's gaze. "Did...did you?"

"Before you came in, I overheard Pa talkin' about it." Prudence paused, dropping her gaze to the floor.

"And?" Zephyr's eyebrows knit together as her brain tried to dissect Prudence's former statement.

Prudence exhaled, the same melancholy expression staining her profile.

"Zephyr, I'm sorry. I...I guess you never heard..."

Zephyr felt a knot forming in her stomach. She didn't like the haunting look in the other girl's eyes.

But once again, and probably to Zephyr's misfortune, her overly-inquisitive nature got the best of her.

"It's...it's alright." Zephyr tried to keep from frowning. Her internal thought processes were screaming the contrary.

Of course it isn't alright. How is it that I am always among the last to find out anything important? If something bad is happening again...

Her heart thumped painfully harder.

Prudence stared at her friend, and Zephyr wondered if she'd let on too much. *So much for putting on a poker-face.*

"What...what is going on?" she croaked.

Several seconds of silence passed before Prudence spoke again. Even though the room was buzzing with activity and the drone of multiple other voices, Zephyr didn't notice. To her, those few seconds were stiflingly quiet, unbearably still. A mixture of relief and pained anticipation surrounded her as Prudence opened her mouth to reply.

"Zephyr, Pa talked to Mr. McIntosh this morning. The Federals raided his property." She paused, her voice still low and quiet. Her eyes fell for a brief second, and then returned to Zephyr with a look that worried her soul.

"They took Silas."

The words pummeled her like a freight train at full speed. The entire world stood still and all sound disappeared from her ears. All that was left was the obnoxious, hateful boom of her heart pounding.

Ka-thump.

Ka-thump.

She felt that her whole head would explode. Her mind slipped into a state of unconscious, involuntary thought, and she wondered for a moment if perhaps she was living in a dream. A nightmare. A strange feeling of delirium crept over her being, as if she had been immersed in the mighty waves of a raging ocean.

She was drowning. She struggled to breathe air into her lungs; and felt her knees lock.

"Zephyr! Are you alright?" Prudence reached out to steady Zephyr, but she didn't notice.

It can't be. This can't be real.

Reality no longer seemed a thing she could grasp onto. Prudence's words hammered in Zephyr's mind like the sound of gunshots, and the implications they left were easily just as painful as real bullets penetrating her flesh.

Zephyr felt a tremble reverberate down her body. Wetness smarted her eyes.

They've taken Silas. Silas is gone.

Chapter Thirteen

HAROLD
September 8th, 1863

A SPARK OF LIFE FLICKERED in Ezra's eyes as he gathered up his few belongings for the march south. Thunder rolled in the distance as Harold watched him silently within their tent.

They'd finally received a new set of orders. Finally, after two months of nothing but waiting, there was a real *mission*.

The Army of Tennessee had been ordered south to intercept Rosecrans and his men at Chattanooga, "the gateway" to the Confederacy. It was pivotal that it remained under Southern control. Their instruction from General Bragg was to cut off the Union's route into the city.

While his brother was somewhat thrilled for the change in activity, Harold felt a myriad of emotions. None of them exactly matched excitement.

He let out a long, restrained sigh, breathing in the humid air. He stood up and moved to the tent entrance, his hands clasped stiffly behind his back.

"What's the matter?" Ezra's voice reached his ears.

Harold remained by the tent doorway, holding open the fabric flap to observe the darkening sky above.

"Nothing," he spoke coolly, concealing all emotion from his vocal tone. Inside, every thought contradicted his spoken words.

"Aren't you at all excited about the news?"

Harry gazed out at the grey landscape beyond the tent walls. Deep down, he felt as dismal as the colors portrayed in the sky. Little did he want to admit, Bragg's order was greatly unsettling.

"Excited, no," he sighed. "I'm not excited about the thought of more lives being wasted."

"It's gotta be done. Somebody's gotta die, so why not let it be the Yanks?"

"I'm concerned for our men. They're not ready."

Even though the 7th already had a bit of experience in campaigning, that wasn't nearly the same as a full-fledged battle. Harold believed the Florida men were in no position for a real fight, and to attempt to go into such would probably result in mass slaughter... of their men.

And it wasn't just the 7th that was untrained. So many other units were made up of individuals who hardly qualified as soldiers. There were twelve-year-olds. Older men. Masses too doped up to care about anything other than their alcohol consumption. Soldiers whose bodies were ruined by numerous illnesses.

"*Harry*. We're a part of the largest Rebel army in the western theater. There's eight thousand of us strong."

Harold nodded quietly, as his brother paused for effect.

"...Not to mention, you've always said that God put us here for a reason. Why would He abandon us now when we're finally given the chance to lay waste to the enemy?"

Harold rubbed his calloused hands across his face, pondering the situation at hand. Finally, he exhaled and nodded again.

"You're right. His promises will not return void."

Ezra seemed momentarily satisfied with that answer. He looked at Harold thoughtfully for a moment longer, and then motioned to the tent.

"If you've got your stuff ready, we might as well get this outta the way too."

Harold knelt to pull up the pegs holding the canvas down.

How quickly things change.

One moment, the group had been stuck, lackadaisical and weary in a muddle of boredom, with nothing to do and seemingly no valid purpose in the great scheme of the war.

But all within the course of one day, that balance had changed.

Harold glanced at his brother.

Somehow, Harold must convince Ezra of something he himself did not agree with. That he had faith in this war. Faith that in the end, this horrendous wager would right the injustices thrown upon the country, restoring peace to the nation.

It wasn't that Harry didn't trust the Lord. He merely struggled with understanding how God would use this conflict for the good of all those sucked into it.

How could one believe in violence restoring order? Chaos restoring tranquility? Bloodshed reinstating prosperity?

No, he didn't believe in this war. Not at all. The thought of encouraging other men to their deaths was sickening.

Death itself was not what he feared. The thing he feared was watching as lost souls perished in the flames of combat. He feared the notion of never again telling Cecelia how much he loved her. Never wrapping his children in hugs or tickling the little boys 'till they squealed.

But what else could he do?

As they finished packing away the tent, he was quiet.

The fact was, Harry was tired - both emotionally and physically— and in no mood for debating what had already been decided. It was out of their hands. He knew he would always be under subjection as long as he served in the army. Only a few got to give the orders, while countless individuals must receive them. Harold was not a man who liked to be under another man's authority, as he had always been a natural leader. It frustrated him when questionable orders came out of nowhere, and all he could do was trust the officer who issued the command.

Harold closed his eyes again, rubbing his face as he made known his petitions to the Creator.

In many aspects right now, Harold realized that his Maker was the only One who truly grasped the situation at hand. It was He alone who could understand the present conundrum and Harry's fears. He alone could Harry confide in, with no concerns of betrayal or misunderstandings.

Perhaps it was foolish of him to fear for the 'inexperience' of the Florida boys. Maybe they knew more than he wanted to admit. Still, what if they were indeed walking into something far worse than they'd ever dreamed?

Trusting You is hard right now. I admit it. It's awful hard. There's so much I don't understand.

Harry's eyes scanned the bustling camp, his tense, achy limbs beginning to relax as he probed for further instruction.

During the rest of the preparations for marching, and deep into the march itself, he kept praying.

I'm not worthy to be called your son. You told me to be an example to these men, but help me accept the leadership of the men above me. My heart wrestles with this order, Lord.

The man paused, listening for several moments. Despite the sounds of many footsteps against the ground mixed with the din of hundreds of voices, Harold's mind felt quiet and empty.

Show me this is what You want, and then I will know to follow it wholeheartedly. That's all I request now. Just show me this is what You want.

Chapter Fourteen

EZRA
September 9th, 1863

HEAT SCORCHED THE SOUTHERN TENNESSEE landscape.

The deluge that existed merely a day earlier had vanished. The grey, overcast sky had morphed into a painfully bright, clear firmament, complete with the blazing sun which the Southern states were so well acquainted with.

Ezra rubbed his arms, emitting a groan. His skin felt like it was on fire.

As eager as he was to intercept Rosecrans' army, he'd never enjoyed marching.

It reminded him of the campaign last year. So far, that had been the most marching he'd done.

Thankfully, Chattanooga wasn't too far south, so he wasn't concerned about a drawn out march this time.

It was so good to be out in the open air for once. Sensations from the old camp still lingered in Ezra's mind, and they were hardly pleasant. He could still smell the rank aromas of bodily discharge, burned chow, and mildewed shelter-half lining.

Ezra noticed young William, who was laughing with some buddies. Even though he was good to see the kid in a good mood, he didn't keep his focus there. The boy wasn't horrible, but his behaviors set Ezra on edge. He figured the kid was still in his days of thinking idealistically about the war, supposing that it was all fun and shooting Yanks once you got to the actual fighting side of it.

But even putting William's ignorance aside, he had a mouth like a sailor and no respect for anyone. Ezra wondered if he too, like

Frances Cranston, had run off from his home without the approval of his folks.

Wouldn't surprise me one bit.

As the day drew on, Ezra's own excitement faded.

The hours passed too slowly. The already blatant heat only grew more oppressive; and was compounded by the lack of trees along the sun baked road. If Yankee soldiers had been marching this same path, anybody wearing regulation uniforms would surely wonder why in the world he'd been issued wool breeches, and a coat of all things.

But these men weren't Billy Yanks. The 7th were ragtag, unfurnished Southerners who'd laugh and shake their heads at the concept of being equipped with an official uniform. It was all for the better that they wore their own clothes, anyway; CSA regulation dress was, just as the Feds' garb, horribly unpleasant during the summer months.

Ezra wanted to tear the sweat-drenched, cotton shirt off his back. It hardly did anything against the sun's rays, so what was the point of leaving it on?

He sighed, running his hand over his wet hair. As much as he was disgusted with the grimy piece of fabric, he forced himself to refuse the urge to peel it off and toss it on the dusty road beneath.

Ezra craned his eyes against the glaring daylight, searching the masses for his elder brother. He wouldn't have minded someone to talk to at the moment – it might just lift some of his awareness from this oppressive terrain.

The thud of footsteps fell like an endless drone against the dusty earthen floor. The group was moving at a snail's pace. Thousands of human bodies, forced to walk in formation at a wretchedly slow stride, some near ready to faint from dehydration.

The only thing that had impaired their progress was the lack of certain necessities--proper footwear, for example. A good number of the fellows were without decent shoes.

Ezra's old boots had held together amazingly well, but he was among the lucky few who could boast of this fact. Many of the boys, like Frances, were going barefoot, and some had simply turned to tying strips of old cloth about their soles when the barefoot practice got tiresome.

Ezra had heard the complaints concerning blisters. They were abundant, non-ceasing. He himself would find several of the nasty things embedded in the undersides of his feet at the end of the day.

While his old boots had saved him on several occasions, they were easily as bad as the cloth strips. Old and battered, their soles were worn thin – just thick enough to put a small barrier between Ezra's heel and the pavement.

Still, at least they were shoes, and that alone was something to be thankful for.

Ezra's mind wandered to graver thoughts. In his midst of thinking about the group's lack of proper shoes, already, hundreds of men and boys had been injured in ways he couldn't imagine.

Ezra could only guess on the numbers, but he had heard stories about how many men had already been killed in this onslaught so far.

It was said that if your arm wasn't blown off by a shell or shredded to pieces by minie balls, you would likely have to get it amputated later on because of worsening in a bullet wound or some sort of infection.

Whatever the case, even the field surgeons did not know everything. Pratchit himself hadn't ever done an amputation. Ezra was a little worried for the man when the time came for him to do so much cutting on so many men.

He'd heard that buckets would become full with human limbs. Some fellows' health slid downward as soon as they had their amputation, some became deathly sick, and some died. Ezra shuddered at the thought of a surgery which could render you even worse than you started out. A surgery which could render you maimed for life or, even worse, dead.

Perhaps this was why many of the soldiers warned to stay away from the surgeons and let your body mend itself as best it could.

Something told his gut that these stories he'd heard were true.

Feeling helpless dwelling on that particular subject, Ezra decided to examine the landscape around him. They were in the midst of acre upon acre of open fields and farmland.

Some fields were full of rye grass, others corn and okra, though the army hadn't passed a citrus grove since they'd left Florida. It was too cool in these parts for oranges to grow.

Ezra whispered a quick prayer. He realized that in his anticipation for change and the thrill of a fight, he'd forgotten to seek God's direction.

The young man's eyes searched the sea of faces surrounding him. No longer did he look for his brother. A discussion with Harry could wait.

No, now his eyes probed for the kid from Jacksonville. The youngster who'd run away from his family, thinking that army enlistment would be lots more fun than slaving on the farm. The boy who didn't look any older than twelve, yet carried an ominous hardness in his leery, blue eyes as if he were twice that age. The boy with the mysterious book.

Frances Cranston.

Ever since Ezra had stumbled upon the boy he'd felt a personal responsibility in reaching out to him. He didn't know how to achieve this, but for whatever reason, his heart had been burdened with some sort of liability for Frances' welfare.

He didn't see him. Either the sun was just too bright, or Frances was elsewhere in the group of tired bodies. Ezra exhaled and wiped away the sweat beads adorning his upper lip.

He's just one boy in a million, why has he suddenly become so important to me?

Chapter Fifteen

September 19th, 1863
The Battle of Chickamauga

5 AM

THE MORNING WAS CHILLED BY darkness. The sun hadn't yet risen, leaving the woods veiled in shadow.

Ezra swallowed. A mixture of exhilaration and trepidation overcame him as he held his rifle tightly, awaiting the next word from Bullock. He couldn't tell if the goose bumps forming on his skin were from the cold or the emotions festering within.

As exhausted as he was, he'd waited so long for this moment. But now it was beginning to dawn on him that he might have anticipated something far more serious than he'd ever dreamed.

"7th! Fall in! We march!"

A shout echoed across the mass of soldiers.

It was now time for the Florida unit to take their place on the battlefield.

The young man set his jaw, his gaze flitting to his brother beside him. He swallowed again, clearing his throat to speak to Harry. But no words came.

The 7th crossed Chickamauga Creek at Thedford's Ford just as daylight broke. For once, Ezra was glad for the sun to return to its place in the sky. A little bit of relief came to his spirit as they marched onward.

Stopping in a cornfield tucked within a bend of Chickamauga Creek, the Florida men formed their lines of battle and the left flank of Bragg's forces.

Warm rays of sunlight fell on the men, but even with the sky awake and bright, it was still dreadfully cold. The smell of smoke drifted into Ezra's nostrils and he looked about to see that some of the men had built small fires to provide extra warmth.

"I reckon I thought a bit hastily…" he thought aloud, rubbing his hands together and glancing at Harry in slight puzzlement. "I thought when Bullock said we were marchin', we'd not be stopping for breakfast." He raised a brow, noticing Pratchit a little ways off kneeling to make a fire of his own.

Harold shrugged, exhaling into the chilly air. "It's hard to know what exactly they got planned for us. But a quick rest and bite of food sure's not a bad thing right now."

Ezra nodded. "That's true."

He decided to go join the surgeon. Admittedly, he'd not had anything to eat since yesterday morning and his stomach was now reminding him of that fact.

"Heyo," He leaned his gun against a nearby rifle-stack and plopped down next to the fire now licking up on the ground. "Mind if I join ya?"

Pratchit looked up, and offered a half-smile. "Go right ahead."

Ezra reached into his haversack, removing a piece of sour cornbread.

"Want some?" He offered a section to the man, while taking a bite out of another fragment.

"No thanks, I've already had my fill of that stuff." Pratchit held his hands in front of the flames, groaning. "Dadgummit, my joints are already stiff and sore to the bone and we're not even a few hours into the day. I'm pert' near tired of all this waiting."

Ezra's mind wandered as he forced down the last bite of cornbread. "How ya think your fiddle will hold up in this weather?"

Pratchit rubbed his biceps, his eyes reflecting a lack of sleep the night prior. "I guess we'll see. I left her in the supply wagon, and she ought to be fine, if we make it through all this. Lord willing and the creek don't rise." The last phrase seemed strangely out of place coming from Pratchit's lips.

Ezra tilted his head forward, and he raised a brow. "I thought you weren't a religious man?"

Pratchit's face was unreadable, and he stared ahead vacantly. "Well, I always tried to be a decent individual. A little religion never hurt a body."

"I guess not...but then again, it would depend on the kind of religion, right?" Ezra savored the warmth on his calloused palms as he held them over the orange and golden flames. It hit him that he'd never actually asked the surgeon about his beliefs before.

"True enough, I guess."

Ezra almost wanted to ask. He studied the small sparks flickering up into the air.

"So...uh..." He cleared his throat.

Pratchit glanced upwards at him.

"What's your idea of 'a little religion?'" Ezra made eye contact with the other man. He decided he wouldn't let fear of rejection take control of him, not when they might not survive the oncoming hours.

"I...don't really know, to be honest. It's not something I think about." Pratchit shrugged and rubbed his forearms, wincing in discomfort. "My wife is more the religious sort in our house, with her being a Jew and all. I never really get involved. I just "pray" with her and let her read her Torah to me now and then, you know?"

Ezra inhaled. Dust coated the inside of his throat, making him reach for his canteen. "So you're not really into it at all then?"

"Into what?"

"God? The Bible?" Ezra took a quick swig, swallowing the cold liquid in relief. There were still small ice chunks floating in the water from the previous night's temperatures.

"Oh, yeah...that." Pratchit's eyes wandered around the camp and he stretched, yawning. "I believe in God. I just don't make Him a part of my life, I guess."

This was an interesting revelation.

"What about the Bible?"

The man massaged his temples. "Well, I don't care a lot for what my Lily reads me—it's fairly boring—but I listen anyway because she's my wife and...well, I love her enough to do anything she wants me to, pretty much. Sometimes the verses are nice, but most of 'em are just rules."

"I'm not too familiar with the Torah..." Ezra glanced in Harry's direction, wondering if his brother had ever covered the subject. "...but I do know there's an awful lot more to the Good Book than just rules."

Pratchit looked Ezra in the eyes for a moment, then prodded the tinder with a tired groan.

"Whatever you say. Maybe there is and maybe there isn't. I just know Lily seems to prefer the rules. That or she hasn't read the rest of the Bible. I guess I never thought about it."

Ezra was quiet for a moment. He himself hadn't read the entire Bible, but he knew enough to say that there were more layers to it than a head of cabbage. The more you read, the more you learned that God was bigger than you thought He was. And not just bigger, but wiser, holier, and downright unpredictable on how He orchestrated lives and events. He seemed to never work the same way twice.

"I guess you just have to read it for yourself, Pratchit. That's really all there is to it." Ezra scratched his bearded chin, offering a small grin of support.

"Maybe someday, Ezra." Pratchit's eyes were still weary, but his lip curved upwards just a tad. "Someday when I decide I've taken a fancy to such things."

The hours passed slowly as the Florida 7th awaited orders.

Noon fell, and still nothing had come.

Ezra sighed. Nothing had happened *all morning*. Not for the 7th, at least. Units like the Florida 6th had already been engaged in battle, since they were closer to the enemy.

But the 7th was further back, sheltered from any contact thus far.

It was frustrating, to be honest. Knowing that there were parts of your brigade already fighting, and you were stuck in the rear, doing nothing. Ezra's spirit yearned to get a piece of the action. The growing wait only added fuel to that fire.

If he listened, he could hear the sounds of gunshots further down the files. The smell of smoke lingered in the air and above the trees. Ezra wondered how much of that smoke had come from the artillery and firearms versus the quiet campfires crackling throughout the 7th's column.

"Ezra!" Harold brushed past the young man, now sitting against a tree with his gear spread on the ground at his side.

"Bullock gave the word. Pack up, we're moving in!"

Ezra sprang to his feet. "It's about time." He slung his canteen and haversack over his shoulder and arranged his blanket roll across his back. Grabbing his rifle from the stack, he followed Harry through the crowd of other men who now scrambled to get their things together and move out.

Three hours passed.

Still, no fighting for the 7th.

But then the world turned upside down. Ezra could see the Federals marching through the woods. His blood heated. As the 7th moved closer, marching steadily through the trees, a clearing was visible - and in that clearing, pandemonium unleashed as the Feds and Rebels collided.

Finally.

The sight came with a mixture of terror and excitement. Each time Ezra's hopes had been raised that they'd finally engage in battle, they'd been forced to wait and those emotions had been suspended. Now, they had accumulated so heavily in Ezra's mind that it was difficult for him to comprehend all that was going on in front of him. His skin tingled, and his heart raced.

It was *here*.

They drew nearer.

And then a new sound filled the terrain. Whoops and hollers exploded from the Southern men, as they grew excited to slay the Northerners.

Fueled by the adrenaline coursing through his veins, Ezra joined his comrades with a fierce yell of determination.

The harrowing Rebel Yell was already well-established by this point in the war. Ezra had learned it by emulating some of the other soldiers. Each had developed his own little flare to it, most without really trying.

Ezra had never heard so many yells at once. The uninhibited chorus of voices around him sent shivers down his spine. It made him glad that he was not hearing it from the Union side.

Sure hope they're listening.

Squinting through the woods, Ezra could make out the forms of men clashing. The sounds of artillery were now close enough to make the ground rumble beneath Ezra's feet as he walked.

The closer they got, the louder the gunshots rang, and the more smoke clouded the woodland canopy.

It was already much louder than Ezra had thought it would be. Thunderous. As to everything else, it was difficult to tell from this distance. But whatever was going on out there, it sure didn't look comforting.

Ezra exhaled nervously, glancing over at his brother. "I sure hope you're praying over this." The words came to his mouth almost without him thinking.

Mr. Darson stared ahead, his eyes vacant and weary. "Little brother, I never stopped."

Ezra swallowed. He felt his throat closing up. His peripheral vision clouded as he took in the reality of the fray. There were hundreds of men out there, just from what he could see, and it was almost impossible to tell Rebel from Yank.

The mere size of what lay ahead made Ezra feel faint out of nowhere. All the excitement had drained from his soul. His heart pounded with intensity, his entire body drowning in a sudden cold sweat.

Forcing his vision to focus, Ezra scanned the impending madness.

Fear engulfed his mind, like the Red Sea must have done to the unsuspecting Egyptians back in the early chapters of Exodus. *What ifs*, questions and sickening notions of failure filled his thoughts quicker than lightning. His head began to spin and he felt his body weaken.

Oh God, help me. I'm dead if I can't even see ten feet ahead.

Ezra swallowed—or attempted to. His throat was still constricted, throbbing with each heart beat. His chest rollicked.

A blood-curdling sensation froze Ezra dead-still.

A bullet had whizzed past his ear, close enough to cause a whisper-like breeze against his skin.

Ezra turned, looking Harry in the eyes. His brother's face didn't look as it usually did. His eyes were steely, cold and emotionless. The middle-aged man brought his rifle to his shoulder in one fluid, practiced movement.

"May God forgive us," he murmured.

Ezra's stomach stirred like the inside of a butter churn. He inhaled deeply and turned his gaze to the camp in front of him.

Forcing the fear from his mind, he raised his rifle above his head with a shout.

"Let's give 'em something they'll remember!"

The following moments passed whirred by. The 7th didn't collide with the Union units in an organized manner. Bullets filled the air, and Ezra was embedded in utter chaos.

He scrambled to cock his gun and squinted down the barrel, searching for a target. With so many moving bodies, it took him a moment to get his bearings. He swallowed and pulled the trigger anyway. His body shuddered at the backfire of the heavy firearm.

Before he'd even finished registering what he'd done, he saw the results of his actions.

A man in blue gripped his head, shrieking as blood poured down what was left of his face. He sunk to his knees, dropping his gun.

Ezra's stomach lurched, his eyes wide. He forced himself to pull his gaze away.

Ezra had never killed a soul before. In his haste to anticipate battle, the severity of it all had never truly sunk in until now. His vision began to blur, the trauma of taking another person's life weighing suddenly on his shoulders. *Oh God, what have I done?*

His fingers quavered as he dumped more powder down his rifle's barrel. He hardly looked at the minie ball in his trembling hand before he loaded it and used the ramrod to pack it down. With the rush and the on-setting panic, he felt as if he was fulfilling the task at half-speed.

The originally French minie balls were infamous for their devastating effects. Upon impact, they shattered bones and shredded through flesh. It didn't matter whether they were shot from a smoothbore or a rifled firearm. They still could cleave a human body in pieces.

Ezra felt like it'd never taken him so long to load that blasted gun. Soon, though, he made up for his clamminess.

As grotesque as it was to see a minie ball rip into a human face, Ezra always aimed for the head, because it insured the target's death. And most of the time, he hit where he aimed to hit.

If not there, then anywhere he could see blue.

He tried not to focus on the masses of men crumpling to the ground, their lifeless eyes glazing over. Blood oozed from one's abdomen. Another had a crimson hole in the midst of his chest. Some cried out in pain, while others fell silently.

The faces of the fallen were painted with a myriad of emotions. Desperation, horror, serenity, anger, pain, fear – it was too much. The culmination of the many ways a human could respond to death. Thankfully Ezra didn't have time to dwell on the haunting faces. He could barely keep up with the mass of Union soldiers that seemed to never stop coming.

One after another, Ezra's bullets found their targets. Somehow, he evaded enemy fire.

Somehow.

The hours passed slowly, and yet they didn't. It was a nightmare, a horrible dream in which Ezra felt anything but lucid. He felt powerless, lost in a torrent of blood and steel.

He had no idea where Harry was. A putrid bile rose in his throat as he realized his brother could be dead this very instant. *No.* Ezra swallowed, his heart pounding against his chest. He refused to let his mind fill with the fear of the worst.

Ezra closed his eyes, his fingers curling protectively around the rifle trigger. The breath in his nostrils was hot and painful, reeking of blood. His throat constricted, and felt as if daggers had been shoved down its passageway.

God, help me.

Determined, the man scanned his surroundings. Bodies lay scattered throughout the woods as far as he could see in the smoky haze. He dared not wonder whose side they belonged to.

Ezra lumbered across the terrain, dropping behind a tree that was thick enough to provide a shield between him and the enemy's firing.

Here we go again.

Relying on instinct once more, he shot at the first Fed to come into view from around the side of the trunk. The fellow had been emptying the contents of an ammunition package into the barrel of his rifle. Another man raised his gun at Ezra but didn't make it in time. Ezra stabbed him in the chest with his bayonet. The man's eyes widened grotesquely, nearly bulging from their sockets. Ezra bit down on his tongue, staring at the Federal as he yanked the blade out in one fluid motion.

If Ezra lived to see the moment when this battle ended, there would be one thing he'd dread. Being forced to stare at the shredded bodies, to pick apart friend from foe in all the gory mess. He didn't want to think about that moment. It dwarfed this present sequence of terror and adrenaline.

These last hours had done a number on him and weary stupor was only a stone's throw from overtaking his body.

It seemed the day would never end. But by sunset, the Confederate attacks in the southern portion of the battlefield had halted. Neither the Union nor Confederates had gained any sort of clear advantage. It was reduced to a stalemate.

But stalemate or no, the first day of the battle of Chickamauga was finally over. God be praised, it was finally *over*, for the day anyhow.

And that was enough for the moment.

The 7th settled down in the woods for the night, north of the Vineyard cornfield.

Cold enveloped the makeshift camp, and there were no fires to alleviate it. Only a fool would light a fire when the enemy was so close.

Ezra collapsed against a tree, feeling like nothing more than a sack of bones and fluids.

To say he was exhausted would've been the understatement of his life.

As much as he knew he desperately needed it, he couldn't make himself eat a bite. His insides hadn't stopped churning. His ears rang from the constant battering of noise, and an ear-splitting headache had settled between his temples. His head swam. He'd run out of water hours ago, and that was the only thing he desired now - other than to erase the gory sights now stained on his brain.

The cold seeped its way through every inch of his body. In a vain attempt to bring some sort of warmth to his aching limbs, he reclined on the bloodied ground and curled into a fetal position.

No matter how he tossed and turned, no sleep came.

As he lay shivering in the dirt, nothing but increased torment met him in the dark.

He could hear voices. And not just voices, but groans and shrieks. In the beginning, his wearied mind was too spent to figure out who they belonged to. Then he realized, it was the fallen. The injured and the dying.

There were men out there, lying helpless and isolated in the blackness - powerless to do anything but cry into the expressionless cover of night.

Cries for mercy, sobs for a loved one and moans of pain pierced the frigid air. Every now and then an ear-piercing scream would send a shiver down Ezra's spine.

This was surely the closest to hell Ezra had ever come.

He tried to ignore the sickening guilt and despair wrenching through his gut, but he couldn't. He couldn't ignore the gruesome sounds echoing through the woods. The atmosphere was so full of pain and suffering, Ezra could almost taste the gallons of blood he'd spilled.

How many of those poor souls crying for help and relief had he shot, himself?

It was impossible to sleep. Ezra wrapped his arms around his chest, praying with all his might that these hours of misery and anguish would end soon.

If this was war, it was the most hideous monstrosity he'd ever experienced.

Now he understood why Harry had never been excited about it all.

Chapter Sixteen

HAYDEN
September 20th, 1863
The Third Day of Battle at Chickamauga

5:00 PM

TENSION SUSPENDED THE FIELD AS time ticked on.

Chaos ensued at a pace no less than before. The sun's warmth had filled the heavens, but all it did was cause the already putrid smell of blood to thicken. Now the sun began to set again as the day waned, bringing the evening chill with it.

Anger surged through Damascus Hayden as he rammed the butt of his rifle against a Federal's head. He'd found the greatest way to survive in this bloodbath was to channel his inner hatred into the enemy.

"To hell with you," he muttered under his breath, stepping back as blood oozed from the gash in the Yankee's cranium. With one last motion, he struck the firearm against the man's Adam's apple, putting an end to his earthly existence.

Hayden had run out of ammunition hours ago, due to his constant barraging and lack of discernment regarding at whom he directed his bullets. Since then, he'd scavenged ammo from any cadavers that were nearby.

Most of the men and boys had replaced their outdated muskets by now with Enfields and Springfields they'd taken from the victims of yesterday's onslaught.

Hayden hadn't. He was awful fond of his own gun, and he knew her like the back of his palm. It didn't make sense to drop her for a

141

different weapon that he'd not been so deeply acquainted with. That didn't mean he wouldn't help himself to powder, balls, and anything else he could find, though. What use would those dead suckers have for their stuff *now,* after all?

The Irishman's typical insensitivity had morphed into a numb coldness, and the act of shedding blood had evolved into nothing more than a sport.

Truth was, he couldn't care less if he died right here and now. There was nothing to live for. His existence was one, long, tragic mockery at all that was *supposed* to be. He'd always been the black sheep, the outcast, the villain. *Always betrayed by those he loved most.* If there was a God, then he sure was a cruel one.

No, killing didn't faze Damascus any more than swatting a fly did. It was a necessity. He quickly stooped to search his most recent victim's corpse for ammunition.

Thank ya, brother. He smiled satirically at the blood-spattered, deformed face as his hand emerged from the fellow's coat pocket, a box of miníe balls in tote. *This'll do.*

He stood, his sharp green eyes scanning the area for another target. He furrowed his brow and raised the rifle to his shoulder, squinting down the barrel at a group of approaching Federals.

So much mingling of the sides had occurred, and Hayden's keen gaze could only pick apart the differences to a point. After that, everyone looked the same. They all held the same expressions: desperation and sheer terror.

Expressions which Damascus Hayden had wiped from his face long ago.

Sweat rolled down his face and back, as he gritted his teeth and pulled the trigger. He was confident in his marksmanship – and was not disappointed. One of the Union men stopped suddenly, flinching in pain and gripping his stomach in horror.

Fearlessness burning deep in his eyes, Hayden glared at the remaining as they raised their guns in his direction. He jammed another ball into his firearm and raised it to his shoulder in the same fashion as before. Once again, he squinted down the barrel and locked his aim on one of the men. A bullet whistled by, narrowly grazing his sleeve. He set his angular jaw and continued to glare in dark rancor.

BLAM!

The backfire of his rifle knocked him back a step. He smiled as, yet again, his bullet found its target.

Several figures raced up beside him, taking aim at the six who still continued onwards, reloading their guns.

Hayden glanced to both sides instinctively as he reloaded and took aim again. His gaze caught a smaller form to the left of him, and out of the corner of his eye, he noticed that it was a child. A boy perhaps in his early teens.

More gunfire rang out as bullets whistled through the air, some finding their marks and some not. Hayden's always did. He considered himself lucky to not have taken any himself, though he always expected it to occur at any moment. An ominous cloud of apprehension always lurked a few feet away.

Hayden found himself glancing over at the boy. Just a small lad. Skinny, underfed and pale.

Looks like a Northern kid with worms. Hayden sighed shortly, wondering who in the world would send his sickly-looking boy off to such a gruesome death.

"You hangin' in there, fella?" he asked throatily, reloading his gun with effortlessness.

The boy's fine, blond hair ruffled as a slight breeze passed through the camp. Putrid aromas of body odor, singed flesh and blood curled up in Hayden's nostrils as he turned his sweaty face to the young soldier and looked him over.

"Already shot down thirty." Feigned audacity masked the boy's response. He didn't turn to acknowledge Hayden. Instead, his eyes locked ahead. He raised his Springfield to his shoulder, taking aim with precision. Damascus realized how similar the boy's shooting pattern was to his own.

Hayden's shoulders rose and fell in a long inhalation. He stared ahead, waiting to see where the kid's bullet would go. "Let's see what you can do, eh?" he muttered dryly.

BLAM!

The young Rebel's eyes widened in shock and confusion, as he stared down at his leg—his lower calf had been mutilated by a miníe ball. It resembled a piece of meat on a hook, cracked bones jutting from skin and blood gushing forth like a fountain. Hayden's grizzled jaw tensed at the horrific wound and a thirst for vengeance filled his soul.

"*Hell no…no…*"

The boy's eyes dilated, his tear ducts filling. He tilted his chin up, staring vacantly at Damascus as his body shook, tremors claiming each limb. His lip trembled as he bit his tongue hard to keep from screaming out in pain.

"We gotta getcha outta here, kid." Damascus sucked in a deep breath, his eyes wide and sober. "Gotta pull ya outta this mess." The man extended a hand out to steady the boy but the young teen pushed it away with bitter resilience.

"No." He spat, his grey eyes fiery. "I have to finish the job." Squinting down the barrel of his gun, he pulled the trigger and stumbled backwards like a drunk man. His small frame was thrown easily by the backfire. Hayden grabbed the boy's shoulders, catching him as his body crumpled. He looked severely into the youth's determined eyes. "You'll make it, kid. Just *hold on.*"

Hayden lifted the small frame in his arms, his gaze scanning the area urgently for a place of shelter and refuge.

Surely there must be somewhere. Anywhere. Desperation filled Hayden's mind as he realized the danger he'd placed the both of them in. They were sitting ducks.

Gotta get you out of here, kiddo. Get you out, and me back to sending the Feds to Hades.

Hadn't they made any sort of dent in the Federal units' numbers? Glancing around, it seemed that the amount of Union soldiers never lessened. More and more always came, as if aroused from some hidden reserve. Hayden's heart sank as he tried to estimate quickly how many of the Florida boys were left.

Well, screw that. There was no way to tell amid this demented madness.

"Come on." There wasn't time for estimations and calculations. He decided to head back toward the woods, out of this field where the fighting was so dense. If he could just leave the boy in a ditch somewhere behind a tree… that alone would be a heck of a lot safer than the fray they were currently in.

"What's your name?" Hayden gasped out, forcing his legs into a light jog and shooting wary glances around at the continuing slaughter and chaos. He hoped that in the ruckus they would not be noticed.

The boy's eyes were distant and glazed. His limbs flopped around in Hayden's arms like a ragdoll. Hayden panted.

"No...don't leave me kid. *Talk to me.*" The muscles in his legs ached as he pushed on, harder, faster.

I will not let you die this way.

"What's your name?" He bit the inside of his cheek, his voice guttural and hoarse.

The boy stared upwards at the bright blue sky, sweat beading on his forehead as he lip continued to tremble.

"Y-York," he stammered, his voice faltering. His misty grey eyes wandered from the sky to his bloody mess of a leg, turned into a crimson hunk of mutton. "D-did I hit 'im?"

Damascus' jaw tightened, as did his grip. He glanced from side to side uneasily.

"York, you hit his blam'd guts *dead on.*" He dared not speak the truth to the lad. There was already a suffocating amount of hopelessness in the air and Hayden determined he would not be the one to add fuel to the fire. He wouldn't crush the boy further with the knowledge that his pluck and sacrifice had been in vain.

Blasted devil of a fight! It felt like he'd been running for twenty minutes, and even though the woods weren't too far off now, the fighting wasn't any less severe. Dryness scraped at the inside of Hayden's throat, making every swallow like fire.

As much as his lungs burned, and breathing became painful, the man kept running. He ran as if his life depended on it – in a way, it truly did. Damascus Hayden had taken so many lives already today. If he could show mercy to one – a child – then somehow the darkness within would not loom quite as oppressively as before. His numb spirit would gain a slight sense of feeling again. A slight form of *life.*

Damascus Hayden determined he would save this boy. Whatever the cost. This boy would get a second chance.

"*York!* Still with me?" He huffed, closing his eyes for a brief second. They burned with the smoke from the firearms all around him. He clenched his teeth, wishing his sense of smell was nonexistent. Death was not a pleasant aroma. The reeking stench of blood was now to the point of being sickening.

This must be what hell feels like. Hayden's muscles rippled as his feet pounded the pulverized ground. Each stride sent painful convulsions up his spine. His biceps quivered, York's weakened body draped between them. The boy didn't respond.

"York!"

Had the miníe ball's expansion in York's leg become lethal? Hayden didn't know anything about anatomy or doctoring but the boy had sure lost a lot of blood. His calf was nothing but a shred of meat and shattered bone. Hayden couldn't imagine the pain such an injury would cause.

This boy... needed help. And awfully soon. It would be sure to result in an amputation of the entire calf, but at least his life could be spared. Pratchit could help him...at least, he could try. That was what the wishy-washy sawbones had come to do, right?

Hayden upped his pace. His throat tightened and restricted, but he soaked in the pain. He allowed his body to be energized by its throbbing power, and he fueled his spirit with its burning vigor. The harder it hurt, the harder he forced himself to run. Determination would be his savior. He could do this. He didn't need a Higher Power to pray to. With all that he had suffered, all that he had pulled his sorry carcass through already, he didn't need anyone. Let alone some jokester in the sky who only added to his torment.

He would not let this boy's life fall to the hands of cruel fate. And if he himself died, it would be on his own terms.

Hayden fueled himself with the longing for vengeance against a God he didn't even believe in.

Zealous. He became zealous to prove this God wrong.

And then, in the blink of an eye, it happened. The man's entire world went black as the deafening sound of artillery blew out his senses.

Darkness filled his vision, even though it was full daylight. His ears registered nothing but the pulsation of his own heart. A numb pain reverberated through his body. He gradually realized that he was no longer running. His eyes burned as he opened them wide, desperate to make out anything in front of him.

Nothing. Pitch black.

The man's head felt heavy and frozen, as if it weighed a thousand pounds.

What the hell...

York. Hayden's heart rate surged and his jaw quavered as he became aware of the cold sweat soaking his shirt and skin – and the fact that he no longer gripped a skinny thirteen-year-old in his arms. No. He was on the *ground*, the blood-soaked ground, and he could feel nothing... *anywhere.* Was he dead? Paralyzed? In a dream? Even his thoughts fell numb and anesthetized.

Where are you, kid? And where am I?

He struggled to regain consciousness. To regain *anything.* Where was his sight? Blackness still filled his vision. His legs had turned to mush, proving useless as he attempted to stand. Hayden didn't care whether he lived or not...but if this was what death felt like, it was pretty crummy. Perhaps succession of life wasn't that much better than being alive in the botched-up world before. Disappointing.

Somehow, Hayden had imagined that death would be more satisfying. Like a long, pleasant slumber in mid-afternoon beneath the sun. A nap he'd never have to wake up from.

This progression didn't even come *close* to a summer siesta. It was as if he was dangling in between somewhere, in a place that made no logical sense. A place that had no name, gratified none, brought peace to none. A place full of those who'd lost their way.

Such a cruel betrayal.

Maybe I am *dead.*

Damascus lay there on his back, motionless. He stared upwards at the darkness, breathing patchy, short breaths. A sticky liquid on his chest and arms made him wonder if he had been shot or hit with shrapnel from the cannon fire. Cannons. How ruthless were these Yanks, to risk blowing up their own men for the sake of a few enemy casualties?

Had the Rebels been able to pack that great of a punch? Were they going to succeed after all?

Gradually, Hayden felt life in his arms and hands again. Good. At least he knew now that perhaps he wasn't dead, and even if he was, his existence didn't dangle in some purgatory place out in the far ends of the universe.

His hands reached up, feeling the warm, oozing stickiness of blood against his shirt. His body was evidently covered in it.

Where are you, York...

Muffled sound began to echo in his ears. Faint cries and yells rollicked against his drums, gunfire exploding in the milieu like distant thunder. Still, he could see nothing. Hayden had never experienced blindness before, but for once, he realized something that was worth appreciation: sight.

The blackness enveloped him, and perhaps that was the worst part of this whole deal. He was helpless. Completely, utterly helpless. Without his sharp vision, he was left to the mercy of whoever found him. Right now, the man just wished that someone *would*. Maybe they could shoot him in the head and get it all over with, since he apparently wasn't dead. He wished he was. Damascus Hayden had no will to live on this hell-hole called Earth.

But no. He couldn't abandon the life he'd purposed to save. York...he was out there in the morass, somewhere. And Hayden had made a promise—he must find him.

I'm coming for you, kid, just hold on...Hold on.

Even though he was still enshrouded in darkness, the man tried to force his body up to a sitting position. Still no feeling in his legs. Now he began to wonder if they were even still there. Shrapnel was almost worse than miníe balls, after all. Larger. And who knows at what distance the cannon had been fired. Hayden and York could've been hit pretty close up – and if that was the case, Hayden could easily have lost his entire bottom half.

But wouldn't he have felt that sort of blow? With all the excruciating pain York was suffering with his one calf, Hayden would have surmised that...well, *this* would be unthinkably worse. He should have felt something by now.

Something.

A vengeful fury rose within his soul and he gritted his teeth. His eyes were widened and craning to see, but nothing came. He couldn't stand this. Nothing was clear, nothing felt *real,* and all he possessed was the sickening knowledge that he *wasn't* dead. He wasn't dead, and somewhere, York was out there alone. Abandoned. Hayden was powerless to save him.

"Just kill me already! Just get the whole damned thing over with!"

A garbled yell arose from his throat as he fought back hot, angry tears. Inside, he cursed his Maker with all the hate he had. He let it all loose, his heart yearning to kill and destroy. All he had wanted was death. Death, or to make a difference in this massacre somehow. Then York had appeared and everything changed. The boy needed someone to guide him. When the bullet hit, he'd needed someone to *rescue* him. Damascus stifled an incensed cry. He had learned to survive without anyone else, but that hadn't come by his choice. This boy needed a better life than existing as a pawn in this blasted war. He deserved better.

I will not let him die.

Livid determination flooded Hayden's system as he choked back the tears. He would get up and overcome this. He would find the kid and get him to safety, just as planned.

Nothing would alter that course. Nothing would get in his way.

He pushed himself up on all fours, as feeling returned to the rest of his body. Pain throbbed in his quadriceps. So he hadn't lost his legs, after all. Well, at least he'd be able to carry York again.

Hang in there, kid...

Fuzzy shreds of light sliced through his vision as, little by little, his sight returned. The tears still swelling in his eyes made everything blurry and muddled. Wiping his forearm across his face, he got rid of the extra moisture.

Have to get to York.

Brightness. It hurt his eyes. As the light crept across his vision, his head pounded with pain. It felt like he'd been hit in the head with a baseball bat at full force.

"York!" He called out, groping forward, still on his hands and knees. Blood had hardened on his hands and arms, painting a dry coat of crimson on his skin. Finally, his eyes began to adjust to the glaring sunlight and smoky atmosphere. He searched with desperation and determination for the scrawny boy who had suddenly become such a high priority in his life.

Men ran about like ants invading a picnic. The disorder and confusion hadn't died, and chaos still ruled the topography. Bodies lay scattered everywhere. Hayden crawled around them slowly, still lacking the strength to stand. He scanned the area for York, his breathing deep and erratic. His head continued to throb painfully as he forced himself to stand.

What happened to you, little man? You couldn't have gotten too...

No.

This isn't real.

Hayden's mouth fell open, forming unintelligible words when the real ones wouldn't come. This couldn't be happening. It wasn't supposed to end this way.

Staring in disbelief at the lifeless corpse before him, he felt his throat constrict. His jaw quivered, his entire being racked with despair. The boy's body was almost unrecognizable.

"*No, no, York. No…You couldn't.*" The man ran both hands through his ragged shock of ginger hair, tears smarting his eyes as he continued to shake his head. He fell back down to his knees and stared at the cannon shrapnel's devastating aftermath. *This couldn't be happening.*

"*You can't be dead, kid. You weren't supposed to die like this.*" Agonizing murmurs escaped the man's lips as his eyes traced the boy's pale, blood-spattered face. The contrast of dark crimson against York's colorless skin wrenched another angry sob from Damascus. He covered his face with his hands, rocking back and forth slowly in misery.

It's all my fault. You took the shrapnel when it should've been me.

Hayden's body convulsed as hot tears mingled with the dried blood on his grizzled face. He gritted his teeth hard, his eyes burning and red. All he could think about was one word, one smoldering, unanswered question.

Why?

Why did he always manage to survive when he possessed not the will? Why had death been forbidden him when that was his only longing, only hope, only desire? Why couldn't his one request be requited? Was it that much of an impossibility, for Damascus Hayden to cease living?

Was it really that wrong to yearn for a cold hole in the ground?

All he wanted was to pass on from this blasted existence. It qualified not as a life; for it had been far too cruel for that term. No. Hayden's life was merely an existence, a cruel and pitiless mess destined to fail from the very start.

There is no God. The man lowered his hands from his face, dropping them helplessly to his sizes. A bile rose in his throat as he fought the urge to vomit all over the place. *And if there is a God, I want nothing of Him. I vow it. I'll never believe in such a merciless being.*

Never.

York's bony, white face stared up at Hayden. His grey eyes remained fixed, frozen. The boy uttered no reply. But of course he uttered nothing; his spirit had been stolen from his body long ago.

Ripped away unjustly, in the most brutal way, by men who didn't care that they'd smothered a child's life. Somewhere, would the boy be missed? Would there be folks back in Florida wondering what happened to their son, the reason he'd not returned by the end of the war? Would *anyone* care that this boy was no more?

If only York had known his accidental sacrifice would leave Hayden greedy for something more. The skinny, short kid with feathery blond hair had conjured up something more vicious than all the rattlesnakes in the Florida scrubs. Hayden's craving for *vengeance*.

The livid Rebel retrieved his rifle, and wiped the blood-mingled tears from his face. Rising from the mess of bone, flesh and blood that covered the earthen floor, he clenched his fists, glaring ahead with a set jaw. He would make the enemy suffer. If there was one thing that would happen next, it would be the destruction of these Union devils. Hayden would kill them all or die trying.

Poor little York was far too young to die.

Chapter Seventeen

EZRA

His eyes were open, glassy and wide. Staring off into the distance, lingering on what might have been one last thought or desire. His mouth hung ajar, a trickle of crimson dried down either side of his chin. No further words would come from those lips.

The man's body was unmoving, leaned against a tree as if he'd been enjoying a summer afternoon's siesta. And aside from the blood and the gun clutched rigidly in one hand, it could've easily been so. Of course, the location was wrong. In the midst of battle, only a fool would steal a few moments of shuteye.

It was an average rifle musket he gripped. A gun that easily might have been loaded or not. This fellow could've been completely armed, ready to fight back. Perhaps he had stopped to nurse an injury and didn't notice the artillery positioned forty feet off. Perhaps he'd noticed it, but didn't think its reach would affect him where he'd stopped. Maybe he'd never seen a cannon before, and therefore underestimated its gruesome power.

Ezra couldn't tell if this was a Fed or Southerner. He wasn't wearing a uniform, only simple civilian clothes, which could've been donned by a soldier from either side. His messy dark hair swept low across his brow, nearly reaching his eyes.

A gaping hole drew Ezra's gaze to the corpse's midsection, where heaps of crimson-colored entrails lay cascading from within.

Intestines. *Yards and yards of them.*

Guts and shreds of flesh were scattered in piles across the man's lap and upper legs. The gaping cavity in his abdomen revealed that this was either the result of a barrage of minie balls, or a single artillery shell. Either would've done the trick.

Ezra's throat closed up and he set his jaw, continuing to stare at the sickening heap of human meat. He swallowed, his stomach lurching as unsavory aromas curled up into his nostrils. He fought off the instinct to gag, not wanting to lose what bit of breakfast he'd consumed nearly fourteen hours ago.

The sight was a ghastly reminder of the tragic results of war. Death had never felt so real and imminent.

Had this man departed into eternity holding to faith in the Savior?

Tight-lipped, Ezra looked at the horrific demise a moment longer. What would it feel like to die in such a way? Having your stomach ripped open? Seeing your own innards spill into your hands?

Finally, he tore his eyes away. Between the man's frozen facial expression and the mental imagery Ezra found himself painting of how this had all occurred... it was too much.

The young man forced himself to get away from this haunting place.

But he couldn't escape death's presence. Everywhere he turned, there were bodies. Hundreds and hundreds of them. Corpses no longer possessing souls.

Flies and other small insects buzzed around the reeking cadavers.

Blood stained almost every inch of the ground, saturating the soil with dark crimson.

Limbs, missing their owners. Fingers, feet, arms, legs; all manner of human flesh tossed here and there as if a tornado had ripped through the camp.

Ezra kept his eyes open and aware as he staggered through the obliterated section of earth, but it was difficult. He hadn't slept for thirty-six hours. The last two days had been a recurring nightmare... sleep was impossible under such conditions.

They'd won.

Rosecrans had been forced to withdraw his army into Chattanooga. Both sides suffered losses, but unfortunately for the Southern boys, theirs were nearly as great as the Union's.

A shudder rollicked Ezra's body as he forced his legs onward, scanning the mangled ground for any familiar faces. Not that he wanted to see any. Not here, at least. He hoped desperately that his eyes wouldn't discover a friend or acquaintance, lying in the heaps of decaying flesh.

Then a thought entered his mind, a chilling recollection that had been forgotten in all the tragic aftermath. A name, which belonged to an innocent twelve-year-old hardly big enough to carry a rifle, much less fight in a battle against cold steel and vehemence.

Frances.

Ezra swallowed, nearly tripping over a mound of yet more bodies.

Oh God, please let that boy be alright. I pray you allowed him to escape this. That he got to run far away, that he'll have a chance to make it back to where he came from. Let him get back to Jacksonville safe. To his family.

Surely they'd be waiting for him with open arms. Surely they'd all run up to him and take his small frame in their arms, kissing his forehead and crying tears of relief and joy at his presence.

How could they not? If Ezra had a family, a son, and the child ran off to war without him knowing…

But he didn't have a family of his own and he didn't have a son. Ezra was just a bachelor, and he had no sights of that ever changing – especially in this present situation. The idea of finding a nice woman with whom he could settle down and raise a family – it was a nice fantasy, but just that at this point.

Ezra's mind drifted back to the young Cranston boy. He continued to pray silently for Frances' safety, that his thin body wouldn't appear among the corpses Ezra searched. If the lad could just get back to Florida, back to his parents…where he belonged. Only then would Ezra be able to rest his mind about the matter.

It was a rather ironic fix, because Florida, despite the fact that it was *home*, was hardly a safe haven. Marauders and looters roamed freely across the northern half of the state and federal troops still occupied the coastal forts. The lower section was completely wild and unknown. It was guessed that Seminoles still occupied a good portion of its terrain.

As a whole, the state of Florida was vastly unpopulated. Compared with some of the other Confederate states, it was an untamed jungle full of all sorts of potential threats. It provided a temporary hiding place for fugitive slaves, deserters, and who knew what else. Malaria was rampant, due to the clouds of mosquitoes.

But amidst all the dangers, Florida was still *home*. It was the only place in which Ezra felt he truly belonged. It was where he'd been born and raised, and it was all he'd ever known—until he'd entered Georgia with the militia.

"Ezra." A firm hand gripped his shoulder, and the young man whirled around.

"Hayden."

Hayden's normally jaded eyes were solemn and blank. Dark circles fell just beneath them, hinting that he too hadn't been blessed with a peaceful night's rest. A certain leeriness hung over the brawny man's visage. Exposure to evil had lent his eyes to a particular darkness, even though their hue was a striking emerald.

The short redhead chewed on the lower inside of his lip, exhaling through his nose wearily.

"You value the company of the dead more than the living?"

Ezra's jaw tensed at Hayden's cutting words, more statement than question. He didn't respond, continuing to scan the area for Frances.

After a moment of stifled silence, Hayden stuck his hands into his pant pockets and shuffled away.

Frustration sank into Ezra's soul. He glanced in Hayden's direction to make sure the man was out of hearing distance. With a huff of defeat, he kicked at the ground. His lip quavered as he stared hopelessly at the scores of human remains surrounding him on all sides.

Would he ever find that boy? Or was it a waste of time to even look? Even if he did find Frances' body, what would he do with it?

That raised another haunting question.

What would they do with all these bodies?

Ezra couldn't even tell ally from foe, Fed from Rebel. The only burial they would likely receive would be in unmarked mass graves. Rows and rows of them. The men and boys here would be forgotten with time, as grass grew on the rows and the terrain returned to its former green, peaceful state.

But even if they received a proper funeral, it still wouldn't change the horror of what had happened.

The young man stifled an angry sob. *God, why? Just why?*

Chapter Eighteen

ZEPHYR
October 1ˢᵗ, 1863

IT WAS FUNNY HOW MUCH you noticed things the instant they were gone. Funny how, once something was taken away from you, it suddenly became so much more desirable.

Only, funny wasn't really the word to cover the emotion. Especially not in *this* case. There were no words to describe *this* feeling.

A thousand could be utilized to explain the sentiment, but none of them would truly do it justice. At best, they would merely scratch the surface.

Zephyr stared at the barn's interior. It looked so empty. At least this could be described with words. The void in her heart could not.

I feel nothing. I feel nothing. I feel nothing.

She closed her eyes, beguiling herself with a lie so bold it could smack her in the face.

Standing here, in the midst of a sea of loss, how could she feel nothing? To say she felt a lack of emotion would be the biggest falsehood of them all.

I think, therefore I am. And I choose to think that I've recovered from it all.

Zephyr took a deep breath as she looked at the abandoned stall where she'd milked Amelia months ago. It felt like just yesterday. The smell of livestock still lingered in the hay. Not that she truly missed taking care of the animals, but in a way she sort of did. Strangely enough, she realized it had brought an odd sort of comfort. Amelia was a good cow. She was tame, quiet, and quite likeable for being of the bovine family. And then there was Daphne. Such a strong, dependable horse.

Those Feds better be treating them right. They were pleasant creatures...they don't deserve to be handled cruelly.

Zephyr's mind trailed off as she listened to the silence, remaining still as a statue. The quiet was deafening between these wooden walls. Even the air possessed a heavy, engulfing quality.

It was so terribly quiet. From a certain perspective, it might have been perceived as peaceful. But not from Zephyr's.

See, Zephyr hated the quiet because it only accomplished one thing – it reminded her of the noise in her head. The contrast between the blaring chaos of her mind, and the deadening silence of this barn was staggering. The longer she listened to the vacant space between these walls, the longer she heard things she didn't want to hear. The longer she stared at nothing in particular, the more she visualized images of the greatest atrocity. The longer she tried to quiet the chaos, the more the opposite occurred.

And the more she tried to banish the clamorous sea of emotions, the more they raged and multiplied within.

It was a battle in vain.

Blood-soaked screams, pleas for mercy. Treacherous whispers, murmurs of condemnation.

Zephyr grinded her teeth, her muscles quaking. Tears welled up in the corners of her eyes, but she held them back.

Please, I can't handle this.

Echoes. Endless echoes. Ceaseless conversations about things that no longer mattered. The searing pain of regret.

Oh, but there are so many things you could've done differently, Zephyr. So many things you ruined, so many ways you failed to live up to what you're supposed to be. So many ways you've proven yourself to be a monster, a beastly fiend. No one will ever understand. You see, you're all alone. And it's your own fault that you are.

There were so many memories. The voices seemed to retrieve them instantaneously and they replayed them without her summons. She heard Silas playing the piano. She saw him smiling at her in his shy little way. Then there was Anson's angry glare. His parting words of malice. Lydia's terrified face, as she watched the federals on their raid. Lydia's cynicism just in general. There was Pa, wrapping his thick arms around her, hugging her good-bye.

And then there was the horrific realization that she could hardly remember what Pa's face looked like. She'd tried so hard not to forget all the little details, but she hadn't noticed how blurry they'd grown in her mind.

No, no. I can't forget Pa's face. Shaking her head, she chewed on the lower half of her lip in panic. She had to visualize it for more than just an outline. She had to remember the exact color of his eyes, because they weren't just green, they were a hazy sort of... wait, they *were* green, weren't they?

She squeezed her eyes shut, as a tremor overtook her body. Her body seized, and she had to lean against the wall to avoid falling. She wanted to argue with the voices, but what was there to say? This time, she actually agreed with them. She was an atrocity. She couldn't even remember the eyes of her own father. Or even the voice that belonged to him.

She couldn't control her own mind. What good was her existence if she was merely destined to be a slave to whatever held her captive? Was she nothing more than a shadow, passing to and fro without purpose?

Zephyr turned toward the door. She traced her fingers through the air until they met a scarred support beam on her right. Pressing her fingertips against the rough wood, a hint of satisfaction warmed her spirit. Splinters pierced her skin, calming her. She took a step forward, feeling her way to the doorframe. Focusing all her concentration powers on this simple procedure seemed to eliminate a few of the voices.

But only a few.

Chapter Nineteen

November 25th, 1863

EZRA
The Battle of Missionary Ridge

GUNSHOTS ECHOED NEARBY.

If it had been miles away, it wouldn't have been nearly as disconcerting. But it wasn't miles away anymore. And it was a lot more than just disconcerting.

The sound of many voices resonated through the terrain, creating a daunting echo of unnatural commotion. The bodies which belonged to those voices hadn't arrived, but they were coming. The valley was occupied by the Union forces yesterday. They'd already taken Lookout Mountain and Orchard Knob.

"Well, here we go at it again," Ezra murmured gravely, looking over at his older brother. His vocal tone spoke of the dread both men now shared.

A month had passed since the battle of Chickamauga. Within that month, the Army of Tennessee had moved to entrench itself at the base of Missionary Ridge, near Chattanooga. It had been another long, monotonous month of waiting.

Harold's face was blank and fixed, his eyes subtly reflecting the drab colors of the barren ridge.

"May God go with us. We certainly need Him." His words fell softly, without any emotion attached.

Ezra let the air seep out of him. His breath felt warm in the chilly autumn air.

The young man felt a strange sort of numbness in his being, and unconsciously chose not to respond to Harry's statement.

This felt like a dream. Stationed in these rifle-pits, waiting for the enemy to release its fury again, Ezra felt as if he were in another dimension outside of reality.

And yet, the war had become his *only* reality.

The two brothers stood in silence, watching the unit approach for a good amount of time. The lack of discussion was coolly stifling. Across the stretch of open shrubbery, the Federal unit came into view.

The Army of the Cumberland. Twenty-three thousand soldiers, advancing in columns of three.

It was a spectacular, ominous sight.

Finally, somebody cut through the silence.

"God let us wind up here for a reason." Harold spoke softly, but with brevity and firmness. His tone was not shaken or altered from its usual authoritative stance. "Therefore, we ought to do our best to fulfill it." There was nothing in his words other than the chill of strict duty.

Ezra didn't respond. His mouth was dry, and no words came to mind which seemed to matter at present. He knew his brother was right.

And nothing else needed to be said.

His jaw stiffened as he gave a very short, abrupt nod, and continued to stare across the valley.

Confederate artillery opened up immediately from atop Missionary Ridge, but everyone at the base of the entrenchment waited until the Federals were much closer before they opened fire.

From this moment on, all focus and energy would be put into what each man and boy had originally enlisted to do: protect his country, defy the government's injustices. But most importantly, all strength and energy would be put into *survival*. The core instinct possessed by each soul in humanity. To attempt to defy death itself.

Ezra couldn't deny the fear he felt splintering through his being. It was a numbing sort of fear that didn't come as sudden horror or alarm. Instead, it subtly twisted his insides into a patchwork of knots and loops, and turned his brain to peach marmalade. He couldn't think straight. His heart pounded like a rhythmic, throbbing drum, echoing dully in the back of his mind and rocking the insides of his chest.

There's no reason to get all in a fuss. We have the upper hand. We won't let them take the ridge. We beat them before, we can do it again. He tried in vain to convince himself that it would be alright. He tried to rally his soul and revive the excitement that had fled during Chickamauga.

But he couldn't. All he could think about was the blood. The limbs and severed bodies.

He couldn't shake the macabre imagery from his head.

Ezra's heartbeat increased involuntarily as a particular boy came to mind. *Frances Cranston.*

He swallowed as his eyes scanned the Confederate entrenchment strip.

Lord God, I wish I could protect him, but at this point, only You can.

A hand gripped his shoulder lightly.

Ezra turned to see who the hand belonged to.

Pratchit's light blue eyes stared soberly back into his, and he removed his hand from Ezra's shoulder.

Ezra searched Pratchit's eyes in silence.

An uncanny emptiness hung in the air between the two men. And yet, at the same time, there was something they shared now which hadn't manifested before. Perhaps a respect for one another's humanity? The knowledge that fear had the ability to encompass every person?

How could death unite souls so seamlessly?

Ezra blinked, his gaze falling back to the valley. "You seen Hayden?"

Pratchit gave a quick shake of his head, his eyes vacant. His mouth opened, but nothing came from within.

Ezra felt his throat closing again. He couldn't swallow. Forcing himself to breathe, he turned to see the faces of his comrades as they too watched in silence.

Lord, please give me strength. Give me the strength to carry on with this.

His eyes focused ahead involuntarily, as the distance between the Feds and the rifle-pits closed. He kept praying silently, his jaw set and tense.

I know it's a strange thing to ask for...helping us to kill people. The young man's lungs tightened at of the sickening thought.

1

Lord, I don't know what this will do to help in the great scheme of things. To end this war, to save other lives, to bring freedom from oppression. How many more men will die before this happens?

The young man closed his eyes for the briefest of seconds.

So Lord, I ask one thing, only one.

They were closing in.

A wave of adrenaline hit his system as he offered one final petition to the Creator.

Make this count.

Ezra took a deep breath, pulled his gun out, and made sure one last time that it was cocked and loaded.

It was. He held the gun at his side, and craned his neck, turning to look at his group.

The 7th was as ready as they'd ever be.

A miníe ball whistled past his ear, close enough that Ezra could feel the breeze against his exposed neck. As daunting as this would have been to an inexperienced soldier, it had no effect on Ezra. He'd felt it raise the hair on his skin before. The only movement he made now was raising his rifle to his shoulder to aim at the oncoming enemy.

The next hour would be one of the worst whirlwinds of pandemonium the Army of Tennessee had ever experienced.

Before Ezra had time to think, his finger was at the trigger and he'd placed bullets in two bodies. Pratchit followed through another two. Blood trickled from one's stomach and mouth. Another suffered a miníe ball to the head, causing the end result to be far... messier.

Crimson was everywhere.

The rifle-pits were in complete disarray. Men and boys were practically fighting at eachothers' throats. More and more joined the unfortunate lads who lay lifeless beneath them.

Death's sickeningly potent odor filled the trenches.

It was a complete massacre. Ezra and his men took down many of the Federal soldiers Killing had evolved into a fluid action that didn't require second thought.

Still, they kept coming.

Ezra's muscles tensed as he raised his gun to his side and aimed at a federal man trying in vain to load his rifle. The man's eyes went wide in terror as he looked up and saw Ezra's barrel pointed at him.

For a brief second, the two soldiers locked eye contact. Ezra inhaled, biting the inside of his lip hard enough to taste blood.

Who would this man be leaving behind? A wife? Children? Where would he be in the next life? Heaven, or hell?

Ezra lowered his gaze, setting his jaw tightly as he unloaded a miníe ball into the other man. The small steel projectiles shredded his arms and upper body on impact, leaving an unrecognizable corpse spattered in red.

Bullets flew around him, ruffling a whirring breeze near his skin. The sound of clashing bayonets only added to the chaos sweeping down the ridge.

Confusion still dominated the melee, and the Feds were far from being unarmed. They too had taken advantage of the chance to replace their weapons back in Chickamauga.

As they continued to advance on the Florida men, Ezra knew it wasn't looking good for the Confederate pickets. They were losing their ground.

His body shuddered as he clumsily reloaded his rifle and glanced about. Suddenly, he couldn't tell enemy from comrade.

The barrage of gunfire, scuffle, and yelling created a throbbing din. Sounds of ensuing death, terror and confusion rang out hauntingly across the topography. His mind inebriated with the adrenaline of the moment, he had no time to think of anything but killing Yankees.

It was a *madhouse.*

Ezra's arms trembled, and his lungs ached. It was late afternoon now, but it seemed so much later. In the midst of battle, time seemed to warp and twist out of the restraints of logic.

Out of the corner of his eye, an unwelcome sight greeted him—a number of southerners now scurried up the side of the ridge as fast as they could go.

No…No, we can't give up now…what are they doing?

Ezra's eyes widened in shock as he watched his retreating comrades. Then his shock turned to outrage.

"*No! We must stand our ground!*" He bellowed into the nightmare, not caring that his shout would fall on deaf ears.

"What in blazes do you think you're doing? *Cowards!*"

The man gritted his teeth, shaking his head in repulsion. He turned around just in time to parry a Union bayonet before it impaled his chest.

He fought with renewed vigor, desperation clawing at him to keep the Federals at bay even if he was fighting in the rifle-pits alone. After what he'd just witnessed, he felt like he was.

More and more Confederates were dropping. Worse, more and more of Sherman's men were assaulting the side of the ridge. The barrage of bullets had become as thick as a cloud.

Ezra was surprised he was even still alive.

But somebody had to stay. If the Feds broke through and charged up the hill, the Confederates would lose their upper hand. The victory at Chickamauga would have been for naught.

More and more men were evacuating, or attempting to at least. The ridge was a steep, seven-hundred-foot precipice. Some of the soldiers were too weak to hoist themselves up and, after several failed attempts, found themselves trapped against the stony earth, facing an onslaught of viscous, cold steel.

Some of the Union men had already begun charging up the ridge as well, right on the tails of the fleeing Floridians.

"*Ezra!*"

A familiar voice penetrated the pandemonium. Ezra's heart pounded harder as his eyes shot up frantically. He squinted into the haze, his finger hovering just above the trigger.

"*Get over here!*"

The voice yelled out a desperate command, and Ezra made the connection.

"*Harry?*" He found himself running towards his brother's voice.

The man was at the base of the ridge, an urgent expression pasted on his face.

"What's happened?" Ezra stared at his brother, his eyes flitting from the steep incline to the army behind them. He didn't want their backs exposed. Still, he exhaled, taking the occasion to catch his breath and wipe a sheen of sweat from his face. *Thank God you're still alive, big brother.*

Mr. Darson's gaze was everywhere but Ezra. "We have to get out of here before any further damage is done."

Ezra swallowed, his stomach churning. Yes, it'd been painfully obvious that more deaths had fallen on the side of the Southerners. But how could they just turn and run?

"Ezra!" Harry yelled. "*Do you wish to die here?*"

Before Ezra had any time to register what his brother had said, Harold was climbing up the ridge along with scores of others, both Southern and Federal.

Ezra scurried up after him. He could hardly think straight. Logic had long escaped his mind, and perhaps sanity itself. His ears rang, creating a relentless din in his head.

God, help me. Help us. The young man bit the inside of his cheek, looking up the crest.

We've only gone from the frying pan into the fire.

The climbing was difficult, but Ezra's body was too full of adrenaline for him to notice or care. He kept his eyes locked on Harold, praying that neither of them would be shot down from this precarious position with their backs to the Feds.

Showered by shot and shell, he saw Harold stop. They were about half-way up the slope now. Bullets whistled past Ezra, pelting the side of the ridge.

Oh horrors, what now?

A beefy, overweight Confederate had also stopped and appeared to be quite winded. It was no wonder, from his size.

Ezra's eyes widened.

Colonel Bullock.

Ezra rushed up after Harry, and saw him hoisting one of the man's arms over his shoulder, attempting to help him up the side of the ridge.

Reaching the two a few seconds later, Ezra grabbed the Colonel's other arm and followed suit. He bit down on his lip, grunting as he helped lighten the man's load.

The three stumbled up the precipice, as fast as they could under their circumstances.

But it wasn't fast enough.

"Down with your weapons!"

Four Union men surrounded them from the back, pointing their guns at the handicapped threesome.

Ezra turned in a mixture of horror and surprise.

"You heard 'im, drop the guns!" One of the Feds poked Ezra in the ribs with the barrel of his rifle musket, boring holes in him with his glare.

Ezra glanced at his brother and Colonel Bullock. The Colonel was still out of breath, and his face was flushed a shade of crimson to match.

"Do as he says." The man's body drooped between them, as he let out a sigh and relinquished his pistol.

Gritting his teeth, Ezra glowered at the Feds as they collected the weapons. "You're gonna regret this," he seethed under his breath.

One of the soldiers laughed. "I can't help that you were stupid enough to try and flee up this hill."

"Take them back with the rest of the prisoners." The other Yank pointed down the ridge a ways.

"Bully! With all the boatkissers we've caught so far? Only the good Lord knows where we'll send all 'em at the end of this."

Both brothers exchanged a look of despair.

Had they really just become prisoners of war?

The Federals would either execute their captives or march them north to a prison camp.

Either outcome sounded just as daunting as the other.

Chapter Twenty

ZEPHYR
November 28th, 1863

A TRICKLE OF BLOOD STREAMED from the side of Zephyr's middle finger. She stared at the sticky, dark crimson liquid. Her hands were already covered in dirt, due to several hours' worth of weeding in the garden. Now, a small bit of red mingled with the great amount of black.

It was just a small cut. Zephyr wasn't even sure how it had happened. Either way, it didn't faze her. The young woman's entire body was filthy, enveloped in dirt and sweat.

Garden work was nothing short of a great exertion.

It's just what Adam and Eve did several thousand years ago. What I'm doing right now.

Zephyr let out a breath of warm air, momentarily musing on the history of mankind, and its connection to the earth beneath.

From dust we were created, and here we are, working the dust.

The sun didn't beat down as overbearingly as usual, and for this Zephyr was grateful. She sent a quick glance to the grey clouds hanging above, which blocked the brilliant rays.

It was amazing how an overcast sky could change the temperature enough to make a difference. They made the heat just a little more bearable, a little less oppressing.

Zephyr returned her gaze to her hands, as they pulled at the cumbersome weeds surrounding a sapling-like okra stalk. She wrapped her fingers around a deeply established root, and tugged, grunting. The weed's roots cut into her skin, causing her face to contort in mild frustration.

Her fingernails had long ago been cut shallow. Digging around in thick, clay-filled soil usually did that to the keratin fibers. Now, the short ridges were full of snags, so that it was almost painful to keep rooting about.

Nonetheless, the girl continued her task. Weeds didn't stop growing because Zephyr's fingers ached a little.

Mrs. Darson and the little boys were all weeding in the same vicinity. This particular plot was the one on the western side of the house and the smaller of the vegetable patches. It was right next to the herb garden, and the kitchen wasn't but about two-hundred feet away.

Zephyr looked up to see Royce wielding a hoe dangerously.

"You have no business with that! It's time for *weeding*, not digging," Zephyr exclaimed as she stood up from her crouched position and wiped a sheen of sweat from her brow.

Ma glanced up from her work and to Royce, assessing the situation. Royce made a low whimpering sound in protest to Zephyr's declaration.

"Royce, no hoes for now—finish your job first."

Zephyr shook her head and sent her gaze back down to her hands groping about in the clay soil.

She dropped to her knees, her spine weary from leaning over for three hours. Her dress was already a sweaty mess, so she didn't mind sitting in the moist dirt. In fact, it felt pleasant compared to being hunched over for an extended period.

The girl heaved a sigh. She was now completely shielded from any sunlight peeking through the grey clouds above. Tall, tree-like okra stalks towered above her head, their wide leaves casting her in cool shadows.

Weeding actually wasn't so bad in these conditions.

Zephyr swiped a dirty finger across her forehead, attempting unsuccessfully to brush some stray hairs out of her face. Her eyes stung as bits of dirt lit upon their surfaces.

He can't be truly gone.

Memories flooded her mind. As she twisted another root around her fingers, Zephyr bit her lip, her heart sinking in recollection.

A weight filled her chest as she tugged the plant loose. She swallowed, pain slicing her insides.

He'd been gone for almost a month now. The tall, dark-haired pianist called Silas McIntosh was gone. Stolen away to help a cause he didn't believe in. Well, Zephyr assumed he hadn't gone willingly. Who on earth would want to join such a thing, after all? Surely Silas didn't favor the northern side. She knew his *father* didn't.

But it didn't matter now. He was no longer here and that was all that mattered. And who knew if he'd ever return.

He would probably forget all about Zephyr. He had no reason to remember her. She'd done nothing marvelous to be remembered by. She wasn't exceptionally beautiful. All the pretty girls were short and small. Zephyr was neither. And though she had skills, there had never been an opportunity for her to demonstrate them around Silas.

Surely he'll forget me.

Maybe it wouldn't be so awful a fate if not for one thing—Zephyr would never forget *him.*

This, you see, was the torture of it all. Silas was gone, and perhaps he wouldn't ever think of Zephyr again. But it wouldn't be so with her. She would think of him constantly. In the distant corners of her soul, his face would appear. In the whispers of the wind, she would hear his voice.

Oh, to forget him would be luxury.

Numbness. Zephyr forced it to wash over her heart again so the emotions would be kept at bay, so they wouldn't ravage her insides and cut her in pieces. Not that this hadn't occurred already, for the very moment Prudence had told her the news that Sunday afternoon last month, Zephyr's world was shattered in ten million tiny shards.

She'd spent that night sobbing into her pillow, hoping that her tears would go unnoticed, but not really caring if they didn't. As long as the red stains on her face were erased come next morning, it didn't matter anymore.

The ache never subsided. She'd been able to mask it well enough on the outside, but internally, it raged like a forest fire…wild, untamed, and utterly out of her control.

How desperately Zephyr desired to put out the flames, to quench the painful fire of burning wantonness.

It was a wish all in vain, the efforts futile. She was powerless to stop her heart from throbbing, her mind from lusting for what she could not have.

Why was it that she always fell for the things that weren't to be hers? There'd been other boys who'd shown interest in her. She could've accepted their invitations if she'd wanted.

But no. No, she'd set her mind on the one that could never be hers.

Zephyr tossed a handful of weeds aside, and cracked her knuckles, listening to them pop. She'd known all along it was foolish to think the way she had. Why did she give in to her flesh? Why did she have to be such a stubborn, irrational thing?

I'm supposed to be a new creature.

Zephyr exhaled, closing her eyes.

I'm not supposed to be focusing so much on this.

A clap of distant thunder shook the ground.

I didn't even know him. He was little more than a stranger.

The overcast sky darkened.

Zephyr's eyes lifted slowly in response to the thunder, and she stared up at the atmospheric forewarning. A wave of numbness again washed over her, causing all feeling to fall flat and meaningless. She set her teeth, taking in the clouds and their foreboding promise of rain.

Rain was a great blessing in so many ways, but there'd been showers nearly every day throughout this last month. Too much water could be equally as troublesome as not enough.

Zephyr felt her throat close up. She hated that feeling.

Maybe it would be easier if I didn't have a heart at all.

Thunder rolled. A warm breeze brushed the loose strands of coppery-brown hair from Zephyr's face as she stood up, continuing to eye the horizon.

The storm was getting closer.

Zephyr wished with all her might that she'd never laid eyes on Silas McIntosh.

She clenched a handful of weeds in her fist, as if attempting to crush the emotion swelling within.

Did you ever think you might wreck a girl's heart so? Did you?

Zephyr swallowed, a foul taste forming at the back of her mouth. A branch of electricity lit up the sky for the briefest of seconds, quickly followed by a low rumble.

The girl blinked, her chest aching as she fought back tears of vitriol.

Silas, did you ever think that I would care for you? Did you ever think that I'd despise you, all in the same?

Mrs. Darson's voice called out in the background. Zephyr stood motionless, unfeeling, as her brothers obeyed their mother's beckoning and ran out of the tall okra stalks. She heard no words, only voices.

Voices. There were already enough of those inside her own head.

I am a selfish creature.

Lightning flashed in the troposphere, brightly contrasting with the various shades of grey in the sky. Billowy, dark, cumulonimbus clouds stirred, and Zephyr became aware of a new sensation.

Wet.

More *wet.*

Zephyr opened her eyes slowly as the rain fell, gently drumming against her skin, cold and refreshing. She made no effort to run from its placid embrace.

Turning her gaze to her hands, the sixteen-year-old raised them in front of her, letting the water wash the dirt and perspiration away. She watched as the trickle of blood on her finger diluted, gradually fading.

Another wave of impassiveness rushed over the girl's body. She swallowed again, forcing back the tears that wanted to flow freely as the rain that now enveloped her.

God, I don't know what to do.

Zephyr blinked, her chest tightening. Her legs began to move, as if of their own will. She was walking out towards the back, the southern field.

I can't stand the person I've become. I have no control over anything. Not even my own feelings. Father, I'm helpless. Completely, utterly, helpless.

Absentmindedly, Zephyr found herself praying. Silently, she offered petitions to the One who had created her. To the One who knew her best, to the One who alone heard every sob she'd stifled and read each thought that crossed her naïve mind.

A spirit of deadness still rested upon her shoulders, but now something else began to form in the sea of her never-ending emotion.

Desperation.

What am I supposed to do? How can I go on, how do I keep myself from feeling?

Thunder rumbled majestically as Zephyr stood in the midst of the Darsons' southern property.

The western woods stretched on a hundred feet to her left, and to the right, a stretch of tomato, okra, zucchini and corn plots. In between and scattered throughout, stood pines and sweetgums.

Zephyr was now completely alone, isolated from any other human. This was how it needed to be.

Here she could hurt no one, and no one could hurt her.

She only had herself to contend with. Her worst downfall, her darkest adversary.

Closing her eyes, the girl soaked in the rain as it continued to fall. Her throat swelled, blocking her airway. Her scarred, dirty hands remained clenched.

I must overcome this. I won't let it take me. I just can't. I have to let it go.

She squeezed her eyelids shut, knowing if she opened them a deluge of tears would escape.

A clap of thunder shook the ground, splicing the eerie silence.

God, I'm trusting you to hear me. Please... just assure me You're listening. Zephyr's lip trembled as she whispered in distress, "*That's all I ask.*"

After several moments of silence, Zephyr released a small sob. Her eyelids opened and her face contorted in anguish as she gazed up at the gloomy sky.

The dam holding back the well of salty tears had broken.

Father, I'm begging you. Show me what the point is in all this. I beg of you, Lord, open my eyes.

Zephyr sobbed. She gasped for air. She allowed the tears to fall and her emotion to have its way. She lifted her face to the heavens, as if searching for the Creator among the billowy clouds. Of course the girl knew He couldn't be found there, but when in desperation it seems automatic that we go to look above.

Tears streamed down Zephyr's rain-washed face. She wanted to scream, to yell out in agony.

With a cry of frustration she fell to her knees in the wet grass. If God was listening to her, she needed to hear something in response.

The morass of her thought processes and feelings had become too much for her tortured brain to handle.

I can't do this, God, I just can't.

Biting her lip, almost to the point where it became painful, Zephyr's jaw stiffened, the tears flowing faster. She forced herself to breath, but the air didn't seem to come quick enough to her lungs.

I'm begging You, God. Please. Just show me I'm not alone. That I'm not just a selfish, uncaring child, wrapped up in getting her own way. See, I have so many regrets, so many thoughts on what could have been. You know that. But if he was meant to go, and me to stay, why do I feel all this? Why can't I let him go?

Zephyr closed her eyes again, sucking in a breath. Why couldn't she let Silas go?

Silas will never satisfy your longings as I am capable of doing.

In the midst of the turmoil within Zephyr's mind and soul, one voice suddenly became apparent.

A still, small voice.

Zephyr let her shoulders fall and her jaw loosen. She let her eyelids remain shut, frenetic for peace and assurance. Was this really happening?

Father. I knew You wouldn't leave me.

I never did.

The girl's heart raced as the rest of her body became numb. Was she truly hearing the words of the Holy Spirit, or was it just her own mind talking back to her as it always did?

Something told Zephyr this was Divine. She didn't know how she was discerning this, but nonetheless, felt it to be truth. She inhaled deeply, desperate to believe it was.

"Lord, please forgive me for doubting. I never should have questioned You."

A whisper escaped Zephyr's lips as her body crumpled closer to the ground. How low and unworthy she felt, to be speaking with the Creator of the universe. With all her shame and the filthiness of her abundant sin, what place did she have even to call upon His name?

"I…I don't know why I have these feelings," she stuttered, her voice still barely audible. Letting her misted eyes fall to the ground, she sighed.

A final tear rolled down Zephyr's cheek, crossing the paths of the many tears which had traveled there beforehand.

Silas will never satisfy your longings as I am capable of doing.

Zephyr found both her body and soul relaxing as the Voice echoed again in her head.

This time, slightly louder.

Chapter Twenty-One

HAYDEN
November 29ᵗʰ, 1863

7:30 AM

THE RELENTLESS PRESENCE OF DEATH shrouded Damascus' soul. Its oppressive stench had wormed through his entire being, gripping his spirit with its vile, bloody claws.

A shiver took the man by surprise, and he rubbed his hands together to ward off the morning's nippiness.

There were bodies to cover beneath the earth, dead men to bury and forget. And with so many cadavers heaped so high, it would take hours to complete this wretched task.

Hayden ran a scarred hand through his shock of greasy red hair and stared vacantly at the nightmare he'd become entrenched in.

Dark crimson spattered across torn wool and cotton, fading dark into the fabric. Severed limbs lay about erratically on the blackened earth. Exposed, decaying flesh. Soulless eyes staring bleakly out at the cold, cheerless world. Porcelain white faces chilled from the winter wind and marred by the fear that likely took their souls as they passed into eternity.

This was a sight no man should ever be forced to become acquainted with. A sight none should ever even get to behold.

And yet, in such a short period of time, Hayden had seen more of it than anything else in his lifetime. He'd seen enough death to last him a million years, to chill his hardened heart colder than the oncoming winter itself.

Damascus Hayden had been so inundated in death that his icy mind insisted *he* was dead as well. And the worst part was, he didn't argue with that sentiment. More than anything, he wished it was true.

Such was life. Reality was what it was, and for whatever hellish reason it insisted he stay alive.

The man exhaled, his body aching due to the dwindling temperature. Florida hardly saw a December day below the thirties, let alone twenties or less. Snow was unheard of, and its few occurrences were monumental and loathed. Snow wasn't welcome in a state where the output of citrus and vegetables was so vital.

But so far, none had been seen in this part of Tennessee. And for that, Hayden was grateful. With what threadbare clothing he had on his back, the last thing he wanted was a blizzard.

In a day or so, the Union forces would move them north to be incarcerated. Rumors had spread that they'd be sent to Rock Island, which was all the way up in Illinois. Hayden had never heard of the place, but he knew it could mean nothing good for the Confederate prisoners.

Out of the frying pan, and into the fire, as they say.

He groaned, and chewed the edge of his lower lip, rubbing his scruffy red beard.

Time to fetch a shovel and get this over with.

Hayden glanced off a ways to where a scattered group had begun digging in the open field.

When questioned on the issue, General Thomas had commanded that the dead not be sorted, but thrown in the ditches together, Fed and Rebel alike. Hayden didn't protest. It would make the job a heck of a lot easier.

The man wondered where he could acquire a shovel. Surely the Union fellers wouldn't lend one of theirs until they'd finished covering up all their corpses.

Scanning the terrain, he exhaled again, wondering why on earth he'd ever wanted to enlist to begin with. He rubbed the side of his temples, moaning to the hundreds of deaf ears at his feet.

Y'all got it lucky.

Footsteps reached his ears, and he instinctively turned to face the figure heading towards him.

It was just a kid in his teens, a Federal boy. A youngster that for once was donning an official uniform.

Hayden eyed him coldly as the boy tossed him a shovel.

The boy looked into his eyes tiredly without uttering a word. His face – and the armful of other shovels and spades he was carrying - portrayed the fact that he knew he should move on, but his feet didn't move.

For a brief second the two shared wearied eye contact.

Dark circles hung around the boy's brown, calloused eyes. Despite the Union victory, this kid had been aged far beyond his years. The bloodshed had turned his visage heavy and forlorn. And what he'd seen and experienced couldn't ever be reversed.

Hell's not a very nice place to venture, eh, kid?

Hayden's eyes were numb and unfeeling as he gripped the shovel in one hand. He inhaled, setting his angular jaw bitterly. A glower crossed his profile, contorting his face into a wary frown.

The boy stared blankly back a second longer, then tramped away silently to the next man.

12 PM
EZRA

Lookout Mountain loomed to the southwest. Even it served as just another reminder of defeat.

Ezra wiped his sweaty brow and looked at what had been accomplished so far, welcoming a moment's rest from digging and lifting cadavers.

One long ditch after another stretched a hundred feet to the south, each about ten feet apart. The scenery now resembled a massive garden bed.

It wasn't the trenches themselves though which were a sight. It was what had been dumped hastily inside their shallow walls.

Endless quantities of human flesh. The vacant, soulless bodies which had been deprived of their lives almost three days ago. They were all here, within *these* rows.

Ezra closed his eyes for a moment, his spirit heavy. No earthly experience could be compared to that of burying a thousand men.

And what was worse, Ezra himself had participated in this bloodbath – he'd taken lives. Dozens of them, in fact. It would have hurt him no more if his heart had been ripped out and crushed into dust. To wrench a soul from another human being…there were no words to describe what that felt like.

Ezra tasted bile in his throat, at the memory of his actions. For all *this*? What was it worth? What had it truly accomplished? And now more men and boys would perish as they rotted away in a ruthless prison camp miles north.

Bitter regret saturated the young man's spirit, causing his eyebrows to remain constantly furrowed and his mouth in a tight frown. He found himself unconsciously weighing the costs of this affair over and over again. Each time his thought processes turned to this, his body sagged and his soul ached. He was so tired.

Even though he'd been one of the 'fortunate' survivors, it felt like his being no longer belonged to him. It was as if he possessed a mere shell of a body that wasn't even his. These arms, these legs, they felt detached, clumsy, distant. His heart kept beating, it wasn't *him*. The real Ezra Darson had vanished with that first bullet he'd fired – the first bullet to mutilate another human being.

What have I become?

A long breath of warm air escaped Ezra's lungs, and he leaned against his shovel wearily.

Lord, I don't even know what to pray. I…can't form the words…

He swallowed, wondering if he'd banished the Savior's presence from his soul somehow. Something deep down told him this wasn't true, but once that dark and treacherous thought had taken root in his mind, he couldn't tell which sentiment to believe.

This isn't me.

3 PM
HAYDEN

"Move out!"

The final command from one of the Union commanders rang out across the valley, and was relayed by Colonel Bullock to the Southern prisoners.

Four thousand men to move north to Illinois. That's what Grant had on his hands now.

Hayden pulled his thin overcoat closer to his body, staring back for a moment at the cursed crest where so much blood had been shed. Missionary Ridge stood bleak and grave, nearly cloaked by the mist-like rain which had begun to fall over the topography. Its stony walls lurked grey and cold behind the massive troop of Federals and their captives.

Just beyond the ridge began the seemingly mile-long stretch of the makeshift cemetery. Of course, it hardly deserved such a formal title. The only evidence left to hint of what lay beneath its ground was the unnatural rising and falling of the soil. The mounds of earth piled unnaturally in hap-hazard rows spoke of the bodies hidden below. Ambiguous rows full of ambiguous faces. Time would soon take its toll on the unmarked graves, and they would be gone, abandoned here. The years would pass, and families would mourn, wondering what had become of their sons, husbands, and fathers. Some would have the privilege of knowing their loved ones' fate, others wouldn't be so fortunate.

But the blood which had been spilled in this sad place, it would wash away. The trees would whisper their grave, winsome stories as the breeze tousled their branches, but these stories would be forgotten, unheard with time. Grass would cover the hastily dug graves, and the thousand men and boys sleeping below would return to the dust which they came.

No name or marker left to pay tribute to their passing, nothing at all. Just a mile's stretch of long, haunting rows.

So many rows. So many men deprived of their honor. What a pitiful way to end an existence.

Hayden hoped he'd never have to lay eyes on this place again.

Chapter Twenty-Two

HAYDEN

WELCOME TO HELL, COMRADES. IT was nice knowin' ya.

They'd only just arrived, but Hayden could already tell Rock Island would be a completely despicable place. It didn't take much time or effort to notice, especially when one was standing in two feet of snow, clothed in little more than rags, and the temperature was thirty-two degrees below zero.

Hayden had never in his life experienced such cold. As soon as they'd passed into this northern region of Illinois, he knew his would be an icy grave.

Twelve-foot-high board walls encompassed the Confederate hostages. Every hundred feet, a sentry tower was posted. Unfazed Union guards stood positioned at each post, watching the new prisoners almost as icily as the dirty snow blanketing the hardened ground. A long walkway was situated outside the top of the wall, which the Federals strode back and forth on periodically.

The camp was massive. Hayden had never seen such a large space for confining human beings against their will.

As he looked around, a sudden sense of impending doom twisted in his stomach.

Rock Island was just that, a single island in the midst of the Mississippi. Three miles long and half a mile wide. Stuck in between Davenport, Iowa, and Moline, Illinois. It was a recently constructed camp, erected just months prior.

Not much to look at, that's for sure.

The barracks were nothing more than eighty-four shabbily constructed shanties lining the inner stretch of the camp. As the men all went their separate ways, scattering like a stirred up ant mound, Hayden examined one of the small structures briefly.

It would do absolutely nothing to keep the cold out. What materials it was composed of could hardly be called even the bare minimum for a shelter.

Hayden trudged onward through the snow, sticking his frigid hands into his armpits.

With all the evident discomforts of this prison camp, the weather had to be the most fearsome of them all. It had been positively horrific ever since the company had passed into Illinois.

Two months ago, the pilgrimage from Missionary Ridge had begun, and the conditions were far more spanking. The mornings had possessed a nice little nip, but nothing wretchedly cold.

Nothing like *this*.

Damascus Hayden had never been in such cruel elemental conditions.

Twenty below and we're here dressed like blam'd beggars.

Most fellows didn't have shoes. Frostbite was growing more and more common, and there'd also been a dozen men who'd contracted smallpox and had to be isolated their own barracks. Death had yet again taken its hold, and no bullets or shell had been fired from this group in sixty days. The numbers had dropped already from two thousand to an estimated fifteen hundred.

Five hundred men lost, just like that.

Hayden didn't find himself daunted by the thought of freezing to death, but frostbite, pneumonia and smallpox weren't very appealing, either. If he was gonna die, the less painful route was obviously to be preferred.

At this point however, nothing really fazed him. He'd seen so much this year. All the blood, death, and hatred had amalgamated together into one giant memory, one hardened wound in his side.

It was all a blur. The only way Hayden could begin to hold on to sanity was to become completely unconcerned about the whole affair, which wasn't hard when he already had nothing to live for or look forward to. He didn't care that he looked like an indifferent shell of a human being, too proud to accept defeat or admit failure. It wasn't pride that kept his mind dulled to the horrors surrounding him. No, it was something far worse. The odium of himself, his life, and everything in existence.

***

Two weeks had passed. It seemed almost miraculous that any of the Florida boys had survived this frigid cold the first night. The days passed tortuously slow, with the daylight hours blending seamlessly into night, uninterrupted by any event to rivet the soul. Any event besides the decease of an old comrade, that is.

The smallpox outbreak only escalated. It was more than a mite unpleasant witnessing its ghastly progression on some of the soldiers.

It first manifested itself with ailments such as fever, aches of the back and head, chills and vomiting. And then, the rash appeared. In the beginning, the wretched condition resembled chicken pox, but it soon revealed itself as something far worse. The bumps spread all over the body. Often, faces were so riddled with them that it was difficult to recognize the poor soul's profile.

Seeing those horrible red bumps appear was an ominous token, and something about the disease stirred a fear in Hayden more than any gun or minie ball ever could. Perhaps because you never knew who the smallpox would infect next. It was contagious, and even with the sick separated, there were men succumbing to the virus' lethal talons.

Never in his wildest dreams would Hayden have thought Pratchit to become one of its targets. The sense of impending doom only worsened when the dreaded scabs began appearing on the surgeon's own skin. Why *Pratchit*, of all people?

Anger pulsed through Hayden's veins. Since the Union wardens didn't provide medicine to their prisoners and the living conditions were so beastly, chances for survival with such a disease were overwhelmingly slim. At this pace, a man would be lucky to make it out alive, sick or not, period. But it was downright cruel that the dear doc himself would be one of the infected, when all he had ever done was work towards healing the others.

Of course, William Dade was missing entirely, and it was very likely he could be found buried in one of those cursed rows back in Tennessee. So many fellows that Hayden had played cards with, got drunk with – so many of those men were missing, completely vanished from the unit. Apparently no one had found their bodies, but if they had, perhaps they would've been unrecognizable anyhow.

The days of idleness back in Tennessee seemed like an eternity past. Within the walls of this island's lime rock shores, time took a new direction and disappeared at a different pace. A much slower, more arduous pace. Like a knife in a sadistic hand, slowly and torturously carving its way into the flesh of the victim.

Slowly, slowly, slowly.

But this was of no importance, because Damascus Hayden was a thick-skinned sort - the kind of man who would rather end his own life than not be too calloused to care.

EZRA

"Well, all else set aside, this is the longest I've seen it ever take to get a fire going."

Mr. Darson stared tiredly at the tiny makeshift fire, sputtering in the middle of the barrack floor. The middle-aged man had assembled a small, metal box which resembled the beginnings of a cook stove, minus the top. It served as a means of containing the flames and was located under one the of the barracks two roof vents.

Already most of the captives had reassembled into their own groups, with their own fellow soldiers from their old units, if any could be found. Several others had attempted creating sources of warmth, and it was a wonder nobody had burned down the shanty yet or smoked the place out.

Thank God, most of the Florida boys had been able to find each other. Hayden, Pratchit, Ezra, and Harold had claimed their bunks in one of the shanties, along with 116 other prisoners. This was where they now attempted to revive their frozen spirits.

Ezra rubbed his hands together, crouching over the small flame that finally licked at the measly bit of tinder.

Snow flurries cascaded from the billowy grey sky, and the temperatures had increased in no way whatsoever. The only way the shanty helped at all was to partially shield its inhabitants from the bitter wind.

"I have to say, it had me worried the thing would never even start at all." The younger Darson licked his chapped lips and frowned, tasting blood.

"What good is a fire if it emits no warmth?" Hayden sat on his bunk nearby, with his hands shoved in his armpits. His voice was antagonistic and wry.

Pratchit said nothing, because he was asleep. There wasn't room for him in the barracks that had been set aside as smallpox houses, so he had been left here.

Ezra glanced at the weakened doctor, considering the chances of getting a bit of shut-eye under these circumstances. They appeared grim.

But before long, night fell on the camp, and exhaustion overcame Ezra's body. He hadn't left the shanty except to do his business, which proved to be rather uncomfortable in the frigid cold. There weren't any sinks here. The hygienic quality of the encampment was already a hundred times worse than anything Ezra had seen when camped with the Army of the Tennessee. No effort of any sort was made in this vile place to maintain proper sanitation, and some sections of the snow were far from white. If one didn't come down with smallpox, it would be a wonder he didn't get dysentery, either.

There was no food. Rations, they'd been informed, would be served the next day. Ezra hadn't eaten in almost a week. Hollowness ate away at his stomach, and he could feel his body weight diminishing. He surmised that he'd already lost a good twenty pounds or so. Weakness poisoned his bloodstream, and he was constantly fatigued. There was never enough sleep to be had. Provisions were so scarce that even hardtack was becoming a novelty to be treasured.

Hardtack of all things.

Wearily, the tall man settled down on the cold ground. Who knew what time it was. Ezra helped his brother reposition Pratchit next to the fire, and then took a seat of his own beside the flame. With a groan, he swallowed, attempting to alleviate the painful dryness in his throat.

"God forbid we exist in this wretched place any longer than a few months." He rubbed his hands together and placed them under his arms in similar fashion to Hayden.

Mr. Darson sat beside Pratchit, a look of equal weariness manifest in his blue-green eyes. The man gazed at his brother with subdued gravity.

As he looked at his brother, Ezra thought the wrinkles on that weathered face seemed more pronounced than usual. Those dark circles hadn't existed before he'd been involved with the war effort, and the sagging skin was almost-nonexistent before the battle at Missionary Ridge.

A lump formed in Ezra's throat, as he thought of what his brother had given up for what he believed. So much had happened since the Darson brothers went to war last year.

No words were necessary to convey what Harold's eyes spoke.

They wouldn't be getting out of here any time soon.

Chapter Twenty-Three

EZRA

"You keep that up, and you'll run yourself plum to the icy grave, cracker."

A shout reached Ezra's ears, but he paid no heed to the useless words. He kept running, his feet pounding the snowy ground over and over. His lungs sucked in frigid air, but he had become used to it now. It didn't sear his throat nearly like it used to.

Thankfully, the human body could adapt to a change in environment – if it survived the process.

He passed one of the two, main double-gate sally ports for the tenth time, staring at its seductive hinges in the same way he always did. It was best not to think about the gates. An exit through that route was only a cruel fantasy.

Ezra's feet were completely numb. And not just his feet, but everywhere else. He ran to keep his mind off the biting cold. It was the only way he could think straight – when he was still, all he could think about was death's claws lingering inches away. Stagnancy was the equivalent of death. He felt it utterly vital to keep moving, as if the snowy terrain would swallow him whole once he stopped. Not to mention, there was no comfort to be found in the walls of the barracks. Not with all the filth and disease running rampant.

At least in the open, there was a measure of fresh air.

Still, the shoes concealing his toes were wearing thinner and thinner. The barrier between his soles and the ground decreased rapidly with each passing day.

He could barely feel his appendages. So many men had gotten frostbite and were losing theirs left and right. Ezra had wrapped whatever areas he could with scraps of fabric, hoping to save himself from the same fate.

This prison camp was a beast of great proportions, swallowing whole men alive. A ravenous wolf, stealing the spirit from any creature it could. It was a murdering entity, claiming more lives than any man would have wanted to dwell on.

Ezra wanted to hope that there would come a time when God would pull them out of here. He didn't care that the odds were so greatly against this event. He only wanted to hope for the sake of hoping. Without hope to stir the soul and warm the heart, there was no purpose for existence. It seemed that the men who deteriorated the fastest were those who'd abandoned it.

A mind without hope was a poisoned one.

Ezra kept running. The icy air stung his cheeks, and the wind whipped at his eyes. If only he had a scarf or some other thick article to shield his face from the searing air. The kepi he'd found did little good as a practical garment. He shivered, closing his eyes for a moment to give them a much-needed rest.

A shudder erupted through his limbs, snapping him back. He longed for so many things that it hurt. He'd suppressed urges and desires for so long now that he was worried he had become less than human. He'd been forced to try and forget, but his body was still intact - and his male parts hadn't forgotten their natural purposes. His mind was still that of a functioning adult man, a curse for the time being. The only things that remained untouched by the cold were his hormones and the... need for female attention, shall we say.

He wondered now, if given the chance, would he even know how to treat a woman respectfully? Would he take a lady in a brutish manner, or settle for the bed of a strumpet in place of the sanctified marriage covenant? He'd never dreamed of following in the footsteps of Hayden or some of the other raucous men, who partook in such scandals.

Scary thing was, now those lines felt awfully blurred. Somehow, it didn't seem so wrong to do those things. Especially if he were to remain a virgin all his life – a thought almost as unsettling as rotting in this prison camp for another few years. Would he ever get married, period? What if he didn't?

His mind pictured scenarios it shouldn't have. He found his thoughts drifting to certain areas of the female anatomy – places his fingers would've given anything to touch. On one hand, it was just out of plain curiosity, and on the other…well, there were other reasons. His imagination roamed further and he soon realized he was lusting after – and even committing fornication with - a body he hadn't even laid eyes on.

He felt as if he were turning into an animal. Losing his ability to retain a sense of dignity and honor, forced to only fantasize about a life denied him.

If only the sun would show itself. It was noon, yet the atmosphere felt like dusk. Tiny snowflakes fluttered down from the dreary sky. Ezra was weary of the grey colorlessness. He missed bright, vivid hues, like yellow and green. He missed the warmth of the sun's rays on his back, and believe it or not, he even missed the oppressive Florida heat and humidity.

His bones ached from never being able to get warm.

God, what's the purpose in this?

The first gate was getting closer again. He'd lost track of how many laps this would make. As always, he stared at the stupid gate. And as always, the stoic Federal guards held their guns firmly and eyed him from their lookout stations. He had to admit, even their pale faces looked cold despite the extra garments wrapped around their bodies. In some ways, they didn't look that much better off, standing there and watching a bunch of men suffering and withering away.

What a life.

Well, at least they could leave if they wanted. And they had sufficient food.

Food.

Ezra grimaced, biting his tongue. He couldn't think about food. That was the worst torment besides the cold. The eternal growling of his stomach was certainly a distraction from the chill, but not a good one.

Maybe I'll just keep running until my body gives way and I freeze to death.

"Ezra! Get over here, you cussed fool!"

A calloused voice met Ezra's ears, and his footsteps slowed. His vision focused on Hayden's form standing outside their shanty.

As he approached the man, he realized how dry his mouth and eyes felt. He blinked, almost stumbling into Hayden. Everything was fuzzy for a moment as his muscles reacted to the sudden cessation of movement.

Hayden grabbed him by the shoulder in a gruff, impatient manner.

"The cold's messing with your mind, Darson."

Ezra looked into Hayden's green eyes obliviously. Hayden's eyes, once so full of charismatic energy and vigor, they didn't look the same now. Their spark was dwindling. Even Damascus Hayden, with his fighting spirit and nerves of steel, wasn't indestructible. He too was succumbing. And if he, one of the hardest pieces of work in this group succumbed, well, Ezra hoped that moment never came, because he feared that it would mean the end was surely in sight.

"Quit starin' at me like that," Hayden growled and shoved Ezra up the steps to the doorway as if he were an unresponsive drunk. "Get in here and talk to your brother. He's preachin' the Jessy out of half the barracks, and I'm bored to tears. And you shouldn't be runnin'. You're a stupid dunce for thinkin' you have the muster to."

Ezra tried to snap himself back into reality as he entered the barrack. He tried to force a frown across his cold-seared face, but his skin felt too tight and numb. H   e settled for merely shaking his head and giving Hayden a weak shove back.

"Why do you care if I have the muster or not? Since when did you start carin'?"

Hayden murmured something unintelligible and his eyes bored holes into Ezra's. "I'm just tryin' to keep another unnecessary death from happenin', alright?"

"You two… gonna kill yourselves…with all that ruckus."

Both men's gazes shot around, landing on Pratchit. He stared up weakly at them, his eyes matching his tone. Exhausted, sick, somnolent. His marred, disease-stricken body seemed detached from his bearded face; lying their limply, depleted of all energy. It didn't look like his person anymore.

Hayden frowned, and coughed, seating himself on a box nearby. The fire-box already had a number of men seated around it, and now a number of them turned to look at Hayden and Ezra.

"I'm sorry, doc. Didn't mean for ya to hear that."

Ezra's throat swelled. He stared at the surgeon, fighting back memories of when everything was good and normal in his little world, as it should've been. Pratchit had been the last one anybody expected to contract smallpox. But here he was, and nothing had made him any closer to recovery.

Glancing at Harold and the rest of the little group, Ezra swallowed, his throat dryer than ever. Harry said nothing, only looking into his brother's eyes, down at the Bible in his hands, and then Pratchit on the makeshift bedroll on the floor beside the firebox.

"You're a blam'd idiot, runnin' around out there like that, Darson." Pratchit's voice was low and guttural, and Ezra could barely hear his words.

Ezra rubbed his biceps, looking at Pratchit with a dismal expression. "I might be, but I needed somethin' to do and felt like I might explode if I didn't get to it." He exhaled, wishing that feeling – any kind of feeling – would return to his achy muscles. The prospect of sitting down like the others wasn't very appealing. In his mind, he could almost picture his joints locking together once he placed himself in a sedentary position.

Perhaps he truly was losing his sanity. When the thought of sitting down made one nervous, even invoking a sense of anxiety, surely something wasn't quite right upstairs. Ezra blamed it on the cold and malnutrition.

"Ezra, if you might settle down and quiet yourself a minute, I was just tellin' these fellas about Jesus and the Samaritan woman at the well." Harold's voice was firmer than usual, and he stared at Ezra with a look of determination in his eyes. Ezra promptly obeyed his brother's order.

He'd forgotten that Harry was trying to get back into doing a chapel service. Guilt twisted in his stomach for causing such a distraction when it was already hard enough to keep the soldiers' attentions. He felt his face redden.

As he sat down stiffly, he caught Hayden grinning on the bunk across from him out of the corner of his eye.

Don't give me that look when you were the one who came yellin' for me. Ezra gave the redhead a look of disgust and rolled his eyes before turning his attention to his brothers' Bible lesson.

Chapter Twenty-Four

HAYDEN

"Did ya ever love anybody, son, or have ya always been this much of a boat-lickin' crab?"

Hayden glanced over in surprise at the older man who had apparently spoken to him, as rations were being passed out.

"Excuse me?"

The wrinkled old fellow was tall and spindly, his back hunched over from many years of toiling in the fields. His long, scraggly beard hid his lips and most of his face from view, but his bright blue eyes pierced Hayden like a Scottish dirk.

"The way your eyes burn with fire, I just was a'wondrin'. Not everyone carries that kind'a bile all the time," the man observed. His voice was gravely and weathered, matching the rest of him.

With a raise of a bushy eyebrow, Hayden looked the old-timer square in the eye. "Life is harder for some than others, I reckon. You look like ya seen a lot, yourself, mister."

"I din't ask if your life was hard, boy. I only inquired if perchance there was ever a source of love, to balance out all that hate." The man's eyes narrowed, continuing to penetrate Hayden with fervent severity.

Somehow, those words seemed harsh, but Hayden didn't let it get to him. Heck, the old geezer was perceptive, no doubt. That or Hayden's emotions were awful more transparent than he assumed. Not that he cared, either way.

"A source of love?" He snorted, his lip curling up slightly in amusement. "You mean, a woman? Makin' love to a woman? Sure, I done that and it was decent enough."

Even through all that facial hair, Hayden could see the man's mouth turning into a frown. "There's a difference 'tweens knockin' a woman up and true love that pulls through both thick an' thin, no matter what happens in life."

"Well, I guess I never found that." Hayden scoffed, bitterly, at thoughts of his past. "Womenfolk an' I don't really get along too well when it comes to life outside the bedroom, and I guess there's more to true love than screwin', right?" A snide laugh escaped his lips as he shook his head in thinly-veiled repulsion.

Catharin, if anybody ruined the idea of marriage and love, it was you. Memories flooded Hayden's mind, and he found himself grimacing at the thought of the years he wasted thinking he was 'in love' when it had only been a cruel masquerade.

What's he tryin' to pull, this bag-o'-bones? Why is he even talkin' to me?

The elderly man let out a sigh as they shuffled forward in the line. His crystalline, clear eyes stared into the distance, as if mulling over an important matter. "Somethin' happened to ya, boy. I sensed the heaviness of your spirit when I caught a glimpse of ya earlier, and that discernment wasn't wrong." His eyes refocused on the redhead, which was disconcerting. Hayden didn't like how the old bat kept staring into his eyes like that. It was as if he was reading Hayden's heart, deciphering the workings of his mind and soul. It made Hayden's skin itch, and his apprehension grew.

"Mister, I don't see how you think ya can step in an' judge a man you don't even know," he retorted, his words sharp as ice shards. If there was anything he hated, it was folks who thought they could just come and judge a body or try to make him better somehow. He fended for himself just fine, and he expected others to do the same for themselves. All was fine and dandy, if everyone minded their own business.

Unfortunately, that wasn't how the world spun itself. People had to meddle, and what could Hayden do about it other than cuss them out and maybe break a jaw or two if necessary? He was only doing what he knew to do, following what he'd been raised on. Kick a dog and beat it for no reason, and chances are you'll end up getting bit.

"It's not hard to tell when a man's hurtin', lad. I just see what I see, ain't tryin' to judge nobody."

Hayden returned the man's gaze with a hardened stare of his own. The line moved up a little, helping to break the awkward moment of silence.

Finally, words worked their way up to Hayden's tongue.

"I'm livin' in a hellhole. And you, sir, are livin' in the very same place. How can a soul find comfort and healing *here*? Talk to the men with smallpox. There's sure a lot of hurt in the smallpox houses."

The old man sighed, exhaustion manifest by the bags under his eyes. He turned away slowly, closing his eyes.

"Lad, in this place, physical comfort will never come. You or I could be the next target of that horrid disease, for all anybody knows or cares. Among many other ailments." He turned his grave eyes back to Hayden. "But, rest assured, there *is* a place to find comfort of another level." With an aura of finality, the man gave a subtle nod upwards.

Hayden's mouth curled up at the corners in the scorning, disgusted, cynical way it always did when somebody mentioned God.

"'Rest assured', that is most certainly *not* where I aim to find comfort."

He rubbed his hands together, exhaling a short breath into the freezing air, watching as it appeared like a puff of smoke in front of his mouth.

At long last, the rations line was waning short. Only a few men to go, and then the devouring hunger would...still not be satisfied. That measly bit of soup was laughable. What was even the point of offering it? Did the Federals *really* expect it to fill an adult man's empty stomach, that miserable teaspoon of scum they were dumping into the tin cups?

Damascus licked his upper lip and frowned, tasting blood between the cracked, chapped bits of skin. His flesh didn't agree with temperatures that extended below the negative threshold. He threw a glance back at the elderly soldier, hopeful that he'd been put in his place and would keep his mouth shut as they approached the cookhouse portion of the barrack.

The combination of odors wafting throughout the shanty was a fetid one, composed primarily of body odor, smoke, and urine. Combine all this with the scent of the thin, greasy gruel being spooned out, and there was even less of an urge to eat anything. Not from *here*, anyway.

I'd put somebody outta their misery for a jug of whisky, and ham with potatoes. And a rhubarb pie. Yeah. I'd willingly kill a body for all that, right now.

If only that was how it worked.

"Well, son, I hope that you are wise enough to keep an open mind. One day, if you do so, maybe you'll reconsider that statement." The barrack rang with the noise of coughing and talk, but the old soldier's low, gravelly voice could still be heard.

Aw, this day be blam'd...

Hayden glanced up to see the man receiving his ration and shambling away, not looking back. Hayden watched for a moment, noticing the long, stringy grey hair which was tied in a braid down his deformed back.

He had a lot of nerve, the old...

"Hey, you hungry or not, mister?"

A grubby tin cup was shoved into Hayden's hands.

Oh yeah, he was next in line.

Hayden took the cup and shuffled on without saying anything to the teenaged server giving him annoyed looks.

He pushed through the crowd, which had stopped up the shanty's center walkway. There were far more people in this shanty than the number it had been built to hold. Now the men that had gotten their rations were searching for a convenient spot to sit, and too many of them were doing this at once for it to occur in an efficient manner. Hayden grumbled under his breath, looking down at the cup of gruel in his hands that he'd already gone through so much effort to get.

This could take another hour. An hour he wasn't willing to spend standing sandwiched between all these bodies, some of which might have already contracted something for all he knew. Not like he had any better way to spend his time, but still. A man had his pride. He didn't like feeling as if he were just another bovine in a herd of cattle.

He elbowed and shoved his way to the edge of the room where he planted himself in a corner on the floor.

For a second, his green eyes scanned the room, watching as the other men and boys received their rations, talked, and found themselves places to sit. A continuous line of newcomers filtered into the room, adding to those already waiting to get to the cookhouse.

He noticed for once that the familiar biting cold wasn't as prominent. Probably because of all these bodies being gathered in one small building, as they were. Hayden looked down at his cup and spooned some of the watery liquid into his mouth.

Completely tasteless, except for the lingering of grease on his lips. As expected. He didn't really care to know what the few ingredients were. It was better to be ignorant of such things.

With a few quick slurps, the soup was gone.

Whoopie-do.

Hayden placed the tin on the floor and closed his eyes, groaning. He stretched his arms and let his achy back slump against the wall. There was no use getting up to go anywhere right now.

When all this was over, what would he do with his life?

Before he'd enlisted, his days had been spent in a blacksmith shop. He had chosen his own profession, instead of taking after his father's which had been the same as George Washington's. A surveyor. It paid well enough, and it gave the senior Hayden a chance to travel which he seemed to like.

Damascus' father was not the type of man who'd like to settle down and farm a parcel of land all his life. His feet were always moving, and very rarely was he sitting unless he was too drunk to do anything but waddle around and urinate on everything.

Hayden kept his eyes closed, allowing his mind to rove where it would. He had nothing better to think about, and he didn't possess the energy to fight away the thoughts. Yeah, he hated the man, but it was still the man that brought him into the world. Of course, that itself wasn't anything very wonderful in particular.

Goodness knew that man had ruined his family. He slept around with other women, drank his own family to poverty, and Hayden's body was still marked by the forceful strikes inflicted at the end of a bad day. Hayden figured the only thing he'd inherited from his father, other than his striking red hair, was the same muscular physique. Hayden, although on the shorter side like his father, could pack a serious punch and was a lethal threat in any fist fight.

At least he gave me something to make up a little for all the piss he threw in my face.

Exhaustion poisoned Damascus' limbs. Weakness had seeped into him like a lethal injection. It disgusted him to think about before the war, when his body was in its prime and actually had some meat on it. When his biceps were thick and toned, and his legs as solid as iron posts. He was a machine when it came to getting laborious work done. Looking down at himself now, he felt like a different man. Atrophy had set in, and malnourishment had eaten away his physique.

It wasn't fair.

Of course, nothing was.

He'd been born into a broken family. He'd picked the wrong woman to love. He'd wasted part of his life just being drunk. And obviously, he'd made the mistake of enlisting. It was all one big mistake.

That's how the world works for me. Damascus Hayden doesn't get a happy ending.

Chapter Twenty-Five

ZEPHYR

ZEPHYR RAN FROM THE HOUSE, slamming the side door that led to the kitchen. It was a brisk, cold night, and the winter wind instantly chilled the girl to the bone.

Now outside, all by herself, she began to cry, letting the tears run down her cheeks. Her eyes stung as the cold reached their wet surfaces.

In broken anguish, she wondered to herself what she was crying about. In her mind, she tried to sort it out, searching her heart for the reasons causing her sorrow. As she looked up at the night sky brimming over with extraordinary constellations, her heart cried ten times more than her eyes did.

But this was not the first time she had resorted to escaping everything, everyone, and all her troubles by running outside where she could cry alone.

Every time, she would ask herself the same question.

Why am I crying?

Zephyr stood against the kitchen's outer wall, staring bleakly up into the sky.

God, help me… what is wrong with me? What have I done? What have I done to have such a broken spirit?

Tears continued to fill her eyes, and she found herself sobbing again.

Jesus, I beg you to come… let your presence be near me. I cry out to you and you alone. Oh, please save me from this despair!

Zephyr knew she was not in her normal frame of mind. Was she going insane? Why was she feeling this way? Her whole being felt tormented by something she couldn't determine, let alone explain.

She dared not think it was about Silas, for she'd pushed aside those emotions months ago. They tried all too often to resurface, but Zephyr would immediately banish them from her mind.

Could it be, she was crying for Pa? That seemed more logical, and yet, she'd not cried for her father's absence for ages. That pain had numbed long ago, and when it revived it didn't come in the form of unexplained tears.

Zephyr cast her eyes to the heavens, stifling a sob. Her mind was heavy, her emotions spent. It seemed ridiculous to weep, and not know the slightest reason why you were doing so.

She wandered out behind the house and the bigger garden, to the open field which led down to the blackberry patch and swamp.

The full moon lit the night with its gentle radiance. Its cobalt beams fell on every tree, building, and post, and they cast their shadows as if it were the middle of the afternoon. Zephyr stood in awe, looking at the illuminated world around her, bathed in blue light.

It was stunning.

All was quiet, except for the occasional hooting and call from one owl to the other.

Zephyr sat down on the cool grass, letting out a long sigh.

"Lord, please give me peace. Show me what I've done wrong. You know how I long for your joy... oh, that your wonderful love would fill my heart again," she whispered.

Cast your cares upon Him, for He careth for you.

A familiar Scripture broke through the chaos of Zephyr's mind.

Was that what she had been missing this whole time? Was she not giving to the Lord all that was rightfully His, not giving Him her all, like she should have been?

And in her despair, she didn't even think to take advantage of the wonderful jewel of scripture, sitting right in front of her blind, disillusioned eyes.

Zephyr's mind began to calm. Sitting there, admiring the greatness of the creation around her, she felt herself letting go of the tensions, burdens and cares which pulled her down before. Or, was it actually her doing? It was as if those cares were slipping away on their own will.

She realized she was powerless. For so long she'd been trying to rid herself of the burdens and sadness, but always fell short of cleansing her own mind.

But Zephyr couldn't do anything by herself. She had needed Jesus, this whole time, to do it for her.

He has promised me new life. I just need to trust that He never fails in his promises.

A quiet, peaceful feeling filled Zephyr's heart and mind, and tears of joy replaced the tears of torment. Zephyr stood up, wiping the dust and grass bits from her chemise, and walked back to the house for a good night's rest.

While most of the world still fell in darkness, treachery, and evil, in Zephyr's soul, all was well again.

For the moment.

Chapter Twenty-Six

EZRA

How many days had elapsed since they had first arrived at this cursed place?

Ezra had lost track. He estimated that it had been at least four or five months, but it seemed like so much longer.

The younger Darson brother sucked in a breath of frigid air, staring out the shanty window. It all felt like an endless loop, an eternal circle that had no end. A bottomless hole. His faith was faltering, but he knew he couldn't let it. Even if he lost all else, he couldn't succumb to the temptation of losing hope. Not when that was all that kept him alive and kicking.

And especially not when that hope was what gave him assurance in where he'd be during the afterlife. He couldn't abandon Jesus, not for anything. Ezra knew that his faith in God would be the only thing he could hold on to and the only thing that would pull him through. Ezra was not a man of great biblical understanding, no, far from it. But he did know this: the God of the Bible, He was a God that kept His promises. He had a reason for everything He allowed to happen, even if the reason didn't make sense at the time.

I know you haven't abandoned us, Lord. You promised you wouldn't.

Ezra's eyes burned from walking in the icy gales earlier that morning. Ever since then, his vision had been blurry and his eyes perpetually wet. He wiped them on his coat sleeve, sniffing. His nasal passages were congested and stuffy, as if he had a cold.

But he could've been a lot worse.

He turned, exhaling wearily, to look at Pratchit lying quietly on his cot. The man hadn't moved since he'd been placed there. It was as if his body had been paralyzed.

Harold hovered over the surgeon, as he had relentlessly for the past several weeks. He had hardly left the man's side. His eyes had become clouded, and his brow constantly furrowed. It was as if he had aged ten years.

But Pratchit was dying, and it was evident by the way his face grew more and more still each day. His eyes were closed far more than they were open. Fewer and fewer words came from his lips.

It would be any day now. At least, that's what most everyone else murmured.

It didn't matter to Harry though, for he'd only ignored them. He remained glued to Pratchit's bedside, whispering prayers over him and attempting to feed him and keep him hydrated.

Anger struck Ezra's heart. Was his brother the only one who felt compassion for this man? Was Harry the only one who thought him worth spending time on?

A man in his forties passed by the cot, standing a good ten feet away with a hand on his hip. He looked at Pratchit with a sad shake of his head. "What's the point? He'll just be another corpse before long."

Harry looked up, the skin beneath his eyes sagging. "You don't know that."

"You're wasting your energy," the man replied, sighing.

Ezra could see Pratchit's eyelids flutter, just barely. Harry's mouth turned into a deep-set frown, and his hazel eyes glared into the man's. "Who are you to judge what man should live and what man should die? Who are you to judge who is worth spent energy, and who is not?"

"I daresay, he's not coming back, good fellow. Just leave him to die." The man's eyes were sunken, his spirit clearly robbed long ago. "Death would've likely been his choice, anyhow."

"Do you claim to be a seer? Can you read his mind?"

The man exhaled and shook his head again, as if cleaning his hands of the matter. Shambling away, he murmured in a pathetic sort of tone, "Well, God save you, sir."

Harry shook his head in disgust, turning his gaze back to Pratchit.

"Hang in there, sawbones. *Hang in there.*"

Ezra shuffled to the cot, kneeling down on the other side and looking across at his brother, solemnly. Harry's eyes met his.

"Ezra, *pray*. Pray harder than you ever have in your life. We need him awake." Harry's jaw was tight, and his upper body looked as stiff as a board. His eyes were ablaze with an extreme sense of urgency, even though his voice was low.

"What should I pray?" Ezra found it difficult to speak.

Harold didn't say anything. He was looking at Pratchit, his face completely focused on one task alone.

"*Harry?* W-what should I pray?" Ezra repeated. A lump had formed in his throat, and his voice sounded cracked and guttural. He didn't have the slightest idea what to say or do. Inadequacy overwhelmed him. His eyes misted and he chewed on his lip.

Harold had already closed his eyes and lifted his hands. He began to pray aloud and a small shiver flew down Ezra's spine as each word rang through his ears. He had never heard Harry pray with such intensity before.

What do I do, Lord? Ezra swallowed, closing his eyes. *Tell me what to do.* His body tingled with something he couldn't explain and his vision had clouded. He wanted to shrink away into the shadows. He was too impure to be praying over a man about to die.

Be still, Ezra.

Ezra's mind stopped racing, and he felt a strange sensation in his heart. What had he just heard? Was that his own mind, or...?

Be still, Ezra.

There it was again! So quiet, almost unnoticeable, yet so clear.

Lord?

His pulse throbbed. He had never heard God speak directly to him before. Or perhaps he had just never stopped to listen.

The next sentence confirmed that the words couldn't possibly be from his own mind.

Pray for Carter's eyes to be opened.

Ezra felt his body go numb, and he let his frame sink against the side of the cot. He found himself clenching the cot's wooden frame as if wrestling with something or someone.

Tears were streaming down his face. He'd not cried in so long, he couldn't even remember the last time it had been. He found himself praying things he'd never prayed before, filled with a sense of power he never knew existed.

Electricity flew through his fingertips. His body shivered involuntarily.

Complete serenity filled his soul as he prayed. The depth of peace washing over him right now was incomparable to any he'd ever felt. He released his grip on the cot frame, letting all tension in his body slip away. The words came instantaneously, as if they were being implanted in his mind supernaturally. He let them come.

In the beginning, it terrified him. It seemed so foreign, not being in control of your own mind in this manner. He didn't know how to react. Soon though, he realized not to react at all, but to simply relinquish himself entirely. When he did, he realized that this was what it was to encounter a small taste of the Creator's presence.

God was giving him the words to speak. It wasn't him, it was God doing this. Excitement flooded the man's heart. Was this all but a dream?

No, it was reality. And it was the most beautiful reality he had ever experienced.

Chapter Twenty-Seven

HAYDEN

SOME PEOPLE GAMBLE TO PASS the time, some write letters, and some fantasize about pretty women. And then you got the Harold Darsons of the world, who spend forty-eight hours chained to the bed of a dying man, praying like a saint that he'll come to 'know the Lord'.

What a world to live in.

Hayden knit his eyebrows together as he lied down on the cot across from Pratchit's, grumbling protests in his mind.

It was amazing how determined Harold had become to resurrect Pratchit from the sickness enveloping his body. And not only that, but convert him as well. The man had practically become glued to the cot and nobody could coerce him away.

The cold clearly was taking his religious craze to a whole new level.

Of course, it was useless to say anything. A lot of other fellas had, and they'd been ignored. Hayden wasn't a fool. He'd rather save his breath than let it fall on deaf ears.

Even Ezra had turned fanatical, leaning over the bedside and praying like the world was going to end.

Should've figured that son-o'-a-gun had it in him too. Had the suspicion ever since he got so hot n' bothered 'bout our trip to that cherry's place. He let out a huff. *Should've figured.*

But the strange thing was Pratchit was still alive. Even talking again. His words were few, but they still came, and he was aware of his surroundings. He hadn't eaten, but who would have guessed a paralyzed, dying man could hold a conversation so well?

Hayden had learned all kinds of new details about Carter's life just by overhearing the stilted dialogue which the doc and Harold had been having the past six hours.

It was regrettable how all this hadn't ever been discovered until now, and that it took a fatal disease to cause him to finally speak of his personal life. Hayden hadn't noticed before, but all the tête-à-tête he and Carter had ever shared... well, it'd never been about anything personal on either side. Just trivial minutia, mutual complaining and dry jokes.

Kinda sad.

Carter Pratchit, thirty-one years old.

He lived in Gainesville before the war and had come from a somewhat wealthy family. The love of botany was what had spurred his vocation in medicine.

He had a wife named Lily, and she was of a Jewish heritage. They'd never had any children, but apparently, it wasn't from lack of trying.

At least the man had a life before the war and a woman that he loved. As to the *offspring?* Well. That was hardly something to grieve over in Hayden's eyes.

To be honest, Hayden had never thought about having children of his own. At least, he didn't think about it intentionally. The idea was ominous at best and terrifying at worst. Not to mention, he was much too selfish, and perfectly content to be that way, without responsibility for another human being.

"Carter, it's good and well that you went to church years ago, but church isn't what saves you." Harold's voice was soft and unthreatening, but it filled the room all the same. Hayden wished he didn't have to hear it. It made him uncomfortable. He couldn't just leave the barrack though, not when Pratchit could pass away at any time. Carter had never confided in Hayden, and vice versa, but he was still a comrade and even something of a friend.

Hayden would wait it out, because that's what any respectable human would do. He would hang in there 'till the end of the line, because Pratchit had been one heck of a man, and he deserved to die surrounded by people that cared enough to acknowledge it.

"I just...never thought...I needed anything or anyone else besides that," Pratchit murmured. "Never really thought about life...after death. It...seemed...unimportant."

"Do you believe there's a heaven and a hell?"

"There probably is."

I sure hope my last breaths aren't spent answering stupid questions.

"Well, you said earlier that you thought you've been a pretty good person." Harold kept going, to Hayden's chagrin. He looked at Pratchit with no less severity than before. "Do you think God will let you into heaven? What reason would you give him to let you in?"

Hayden turned to lean on his side so he could watch Pratchit's reactions. Even though he displayed little of those, a lot could be said with just a turn of the lips or a narrowing of the eyes. It didn't take much to manifest an emotion.

Pratchit's face was mostly stoic, but it appeared that he was thinking. After a few moments, he coughed a little, his voice low and groggy. "I know what you are going to say, Harold."

Oh, this should be interesting. Shall we see a dying man debate his proselytizer? A flicker of interest sparked in Hayden's eyes, and his ears perked up.

Harold's voice remained even. "Oh? Pray tell, then."

Pratchit closed his eyes, exhaling through his nostrils.

"Y-you are… trying to tell me that I can't get…to heaven…on my own. And…that being a good…person…isn't…enough."

Harold nodded. "You're right."

A moment of silence passed.

"It's…strange. I never…" Pratchit continued, his voice barely above a whisper. "I never…wanted to admit it. But…it was always there. In the…back of my mind. I didn't want to listen. It was… more comfortable…to ignore."

Oh, come on. Please tell me that's a lie.

Hayden couldn't believe the surgeon was opening up about this stuff. That, or he was making it up to appease Harry. Maybe— hopefully—it was the latter.

"Sometimes listenin' to the truth is the most uncomfortable thing you can do." The mellow, baritone of Ezra's voice reached Hayden's ears.

"And acknowledging it ain't for the faint of heart," Harry added. He looked back at Pratchit, exhaling quietly. "Carter, what makes you want to admit this now?"

Because he's dyin' and his mind ain't in the right place, naturally. Or maybe he's just tired of hearin' you jaw. Hayden rolled his eyes, shaking his head.

For another five minutes, it was quiet, all eyes locked on Pratchit to see what he would say. Finally, he satisfied them with a response.

"I…I know I don't have much longer." Pratchit's breath hitched, and he looked around the room in a melancholy manner, as if it had been his own home he was departing. "But there's too much… I… need…" He paused, closing his eyes. His Adam's apple bobbed once as he swallowed.

"I just need some *hope.*"

Hayden watched as Ezra's eyes seemed to brighten, matching his brother's.

Reaching over carefully, Harold took Carter's bony hand in his own. "We *all* do, my friend." He glanced at Ezra, before returning his gaze to Pratchit.

"That…is why Jesus suffered and died for us." Ezra's posture straightened a little. He smiled at Carter, who stared back at him with a somber grievance in his eyes.

This had to have been the most cumbersome conversation Hayden had ever witnessed. He still was amazed that Pratchit's interest had held for so long. The man had never shown an ounce of religious desire, in all the time Hayden had been around him.

Not much had even been spoken, yet it seemed like far more had taken place. It was a strange feeling, one that Hayden didn't exactly like.

Harold exhaled quietly.

"Carter, I believe you know in the depths of your heart what you need to do next. No other man can make that choice for you. Only God can read your mind and know your heart. It's up to *you* to decide what you believe."

"Nobody can force you to give your heart to Him. It has to be entirely out of your own desire. You know what you have to do," Ezra added, glancing at Hayden out of the corner of his eye.

First time anybody's acknowledged my presence today. Hayden's throat constricted as he raised a brow in mockery. He resituated himself on the cot, attempting to ignore his aching spine. Why did his skin crawl? The more he watched Pratchit, the more he wanted to get as far away as he could. If only he could've numbed himself to seeing Pratchit die, like he'd done with all the other casualties so far. It just wasn't happening. He sighed. His heart wasn't as hard as he'd hoped.

The halt in the conversation was stifling, even though there were plenty of other voices carrying on in the barrack. Hayden tried to distract himself with them, but it was in vain. It was as if the four men were the only ones in the building. And it made no sense at all.

Still, he was stuck here. He couldn't leave. He dragged his gaze back to the withering surgeon.

Pratchit closed his eyes slowly, emitting a breath of spent air. His face wrenched and his mouth quivered, contorting into a frown as a lone tear slipped down his unshaven cheek.

Oh, for the love of… is it finally over? Hayden's stomach turned. Something was happening. The furrowed brow, the eyes squeezed shut – the tortured expression on Carter's face seemed to imply that he was fighting with some sort of being or thought in his mind. Was he fighting to believe in a God he couldn't see? Was he struggling to obtain his sanity before he departed? Was his body simply shutting down for good?

Then the man's lip trembled. His mouth curled, and in the beginning it almost seemed he was growling. But it wasn't that. He was murmuring quietly to himself. *One last protest to the unfairness of it all?* Hayden swallowed, searching for answers in the creases of the man's furrowed brow. Unintelligible words were etched in every line. He couldn't figure out what he saw, and that frustrated him in a way he'd never felt before.

And then, Carter's facial muscles relaxed entirely. All movement stopped gently, as if his spirit had finally been given permission to depart from the mortal cage of his flesh and bones.

It was over. It was finally over.

Dryness filled Hayden's mouth. He couldn't take his eyes away from the lifeless profile.

In those last few seconds, he'd never seen Pratchit look so happy, so *alive*.

EPILOGUE

ZEPHYR

DEAR GOD, IT'S HARD TO know who's in the right and who isn't. I'm at a loss for words, and to say I can think straight right now would be a lie. I look down at my body and wonder who I have become. I look at my hands and question what life I'm truly living.

I think of all the blessings I've been rewarded with, and the losses don't seem so large. That's because I know, in comparison, they really aren't. Sometimes, I feel like you've given me far too much. Well, alright, more than sometimes. It's true. I've been given far more than any human is worthy of.

There is a voice though, and not my own, telling me that I am a useless daughter. There is a voice echoing in my head, telling me I will make a wretched wife. My husband will surely grow weary of my endless storm, my hurricane of emotions that I can't control.

I can't keep things together with Ma and the boys. I handle criticism poorly, and I'm far too sensitive.

Honestly, I'm tired of myself. I'm tired of not being able to live up to my own expectations and those of my family. I am scared to think of how You must see me, even though You can forgive, and You forgive us when we certainly don't deserve it. The thing is humans don't forgive. And there are several who won't forgive me. Why should they? I haven't given them reason to. My words don't line up with my actions.

This constant cycle, it repeats itself again and again. Perhaps this is to keep me from ever getting lost in pride. Maybe it's to keep me from letting the praise of others go to my head.

I don't rely on others to make me feel like a beautiful individual worth loving and listening to. I don't need their flattery to make me feel accomplished. But when someone looks you in the eye and tells you, "God is powerful to forgive, and thankfully He is, or we'd all be doomed. But, I'm a human, and I can't forgive you," you get this powerful sort of hurt inside and it doesn't go away. You kind of want to reach inside and tear it out before it eats away the rest of your innards.

Somehow, I think Pa would say that, if he could see all that's been going on while he's been gone. If he could see how we got raided and how I didn't make any extra effort to go find work or help in Reddick or Micanopy. How I only stayed, cried, tried to pick myself up and clean up the destruction left in their wake. We wouldn't be struggling so much if I pitched in more. Ma's eyes wouldn't look so tired. Clarence wouldn't give me angry looks and I could be a better example to the little boys.

The little boys. Sometimes I forget how it must all look to their small eyes. I feel ashamed to have let so much slip in front of them, as if they are invisible. How much of this will they remember when they are older, when their personalities have become set in stone and they have their own opinions and say in life? It's a scary thought.

If only I could take an invisible knife and cut away all the parts of my soul which are tainted by the poison of my wickedness. Ah, but since I know I can't do that, this is where You come in. Lord, I'm so thankful you are there. It gives me peace to know I will never have to trouble myself with the task of washing my own soul, or remedying my own spiritual illness. The only thing that keeps me sane— erm, saner— is knowing it's all in Your hands.

To be honest, I hate myself a lot. I know I shouldn't, because You made me, but I messed up the creation you crafted. I soiled something good and dragged it through the dirt, like a child messing up the new church clothes their momma made them. I hate how I have slapped you in the face by disregarding your instructions for my life.

It's hard because there isn't anyone I can talk to, well, other than You. What would I do without You to vent to and guide me? Still, it would be nice, I reckon, to have another person in front of me to listen and understand.

Alas, there isn't a body that can do that for me and my condition. Nobody understands the things that go through my mind. It would probably scare the living daylights outta them to know what goes on up there. I can't tell if I'm just being dramatic or if I actually have a point. I wish I could see it from another perspective, but the problem is there's no such thing as an unbiased viewpoint. So I probably wouldn't be able to trust that extra perspective anyhow.

I'm alone in this war. It's not my family to blame and it's not the Rebels or Feds. It's not me against the world and it's not me against the elements. It's me against me.

I want to take my feet and go far away where nobody can observe this conflict. I want to walk along the dirt road, just keep walking and never stop. I want to explore the world and see what else is out there. I want to feel the fresh air on my face. I want to look up and take in the beauty of your glorious night skies and sunsets. I want clarity, clarity of mind and thought. I want to know who to listen to and who to trust. If my feet ever stop, it will only be to get a few hours rest. One day, perhaps I'll build myself a cabin in the woods all by myself and live like a hermit until the storm inside passes. If it ever does. But what if it always remains?

I have nowhere else to go.

No one else can fight my battles for me. Pa and Uncle Ezra might be up north defending the Confederacy, but they can't protect me from myself.

Only You can.

TIMELINE of ACTUAL EVENTS PERTAINING TO THE 7TH FLORIDA

Late 1861-Early 1862 – Florida companies first organized.

April 16, 1862 – Confederate Conscription Act is issued.

April 1862 – 7th Florida Infantry organized at Camp Lee, Gainesville.

Early June 1862 – 7th FL leaves Jacksonville.

August-October 1862 – Lt. General Kirby Smith's forces (which the 7th FL was a part of) journey to Kentucky - the Cumberland Mountains.

April 1863 – Both 6th and 7th FL units have their regimental chaplains resign.

June 1863 – Small skirmish at Knoxville.

September 8th 1863 – The Army of Tennessee marches south to intercept Union General William Rosecrans.

September 11th 1863 – South of Chattanooga, the Army of Tennessee forms lines in preparation for battle – but the Union has already left.

September 18th – Preparations begin for the battle of Chickamauga.

September 19th – Battle of Chickamauga. Colonel Robert Trigg's Floridians fall in and march off at 5am.

November 12th – Colonel Trigg is replaced by Colonel Jesse Finley before the Battle of Missionary Ridge.

November 25th 1863 – Battle of Missionary Ridge. Colonel Robert Bullock is captured. By 6pm, the center of General Braxton Bragg's line has been completely broken and left in retreat, heading towards South Chickamauga Creek.

November 26th, 1863 – General Bragg orders retreat of his remaining forces to Dalton, Georgia.

For more information on the 7th FL Infantry and Florida's military involvement in the Civil War, the author suggests "By the Noble Daring of Her Sons: The Florida Brigade in the Army of Tennessee" by Jonathan C. Shepherd.

THE REBELS OF FLORIDA BOOK TWO

FRAYED HORIZONS

Several months have passed since the Florida Brigade's horrific loss at Missionary Ridge. Harold, Hayden and Ezra slowly wilt away, trapped in the earthly hell of Rock Island Prison. As disease takes more and more lives, the Florida men plot an escape from the madness – but time is not on their side. Harold's mental health is not what it was and with each day it's deteriorating further. With every odd against the Florida trio, will their efforts be in vain?

Meanwhile, back in Florida, the Darson family struggles to stay afloat. Left in the aftershock of the last Union raid, they have no livestock and no money to replace what they lost. Too much rain has left their crops useless for selling, so Zephyr and Lydia take work at a hotel in Micanopy to help with the family's debts. Not long after, Zephyr meets and begins a courtship with Niles Kimball, a respectable young surveyor. Will Zephyr's battle with her alleged hysteria ruin her chances of a happy marriage? Is it possible to experience true love untainted by war and strife, or by the tempest of emotion itself?

About the Author

Ambitious. Rebel. Hippie. Just a few words that describe Leah and her vivid life in the farmlands of North Central Florida!

Leah has been writing, drawing and creating ever since she was little, and enjoys presenting living history demonstrations at American Civil War reenactments. As Florida's one-and-only girl infantry snare drummer, she is also very passionate about music and can play 9 different instruments, including piano, which is her favorite. She lives to be more like Jesus Christ and to glorify Him in all she does. She is a certified fitness trainer and especially fond of tea, strength training, exploring, and spending time with friends and family!

Visit Leah's blog: www.leahoxendine.blogspot.com

41249349R00135

Made in the USA
Middletown, DE
07 March 2017